Enjoy the
read!

Circle of the Hawk

By
L. J. Mannon

Copyright © 2004 by L.J. Mannon

All rights reserved. No part of this book shall be reproduced or transmitted in any form or by any means, electronic, mechanical, magnetic, photographic including photocopying, recording or by any information storage and retrieval system, without prior written permission of the publisher. No patent liability is assumed with respect to the use of the information contained herein. Although every precaution has been taken in the preparation of this book, the publisher and author assume no responsibility for errors or omissions. Neither is any liability assumed for damages resulting from the use of the information contained herein.

This is a work of fiction. Names, characters, places, and incidents either are the product of the author's imagination or are used fictitiously. Any resemblance to actual events or locales or persons, living or dead, is entirely coincidental.

ISBN 0-7414-1941-6

Published by:

1094 New DeHaven Street, Suite 100
West Conshohocken, PA 19428-2713
Info@buybooksontheweb.com
www.buybooksontheweb.com
Toll-free (877) BUY BOOK
Local Phone (610) 941-9999
Fax (610) 941-9959

Printed in the United States of America
Printed on Recycled Paper
Published September 2004

I would like to gratefully recognize the efforts of Charles Swannell and Carol Nazzaro, whose thoughtful insights and suggestions brought this story to fruition. And a very special thank you to my dear friend and riding buddy, Alex Kilger, whose friendship and enthusiastic support has propelled me to finish this project and begin the next.

Several South Jersey locations serve as a setting for this story. However, the characters and events are completely fictional and part of the author's imagination. Any resemblance to people living or deceased is coincidental.

For Bob, Craig and Jake:

*A mother teaches love.
A father teaches discipline and later - respect.*

Anonymous

Chapter One

"Do you have him?" His voice bellowed in short breathless waves from the static of the radio.

"Not yet! Repeat...not yet!" She answered back, then released the button and let it drop carelessly from her grasp only to be caught by the rope around her neck. She pressed the heels of her boots firmly against her horse's side, tugged on the rim of her baseball hat, turning him off the path and into the thick cover of the woods. "Come on boy," she whispered, "he's here somewhere."

The heavy evening haze slithered across the fields and left only fragments of fading amber streaks to the west. A deep gray hue dominated the trails and blackened the woods while objects seemed to undulate in darker shadows from the corner of the eye. The last thing they needed was to lose Toby before dark. There was no telling how far he would be by morning and neither of them would sleep knowing he was left behind.

Mary's horse saw the motion first and instinctively came to a halt signaling her to change direction. She only needed to look at his ears to decipher his body language. Shortstop was a seasoned veteran of this sport. He automatically changed direction and picked up his pace toward the flash of illusive movement. Her horse's senses were far more astute than any humans. He knew what to do. There it was again. A brief flash of white swallowed up by the tentacles of deep brush as quickly as her mind had acknowledged its presence. Leaning forward, she pressed her head against the side of his neck and urged him on, picking through the tight mesh of overgrowth and gnarled scrub pines as they made their own shortcut. The low branches scraped against them as they fought, but finally they broke free of the gloomy grayness and stumbled into an open field.

Happy to be loose from the murky confines of the woods, Shortstop immediately slipped into a rhythmic gait toward the small patch of white on the edge of the hedgerow. The thin gathering of trees that separated one open field from another was the perfect place for a covey of quail, and a pointing dog at work.

She breathed a sigh of relief as she pressed the button and reported into the radio. "I have him! He's on point by the high-tension tower. I'm going to use this bird and call it a night! Do you read me? Over!"

There was no response, so she repeated the request again and waited. Still no answer. She looked nervously up at the sky. She had to hurry; it was getting too dark to continue. "Damn radios," she muttered, "such short range."

Mark Winters sat high on his horse scanning the fading landscape before him. He listened for a call, an echo from the distance, any clue as to the location of the dog. His large strong shoulders appeared even wider under the flaps of his brown oilskin coat. He turned his horse past a broken down foundation; the skeletal remains of a building from another century. There was no trace of wood to reveal its history. All that lingered was a low stonewall that poked through overgrown foliage and haphazard piles of rubble.

Autumn was crashing in like a rip tide and the onslaught of night was ending their training sessions far too early. Toby would be ready for spring field trials if he could just stay near the course and stay out of the woods. He had finally started to hunt with enthusiasm and purpose. He had moved past his puppy instinct to chase the fluttering birds that teased his senses and was working hard for his master. He could be a field champion. He had the breeding and the desire. He just needed a little more time…a little more practice…a little more maturity – and a little more daylight.

Mark guided his horse toward a wide muddy trail that led away from the fields and into the heart of woods. *The tunnel* was a fitting name for the pipeline trail through the training grounds.

He spoke into the receiver, "I'm at the tunnel. Where are you? Over!"

Nothing but static responded.

The tunnel was a corridor of trees whose wide fall canopy completely eclipsed the remainder of useable daylight. In the darkness its path appeared to be endless, ominous and alive. He entered it willingly, but the movement of the cold wind through the dry autumn leaves seemed to taunt him and put his horse on edge. Butch snorted and perked his ears toward the front in anticipation. His normally high stepping Tennessee walker gait slowed to a cautious, uncertain, and leery stagger.

"Just a deer, boy," Mark mumbled reassuringly, all the time looking around him at the shadows that enveloped them like a blanket. He felt it too. It was a sensation of fear that reality couldn't define. It crept down his spine and made him feel foolish in its presence. He refused to give into it. He urged the horse forward. It had to be nothing.

Butch reluctantly took a step, and halted. Mark pushed him harder pressing his legs against the animal, speaking in low tones of firm reassurance, but the horse stood like a statue blatantly ignoring his rider's request. His attention was elsewhere.

Suddenly, Butch's body jerked and went rigid with fear, his eyes wide with anticipation. Mark tightened his control preparing for the wave of blind panic that he knew was next to come from the terrified animal. His eyes scanned the fluid tree walls of the path as his steed began to spin nervously beneath him edging toward an escape.

With a sudden bolus of adrenaline the horse began to thrash against the bit, pulling and twisting his head from side to side, using his powerful neck to propel his body, desperately fighting the control of his master. Mark fought against him, a powerful man against a powerful animal, opponents in a battle of instinct. Mark's eye caught something in the shadows that he could not make out in form or motion. He yelled in its direction as he tried to regain control, "Show yourself! You're spookin' my horse!" But the reply was a high-pitched sound driving out of nowhere.

Butch reared onto his hind legs to strike the unseen demon, just as a sharp deep pain pierced Mark's upper chest, nearly knocking him from the seat. His body began to fall backward as he struggled to hold the reins, but instead of gaining control- he forced his horse down onto his haunches then onto his back, crushing himself beneath the animal's weight.

It seemed like forever…a blanket of cold and pain swept over his body as the horse rolled, fought to his feet, and lunged forward at breakneck speed obeying his need to escape. Paralyzed and struggling to breathe, Mark felt the earth pass beneath him in waves of hard terrain and choking dirt. He opened his mouth to yell, but his voice was replaced by a suffered whimper. In the seconds that followed, he felt nothing except the numbing motion beneath him and the conscious realization that he was going to die. He slipped farther away from reality and physical pain, sucked hopelessly into a whirlpool of suffocating gray and bitter cold; fighting for his life with every gasp he could manage.

A calm chill swelled inside him as images and voices clouded his sight. Mary's youthful smile mingling with her playful, giggling laughter; Bob's first baby steps as he toddled toward his waiting arms; Steve's first home run and the cheers that filled him with pride. And finally, he and a grown up Bob, face to face, fists clenched in blind distorted rage, Mary helplessly struggling to separate them.

Each pivotal sequence of his life played frame to frame as the earth relentlessly throbbed beneath him and the sky stood still above him. There was so much left undone. So much left unsaid. The gray surrounded his view of the past and pulled him methodically into its undertow. His foot fell away from the tangled stirrup when his body went limp.

Mary rode up on the dog. Toby was motionless and yet he trembled with excitement. The white of his coat and the statuesque instinct of his point made him look like the classic pointing dog cartoon, a white-gloved finger pointing the prey to its master. It was a thing of beauty to watch him work; this is what they were born to do. She dismounted and walked over to the dog.

Toby was a strong looking Brittany. He had the classic orange mask and large spaniel type ears. His body in motion was that of an athlete, with a broad chest, muscular frame and long graceful strides. He had several orange spots on his coat but was predominantly white in the torso. Mary took the blank pistol from her holster and walked slowly around the front of him. Toby's eyes were locked onto the target and his nose swelled rhythmically with each breath of the quail's sweet scent. "Whoa boy," she whispered, looking for the hidden bird among the leaves and the branches. A sweep of her foot released a sudden flapping of wings and the bird was up and away, chirping as it flew. She watched the dog carefully as she fired the blank gun. The dog stood still and watched the bird fly into the shadow of the woods.

She leaned down and stroked him softly, "You're on your way pal. Good boy!"

The dog waited patiently as she took a long rope out of her saddlebag, hooked one end to his harness and the other to the ring of the saddle, mounted her horse and let Toby trot happily back to the horse trailer leading the way. It had been a good day and Mark would be pleased that it had ended with a good find.

There were still a few people training at the club. Most had finished and packed up to go home, but a few stragglers remained. Mary waved and made idle conversation as she passed on her horse. All the members had pointing or flushing dogs and most rode horses over the acres of rough terrain. The club members came from many different backgrounds, but those that could successfully train a champion bird dog, had an aura of mysterious power that seemed to give them god like status to the amateurs.

Kevin Alston was one of the mysterious gods of the sport. He came from generations of great dog handlers and breeders. After wining four national championships, he turned to training and handling as a full time profession. Pictures of Alston's pointers, took up plenty of wall space in the old clubhouse dining room. Now in his fifties, he chose to merely train the future field trial champions, then return them to their owners to campaign around the country for prize money. His wife Susan had changed his life forever. He had settled into a working routine of rising at dawn, running his kennel business, and training bird dogs. It wasn't about the winning or the money with Kevin, although that was good, it was about working in the outdoors and making a good dog - great. It was the fruition of a family tradition, trade secrets passed from fathers to sons, and having a gift with bird dogs that was born from love and respect.

Kevin sat on the gate of his pickup and tugged once at a thorn stuck in the paw of one of his pointers. There was not so much as a whimper from the dog, only a thankful licking across Kevin's face. He chuckled as he playfully pushed the dog away, saving himself a bath by whispering the word, "kennel." The chocolate and white pointer immediately turned and took its place in the row of dog boxes that lined the bed of his old blue pickup.

He laughed heartily as he wiped the slobber from his face with his dirty shirtsleeve. He was a tall, lanky man with jet-black hair and a smile that spread to a sparkle in his eyes, especially when he was working his dogs. His large green four-wheeler sat along side the truck. He tossed the thorn to the wind and poked the pliers into the leather pocket of the four-wheeler's saddlebag.

"Where's your other half?" He called to Mary. "He owes me money!" His large wide grin revealed a space between his two front teeth. He closed the kennel box door and reached for the open beer in the bed of the truck. The end of a workday signaled the start of cocktail hour and the recitation of bragging tales that accompanied every proud dog owner.

"He's around here somewhere. Make him pay up. And get a little extra for me too!" Mary called back. She spotted Susan in the field and gave her a distant wave. Susan returned it with a smile.

Kevin and Mark had a history. They were equally strong willed and had open arguments about whose breed of dog was better. After a few bourbons, their arguments would escalate into open, playful insults. Kevin felt that pointers were better hunters from birth – a product of centuries of great breeding. Mark felt that pointers were fine if you didn't mind your dog being as dumb as a fence post and too ugly to bring in the house. It was an age old argument that only a first place ribbon would settle. My dog is better than your dog.

One night they had run out of *your dog is so ugly, so dumb remarks,* and had fallen asleep in the clubhouse dining room. Mary and Susan had decided to teach them both a lesson and their husbands awoke in the middle of the night with no vehicles to drive home and nowhere to sleep. After the incident, the two men decided to call a truce, and had remained good, but competitive friends. The two women still secretly gloated about being able to bring the two tough guys to their knees.

The old stone clubhouse rose in front of Mary as the gradual rise in the property led them up to the parking area with its scattered trailers and dual wheel horse pulling trucks. Toby led the way as they trotted up the hill, his strong body pulled toward the large gray tub filled to the brim with water for the livestock.

With one graceful leap he was into the tub splashing and shaking water onto Shortstop. Her horse shook his head and gently started to sip from the tank. Toby lapped the water greedily and noisily while enjoying the feel of it slosh over his back. Shortstop tolerated all the commotion and sucked the water in silently, barely breaking its glassy surface. She patted her horse on the neck. A good horse made training easy and fun.

Shortstop was a small chestnut gelding with a beautiful head, dark gentle eyes and a curious nature. He was bred from champion bloodlines but sold when it was obvious that the show ring was never going to be his place. His small stature and oddly husky conformation had taught him to be submissive to humans as well as other livestock. Like the little kid who gets picked on in the schoolyard, he learned to avoid conflicts. Mary had taken to his easy disposition and smooth shuffling gait the first time she rode him. His lope was as deep and comfortable as Grandma's rocking chair, and the short muscular build that was unacceptable to his breeders seemed to be the very trait that could outwork and outlast the other field trial horses - with far less physical effort. But most of all she believed this little horse took care of her. He would slow and warn her of obstacles, stay still for mounting and dismounting, and seemed to anticipate her every move before the pressure of the reins urged him.

Shortstop lifted his nose from the water tub making a deliberate reaching motion to drip over Toby's head. The dog shook wildly in retribution and jumped out of the water. They proceeded toward the trailer where, once unhooked from the rope, Toby curled up in the cedar bed warmth of the dog box, awaiting his transport home and the warm meal that followed a good run.

Mary closed the kennel box door. She pulled off her hat and combed through her long black hair with her fingers. Strands had fallen free of her ponytail and she watched the remaining sunset as she tugged at the reluctant rubber band.

It was a beautiful sight from the top of this hill. This is what she loved. It wasn't the test of the actual field trial, although a win would occasionally be nice. It was the beauty and solitude of this place and the willingness of the dogs to work for their masters. It was fun and exhilarating. For a while she could forget about the politics at work and the problems at home, and admire the natural instinct God had given these animals.

Open fields spread out before her like a patchwork quilt. Layers of milky haze hovered over the high grass and soybeans, finally reaching the last crack of sunset that blazed one thin final streak at the western edge of the earth. The heavy dusk was rapidly consuming the trees and she watched her horse graze restfully near the trailer. It would be completely dark within the half-hour. A chill began to bite the air and body heat rose slowly from the nostrils of her horse.

The plateau where they parked was part of the original clubhouse, an old stone and brick building that dated back to the 1600's. It was the highest part of the property. The massive elevation seemed out of place in contrast to the flatness of New Jersey. The old house was dilapidated by today's standards, but still unique in all its rustic, simple beauty. Attempts had been made at minor improvements over the years and from some angles the house seemed out of place in history. Behind the clubhouse stood an old wood storage barn with a tractor and a few of the club member's four wheelers. Behind that, a small wooden coop softly clucked with homing pigeons. She strolled behind the buildings and up a narrow path to a patch of field protected by a circle of trees. It was at the back of the plateau, an area of the grounds that went unnoticed by many who trained there.

The cemetery was slowly being taken back by nature and hadn't been tended to in years. Its inhabitants were the fallen dogs and horses that had been faithful companions to their hunter masters. Trees and brush were beginning to up heave the monuments and no one at the club was old enough to remember any of the champion dogs and companion horses interred there. What better resting place than the training grounds where they saw their greatest victories.

There were all kinds of old head stones and make shift markers being reclaimed through downed branches and overgrown brush. It was a reminder of a time when laws permitted the burial of both large and small animals on the property. Some markers were made of stone and concrete, others were mere posts stuck in the ground.

The largest and most elaborate marble head stone read; *"Bucky, my faithful field trial companion for 30 years."* It was amusing to her that anyone would name a horse "Bucky." Seemingly the rider enjoyed tempting fate. But there was no mistaking the love they held for their horse. There were hand painted crosses and a variety of smaller head stones with sayings like *"Here lies, FC Barreling Baily; at rest where he was happiest - hunt with God, my friend."* One owner had placed a cement dog on the grave. The years and the weather had wiped away the inscription along with half the face. It was barely recognizable as a dog anymore but looked more like a statue of a ground hog.

The evening gave the old cemetery a surreal kind of look, but more surreal to Mary was the devotion and gratitude seen here from men who rarely knew how to express it. She had seen these men lose their homes and lose their wives, but tears only came when they lost their dogs. This place was a tribute, a kind of hall of fame to the animals revered by men.

She looked at her watch and strolled back down the path toward the trailer. She was anxious to tell Mark about Toby's last find and how well he stood for the flush of the bird. The stars were starting to come out and she began to pack up their things. As she swung open the back of the trailer doors and emptied Toby's water pan, her attention slowly began to shift to a commotion down in the field. At first she thought it was just someone yelling for their dog, then the words became pieced together in her brain.

"Where's Mary! Get Mary!" It was Susan, frantically yelling from a distance. Her voice strained as it echoed over the hill.

Mary dropped the pan and ran to the edge of the plateau, her eyes locating the direction of the voices. Susan stood at the base of the hill, waving her hat and pointing down toward the tree-lined end of the cut field. "Isn't that Mark's horse?" she called, cupping her mouth with one hand and pointing toward the field with the other. "He looks hurt!"

Mary squinted through the last of the evening haze and vaguely saw a shadow of a horse in the distance. She raised her fingers to her mouth and let out a long sorrowful whistle that she used nightly to call her horses in for feeding. When the horse stopped and lifted its head, she knew something was terribly wrong. Butch carried his head low and limped badly in an effort to come to them. The saddle looked like it was off to one side.

Everything stood still as if time defied her. Her movements seemed slow and clumsy, paced by the pounding of her heart. She ran to the pickup, snatched up the portable phone and stabbed it inside her jacket pocket. She startled Shortstop as she grabbed the reins and hurled herself onto him, cracking the leather against his side, pushing him into a full gallop down the hill. Kevin had already fired up his four-wheeler and together they sped out in the direction of the injured animal.

"I'll go this way!" He shouted, pointing over the roar of the machine.

She nodded and began to search in the opposite direction, darting through the trees. "Mark! Mark!...Answer me! Where are you?" She sat up in the saddle and screamed his name with all the voice she could force from her lungs. Her eyes searched for a sign, her ears hoped for a call – all her senses struggled to stay calm and alert.

What she noticed was a sudden silence, and she felt a coldness claw at her chest. The roar of the four-wheeler had stopped.

"He's here! The tunnel!" Kevin's voice echoed from the opposite direction.

She thundered toward the sound of his call, past the high-tension tower, through the soybean field, and down the trail into the waiting darkness of the tunnel.

Minutes seemed to tick in her head like a slow paced metronome. First she saw the hat. Then ahead a twisted form lying in the mud. Kevin was already standing over the figure, staring. Mary jumped from her horse and punched 911 into the phone as she stumbled toward the motionless form. Mark's leg was twisted and the heel of his boot was turned starkly upward to the sky. Kevin rushed toward her saying something that she couldn't understand. Her eyes were focused on her husband. He was face up, mouth and eyes wide and blank. There was a jagged gash across his head and blood soaked his chest.

She spoke breathlessly into the receiver of the phone, "Yes...I have an emergency at the Semi Wild Club. Yes, off 481 ...that's right! It's a riding accident, looks pretty bad, may need a helicopter..." her voice cracked as she pushed Kevin away and knelt down to check Marks breathing. "He's in arrest! She plunged the phone into Kevin's hands. "Get them out here, now!" she cried.

Some other part of her took over as she pulled open Marks coat to do compressions. She saw the searing puncture wound under the clavicle near the heart, but knew it wasn't the worst problem at the moment. She had to keep blood circulating and air to his brain until help arrived. His skin was dark and his eyes were bulged and bloodshot, his face grotesquely distorted. Blood had spilled from his nose and mouth - the streams now silent and drying. She pinched his nose and blew into his mouth, but the airway was obstructed. She tilted his head slightly, knowing he may have a neck injury and suspecting the worst, but there was no choice. She had to get air to his brain. It was a decision she had to make with no supplies and no support. As soon as the weight of her hands applied pressure to his chest she jerked them away. Shocked and stunned, she felt the crushed protruding bones of his sternum and ribs move freely beneath her hands. The tactile sensation of air bubbles crinkled beneath his skin and up his neck.

Flashes poured through her mind; pictures of twisted, torn bodies and swollen plastic faces. She was always on the sideline waiting to obtain their x-rays among a sea of ripping packages, hurried nurses and shouting physicians. Face after face passed before her memory, the passages unfolding as if she were fanning through a book; residents, frantically banging on the dark room door, demanding films that would define their patient's chances. Trauma radiology was her life and now Mark was a new mental landmark in the worst trauma she had ever seen. He fell into a tragic category, justified by a list of clear medical failures. Her mind started to itemize the probable extent of his injuries as if she were evaluating a chart. Massive crush injury to the chest, multiple fractures involving sternum, and ribs, massive hemorrhage, and air into the subcutaneous tissue. Open head wound, eyes dilated and unresponsive, respiratory and cardiac failure. She had spent enough time next to nurses and doctors to know that there was very little she could do to intervene. She was helpless and stunned.

For a moment that list of injuries defined the man she knew as her husband. She knew what she was seeing in front of her, but the reality... that was something else.

"He's dead," she said, as if hearing it out loud would make herself believe what she was seeing. "He ....he was crushed."

Kevin was still on the line with 911. Mary couldn't hear what he was saying, but heard his voice without word recognition, like someone speaking a foreign language. In the distance there were approaching sirens cutting through the dark.

She slowly stood up in a trance-like motion and extended her blood stained hands toward the sky. "WHY!!!" She screamed at the heavens - screamed at God.

That one word question turned into a long mournful wail that spilled from her throat into an agonizing bellow. It painfully resounded across the fields and pierced the souls of both the men and beasts it touched - until there was no more air left in her lungs.

Chapter Two

At 6:22 P.M., Mark Winters was pronounced dead at the scene. Detective Tate and his men had detained everyone at the club and were systematically interviewing each individual. While this process was taking place, the crime scene was taped off, lights were set up and photographs of the area were taken. Police officers spoke in low tones and dotted the area with their uniformed presence.

Nathaniel Tate had come highly recommended from the Philadelphia Crime Force. His short blond military haircut and muscular arms gave the young detective an intelligent look that cooperated with his slow deliberate personality. His disgust of senseless inner city crime had brought him to this small suburban life, boring but pleasant by comparison. He had a theory about these things: the simple answer was probably the correct one. Sketchily acting out the events in his mind, and based on the victims wounds, he came up with two possibilities: someone was hunting out of season, and Mark Winters got in the way and was dragged to his death, or it was just an unfortunate riding accident, and he was somehow impaled through the chest as a result of the injuries.

Kevin had given his rendition of the story and had started to load up Mary's horses to drive them back to her house. He left Susan with Mary, sitting on the crumbling stone foundation with their arms around one another. As they sat with their backs to the lights, the detective moved in front of them and knelt down to face Mary.

"Mrs. Winters," he started gently, "about what time did you say you found the dog and couldn't reach your husband on the radio?" He was sure this woman was in shock. He couldn't get more than a few words out of her. She stared sadly into nowhere with dark almond shaped eyes that were glazed and blank and stolen. It was as if her soul had been taken. He had seen that look many times before in the face of victims. Tears laced with dirt and mascara had run down her tan face giving her an almost harlequin appearance. She smelled of horse sweat and leather. She kept looking down at the blood on her hands, draped limply over her muddy chaps as if she were seeing it for the very first time.

"I...don't...know," she said in short exhausted words.

"Detective, can't we do this tomorrow?" Susan protested angrily. "She's been through a lot tonight. I don't think she's in any condition for an interrogation."

"This isn't an interrogation, Ma'am," he replied, nodding his head in acknowledgment, "but I was hoping to clear a few things up before we move the body. I'm trying to establish a time of death here."

"I don't...keep track out here," Mary spoke slow and mechanically. "I just don't know..." Her eyes didn't move and it was clear that the incident could not be retold at that moment.

"I think she should see a doctor," he added, locking his eyes with Susan's.

"He's coming out to the house later. Really, she's not doin' too good. Can't we pick this up after the shock wears off? Maybe in a day or so?"

"Just a few more things. Maybe you can answer them for me, Mrs. Alston. Was Mr. Winters a good rider? I guess what I'm asking is, do you think this could have been avoided?"

Susan thought carefully, her eyes scanning the air as if reading the answer. "You don't understand. When this sorta' thing happens, it happens fast. It's not like riding in a ring...under controlled circumstances. You don't get a lot of time to react and you can't anticipate everything you might be faced with. I guess what I mean is, if Mark could have avoided it, I'm sure he would have. He's a good rider and his horse is solid. No...something else happened out here."

"Are there many horse related accidents on the grounds…obviously, something this extreme doesn't happen often, but how about other injuries?" He was trying to get a feel for the amount of risk involved in their pastime.

She sighed heavily and acted annoyed at his question. "No matter what sport you like, you're gonna' get injured. Doesn't matter if it's skiing or…or walking. Do it long and hard enough and your chances of getting hurt increase. But your level of expertise also gets better, and these people know their horses. To answer your question, no…everybody occasionally takes a minor fall, but you learn how to fall, to let the horse go and to avoid anything major. Mark's judgment for some reason was not to let the reins go. He was a good rider. He must have thought he could get control." Her attention went back to Mary, who was still staring blankly down at her hands.

Mary mumbled, "Why, Susan? Why did this happen?"

"Can I take her home now?" Susan's voice was almost pleading to the detective.

"You've been very helpful. Will she be staying at your house then?" He jotted another note onto his pad.

"As long as I can keep her with us," she replied. She helped Mary up and walked her to Kevin's blue pickup truck.

Kevin drove Mary's truck and trailer back to her house. The road was isolated and there were no streetlights where she lived. The headlights of the truck seemed to illuminate the white broken lines down the center of the road like an old Twilight Zone episode. Its rhythmic effect was hypnotizing. The occasional wide eyes of deer reflected his headlights and he slowed to a cautious speed. He needed to tend to Butch's injuries. His plan was to unload and care for the animals, disconnect the truck from the horse trailer and drive it back to his house. Mary would have it when she was ready to leave. She was a tough woman. She would get through this.

He swung the silver horse trailer down the long access road beside a modest ranch house. It was a small six-acre gentleman's farm that Mark had kept well maintained. It had four paddocks of newly painted fence and one large barn that the access road led to. The house wasn't much, but they hadn't bought it for the house. It was the paddock and the barn that had made the sale. The house was just an accessory to be fixed up at a later time.

The barn light cast a dim glow on the front of the metal doors as he backed in the trailer. He let Toby out of the kennel box and the dog ran first to his favorite tree, then to the tall wooden box filled with training pigeons that stood outside the barn door. He sniffed the wood door and listened with intense interest, cocking his head from side to side as if the cooing was a language he was trying to understand.

Kevin flipped on the lights inside the barn making a mental note to feed the homing pigeons before he left. The sudden surge of electricity hummed gently overhead as he unloaded Shortstop and led him down the center isle past four redwood stalls to the gate at the end of the barn. Mark had removed the last two stalls and opened the end of the barn into a spacious walk-in shed. The walk-in lay open directly to the fenced pasture. The couple rarely stalled their horses except in illness. The walk-in provided shelter that let the horses decide when they wanted to come out of the weather.

Butch and Shortstop were well cared for, but low maintenance animals. They grazed day and night and only came in the barn for occasional shade or relief from the cold. The method worked well and kept the horses healthy with the added benefit of far less daily clean up for the owners.

As Kevin walked back to the trailer, the little horse stood in the open end of the barn and whinnied nervously over the gate for his missing partner. Butch answered back from the trailer in a deep throaty grunt of a refrain.

He knew a horse with this kind of history was no good to anyone. It couldn't be trusted with another rider. If Butch were his, he would put a gun to his head personally and without hesitation or remorse. Mark might still be alive if the animal hadn't rolled on top of him, regardless of the other circumstances. But it wasn't his decision to make.

Butch limped painfully into the stall, his leg straining to support his own weight. His front right foreleg was swollen and his movement was difficult to watch. Kevin set down a water bucket and started to check him over. He was a massive animal, his head well above Kevin's. The brush wounds from the saddle swept down his light brown coat and exposed large tracks of oozing raw skin. His mouth had bled profusely, but the stream was beginning to slow, and his left eye was tearing and half-closed. Kevin evaluated his injuries suspecting that the cornea had been lacerated in the struggle, and the extreme pressure of the bit had cut the animal's gums.

His callused hands put gentle pressure across the spine, and Butch tensed up and reacted with a threatening gesture, flattening his ears against his head and lashing his tail toward him like a whip. He examined the deep gash on the left side, about the height of the stirrup, and decided that it wasn't gaping enough to need stitches. The image of Mark's twisted leg flashed before him and he could feel himself getting angry. These injuries could all wait for the vet in the morning. None of it was an emergency. He would just keep him quiet and comfortable tonight and confined to a stall. That's what Mary would want.

He searched noisily through the metal locker in the corner of the barn pulling out medical supplies. He flipped opened a saline eyewash and approached Butch with the bottle. His plan was to sneak the tip of the dropper up to the corner of the eye. Butch anticipated his plan and reacted in a wink by clamping his eyelid shut.

"C'mon you old one-eyed mule!" Kevin muttered, as he tried to pry the eye open with his thumb and index finger. After a struggle and some creative cursing, he sufficed to get a few drops in and most of it on his hands. Butch blinked repeatedly and turned his head away.

"The hell with ya then." He finished dressing the open wounds with ointment and turned his attention to the injured leg, packing it with cold packs and securing it snugly with adhesive vet wrap. Then he opened a syringe of analgesic and coaxed the horse to accept the milky paste squirting into his mouth. Butch stuck out his tongue over and over again, like a disgruntled child forced to eat his vegetables.

Kevin turned his back on the animal and bent over to recheck the wrap. He wanted to make sure it was secure before he left the horse alone for the night. As he bent down, the exposed track of pale skin between Kevin's jeans and the bottom of his jacket proved too tempting. Butch's ears went flat against his head and his eyes widened. He tossed his head in a spiral motion and with teeth bared, came down on Kevin's exposed butt cheek with one quick striking motion. Kevin jumped back, fuming with anger, "You son of a... If you were mine, I'd rename you dog food! Do you hear me horse? – DOG FOOD!! He was up in the animal's face, fist clenched.

Instead of looking away in submission or fear, Butch's ears perked up and forward in a curious fashion, as if amused by the actions of his prey.

Kevin relaxed his hand and moved awkwardly around the stall rubbing his rump and cursing. Both horses now watched him intently. He had received a pretty good bite, but there wasn't any blood. Still cursing under his breath, he continued about his chores tossing a sliver of hay in the rack. But he did so never turning his back on the horse.

As he prepared to leave, he glanced over the barn one last time. The gates were locked, everybody had hay and water, the feed room was closed, the pigeons fed. Acknowledging this, his eyes fell again upon the once high-spirited elegant horse, Mark's pride and joy - now broken and pathetic, with his wrapped leg, lowered head, open wounds and his one tearing half closed eye. Fishing through his pockets, he approached him again. Butch promptly squeezed his left eye shut, and Kevin smiled extending his hand with a few horse cookies.

"You're obnoxious all right. Just like your owner." He spoke softly, patting him on the neck and realizing he had used the present tense as if Mark were still alive. The horse nuzzled his hand as if all were forgiven, taking the cookies in one gulp.

"You've had a bad day boy...and you're the only one who really knows what happened out there." As Kevin turned from the stall and walked toward the door, Butch tossed his head and snapped at the air - just a reminder that he was still the boss.

Susan Alston sat at the kitchen table stirring her tea. She looked up when Kevin entered the back door with Toby bounding behind him. Her eyes were blood red and her lips were trembling. Her fine blond hair had fallen into her face and she let the spoon hit the sides of her teacup in rapid irritating pings. Kevin hated to see her cry and it pulled at his heart.

"Are you doin' O.K?" He asked, resting his hands on her shoulders and kissing her lightly on the cheek.

She squeezed his hands reassuringly and nodded. "She's resting now. She was in the shower for almost an hour. I'm really worried about her. Can't get a word out of her. I left a message with Jack's answering service and he's coming after surgery ...at least that's what they said. I hope he can help her." She shook her head disapprovingly and continued to stir her tea.

"He'll help her," he assured her. "She needs friends right now, even the ones you don't approve of." He turned his back to her and washed his hands at the sink. "I know you don't like Jack, but give him a break. If I came home and found everything I owned gone...well, I'm not sure I wouldn't go a little crazy too. The man idolized... what's her name...Annette?"

Susan rebuffed his comment, "He burned down that house they were building. I just know it!"

"C'mon Sue, you can't be serious."

"...and I think he would have been happy if that little stuck up snot he married was in it! I never liked her, and I don't trust him." She went back to stirring her tea.

Kevin dried his hands on the dishtowel and threw it casually on the counter. "It's ancient history now. Besides, the police didn't find arson and from what I understand Annette shacked up with someone in Jack's own practice. Like I said, give the guy a break for Christ's sake. Everyday, all the hospital gossip as if his life were a soap opera. Mary says he's been through a lot. I'm sure we don't know the half of it. Worst of all, he's still paying for it." Kevin leaned against the counter, then added, "Speaking of soap operas. Did you call her boys? God knows that's all she needs right now." He looked down at the floor and shook his head.

"I got a hold of Steve. He'll call Bob and get a ride down from college sometime tomorrow. I told him there was nothing they could do tonight and she was in good hands."

"How'd he take it?"

"Real bad. Broke down terrible. I hope he's gonna be all right. Listen, I think it's best if they all stay here tomorrow night too. No sense facing all the memories in that house before they're ready."

There was a moment of uneasy silence between them as their thoughts drifted back to the accident. Toby made his way to Susan's side, and she stroked the dog affectionately. The dog closed his eyes and enjoyed the attention.

"I've never seen anything like that," she whispered, "every time I even think about it I start feelin' sick." She lifted the tissue to her eyes. "How's Butch? Do you need me to go over tomorrow and check on him when the vet gets there?"

Kevin fought the urge to yell, *Screw the horse! A man died tonight!* But he knew that nursing an injured animal was her way of dealing with the tragedy. He tempered his words. "Butch is feeling pretty bad, but not that bad. He bit me on the ass the moment I wasn't lookin'." He turned around and tugged at the back of his pants until the ring of semi-circular teeth marks were visible on the milky white skin of his

21

buttock. "Damn horse...he tattooed me....look, but you'd be proud, Sue! We had a little talk and reached an understanding."

Susan laughed out loud covering her mouth with her hand letting the tears run down her cheeks. It was a nervous restrained kind of laugh – an acknowledgement of the ridiculous under tragic circumstances, like a joke told at a funeral. She slapped the reddened area. "You probably deserved it! What did you say to him? Ya know he's sensitive!" He caught her hand and pulled her close, hugging her tight while her laugh diminished into a series of uncontrollable sobs.

A tap at the door startled them both and Kevin quickly pulled at his pants and tightened his belt. Susan mopped at her eyes as she hurried from the kitchen to open the door. "Hello Jack," her voice was low and again strained. Jack came in and sat down at the table. He looked exhausted in the fluorescent light of the kitchen. His face had far too many lines for a man in his forties, his once rugged good looks seemed to gravitate steadily towards tired old age.

"Got your message. Thanks for calling me. How's she doing?" He asked, searching for the answer in their faces.

Kevin took a glass from the cabinet. "Can you have a drink?"

Jack shook his head no, glanced at his watch, then suddenly changed his mind. "Yeah, I think I will...something strong. You know they brought him through the emergency room? The police were taking more pictures of him. God, I can't believe it. I hardly recognized him. I was just talking to him the other day about Club business. His eyes drifted to Kevin's, "So how'd you say Mary was doing?"

Kevin poured a little Southern Comfort into a glass and set the bottle down on the table. "I don't know how someone in her position should be doing." He pulled the chair out and sat down with slow deliberate care on his injured rump."

Jack watched his tender descent and took notice, "Are you hurt?"

Kevin's eyes met Susan's, "I'm fine, just a bruise. I can tell you she isn't talking, very little eye contact... no emotion. I guess it hasn't hit her yet. She was mad as hell at first, screaming and crying at the sky, like God was takin' revenge on her. Then she just went silent. Now she looks like a zombie."

Jack took a sip and rolled the glass between his fingers. He stared at the movement of the liquid in the short bulky glass wondering how his visit was going to make any difference. "Has she taken anything, or drank any alcohol?"

"No, she's resting," Susan answered, nervously stirring her tea again. Their collective gaze focused on the annoying pinging of the cup.

Jack took another sip of his drink. "She just needs some time to get over the shock. I'm sure she's in overload right now. Most people go through this after witnessing a serious trauma to someone they love." He heard himself sounding more like a disinterested scientist reading a definition from a book than a reassuring friend offering comfort. He hated himself at that moment. Another quick sip, and he started down the hall to look in on her.

Jack knocked softly on the bedroom door knowing he didn't have much to offer her right now. He could give her medication to get her through the night, but he felt flat and drained as a human being, helpless to console her. He relived the pain of his own loss every day- every moment. How could he tell Mary that her pain would eventually subside with time? He would be lying ... he took a deep breath ...a friend needed him. Put it behind, and find a way to help her.

The sharp click of the lamp sent amber shades of light bathing the room in artificial warmth. He went to close the door behind him, but Toby got between his legs and was up on the bed nudging his mistress. Mary had wrapped herself in a quilt and lay facing the window, her deep slate eyes staring blankly out into the darkness. She didn't acknowledge his presence.

He sat down on the edge of the bed next to her. "I know this is hard," he started, stroking her wet hair, "but you have to be strong. I brought you something to help you rest."

He helped her into a sitting position and handed her two pills, and a glass of water. Her movements were slow and her face expressionless.

"Don't try to think about things. It all has no rhyme or reason. Don't try to figure it out. Just take each day as it comes and we'll deal with one thing at a time. We're all your friends, we'll help you through it." He rambled on in vague clichés not expecting an answer, and knowing full well that she would be facing the pain alone. Still it was his need to fill the air with words of comfort if not for her, then for himself.

"Turn out the light," she mumbled in a tired voice, her eyes still on the window. Their images stared back at the both of them like a dark endless mirror.

Jack reluctantly obeyed, and soon the room was filled again with tones of gray and blue. Mary became only a dark silhouette on the edge of the bed, a shadow of herself with her dog at her side. Toby had given up trying to get her attention, and was content to stare curiously out the window with them. Jack put his arm around her. Her hair was damp and she smelled like Ivory soap. Her tanned skin seemed luminous in the moonlight that cascaded from the window.

He held her in silence for the longest time watching the trees bend to the cold October wind. They had been friends and co-workers for many years and had met when he did his orthopedic residency in the E.R.

His mind drifted back to their first meeting ten years before. He had been awake for thirty-six hours and was paged from a brief slumber to assist in an early morning parachute accident. He had walked over to radiology to find a woman pulling films out of a processor and evaluating them on the lighted view boxes. She didn't seem to notice him, but spoke to one young girl carrying armloads of cassettes into the darkroom. "Did you get a cross table lateral lumbar?" She asked the young woman.

"Wasn't on the order," answered the girl.

Mary responded, "I'll call and get it added. Take an AP and cross table lateral of his lumbar spine while he's on the table. Use the best grid we have on the lateral."

Jack walked up to the films as the young girl scurried away. "I didn't order a lumbar. The guy has fractures of his ankles and his hips and pelvis. But he didn't complain about pain in his back. It's a wonder it isn't a lot worse. But he doesn't need a spine. At least not right now."

Mary smiled at him. "You're new here aren't you? Are you Dr. Moen's new resident?" She shook his hand with a confidence that he wasn't expecting.

The young technologist returned with more films, slamming the darkroom door behind her. He turned his attention back to Mary, "I didn't order a lumbar. He's got bigger problems right now. I need to start treating this guy, and I don't want him down here any longer."

She nodded, "I understand, doctor. I have a little leeway when it comes to this area. Believe me, he has a nurse with him now and we have several people taking and developing – it's best to get it while he's here. Have you seen this kind of injury before?"

"I've seen lots of injuries before," he wanted to establish authority and was in no mood for a pissing match with an x-ray tech. He leaned forward and examined the multiple fractures that spread across the patient's pelvis like a road map, "When you go back to school and get your M.D, you can tell me what to order." The thought of those words embarrassed him now even in retrospect.

Her demeanor didn't change, "I trained near an army base – coincidentally, so did Dr. Moen. I've seen this pattern before. The chute fails at some point close to the ground, they land on their feet and the percussion produces fractures above the ankles, necks of the femurs, shattered acetabulums as well as the lower pelvis – and then a compression fracture of L-2." She turned to face him, "it's a physics thing…has something to do with force and impact, but that's what happens."

Before he could answer, Dr. Moen turned the corner. He acknowledged the technologist with a nod, but seemed to take on a scowl as he started pulling down films with a posture that spoke of years of experience, and little tolerance for orthopedic residents.

"What's the story here, rookie?" His authoritative voice boomed in his young resident's ears. He was a hard man, but Jack knew he was lucky to have been selected to work under him. He couldn't make any mistakes.

"Parachute failure. Landed on his feet with enough force..." his hand started to sweep across the injuries on the film when Mary interrupted them, "Good call Doc – L2 it is!" She snapped the lateral lumbar film up onto the view box.

Dr. Moen examined the image and just a hint of a smile curled his lip, "Good work, rookie; I think you'll do just fine."

Mary winked and disappeared around the corner to help transport the patient back to the E.R.

That night he had found a friend in the hard cold world of his training. She had saved him many nights during his residency - directing his inexperienced eyes to barely foreseeable disruptions in bone cortex, widened growth plates in children, and displaced fat pads that would later be viewed by a radiologist as clues to fractures and tears. She never pretended to know more than she did, but gently passed knowledge to him that he used every time he looked at a film. *Notice the obvious,* she would tell him, *but look hard for the subtle.* They shared a bond through their work that in some ways was closer than man and wife. When she heard he purchased the ranch house on the edge of the Semi Wild grounds, she and Mark invited him to learn about the sport of field trialing. It changed his whole life and his whole attitude. He liked the people at the club. They had a single purpose, disconnected from the social order to enjoy a sport that few rarely participated in. His dogs and horses took him away from his rigid, stressful world and reminded him of the purity of nature's instinct. He owed her. He owed Mark. So why did he feel so crippled now that she needed help in return?

"Jack," she whispered, "do you remember the kid who was brought in...the one with the crushed legs?" Mary's voice startled him from his memories. Her speech was slow and deliberate.

"Oh, the tractor accident. Yeah, I remember him. He's one you don't forget easily. I remember that he wouldn't let your hand go and kept begging you not to leave." His arm tightened around her as he recalled the pleading teenage boy, knowing that the young deaths were always the hardest to come to terms with.

Mary took a ragged breath. "He knew he was going to die that day, Jack. All he wanted was to focus on someone, anyone that he could cling to...I was that thread...a conduit that connected him to his mother for the last few minutes of his life."

"I guess women have that power. I remember you shouting at him to look into your eyes and not to look away, to hold on. Letting your hand go...well, might have given him reason to slip away and he was a fighter that boy. You just can't control everything, no matter what you do. What made you think of him?"

"Mark's leg and the look on his face, like he knew he was going to die. It was the same kind of look - like he was struggling to hold on with every part of his being and just couldn't. Like he wanted to say something. I wasn't there for him, Jack. Like that boys mother just couldn't get there for him." She closed her eyes. "Sometimes ...what we do - it's like having a fight with God. We're trying to keep them and he's trying to take them... there was nothing I could do. He was already gone."

Jack didn't know what to say or how to console her. His own emptiness burned inside him and made him feel branded and helpless.

Soon her head weighed heavily against his shoulder and he laid her down, wrapping the quilt around her. Toby watched intently and curled up in a ball beside her. The dog lay still against his mistress, but his eyes followed Jack all the way to the door.

Chapter Three

Steve lay sprawled across his bed staring at the exposed bunk above him, one arm resting behind his head and the other clutching a baseball. He'd turn it in his hand, unconsciously tossing it into the air, snapping it back with his fingers and finding the smooth predictable threads in the leather. He had done it for years; the raised red tracks were a guide to the perfect throw down to second - a bullet that thrusts downward and to the right, at the feet of the flying runner. Finding those threads was so much a habit and a part of him that he no longer had to think about their position. The ball seemed to turn naturally in his hand as if it were an extension of his being.

He and his dad were tied up in all of this. Baseball and the two of them had been their bond and been their breaking point. *You gotta' change your stance then!* He could envision his father speaking as if replaying a home movie. *I'm not changing my stance!* He had yelled back defensively. *I haven't struck out in two years. I'm hittin' seeds -they're solid hard hits...they're just gettin' caught! They'll come around- they'll find the gaps.* Those were the last words that passed between the two of them. It had been a brief angry phone call. He couldn't stand it when they were together, but somehow the man's approval meant everything. He supposed Mom was right - they were too similar in personality. He was overbearing and argumentative. He thought he knew more about baseball than the people who played it. Dad was so proud that he was playing college ball that he was embarrassed by his enthusiasm.

At least he wasn't alone there. All the guys on the team seemed to have similar problems with their fathers. None of them realized that it was just a game in which the scale could tip so easily in the opposite direction. It had for him. His batting average was flailing, not because he wasn't seeing the ball, but because he couldn't find the gaps. Why was it that they would fight when together, but when they were apart he always missed him. And now he was gone. All those years of practice, clinics, camps and drills, and now he was gone. Dad would never see the end result of all his work, whatever it happened to be. He wouldn't be in college if it weren't for him. The man had sacrificed every summer vacation to get him to All Star games and tournaments. He had always bought the best catchers equipment even when he couldn't afford it. And he never missed a game. The single biggest influence in his life was no more. Who would help him now? Who would tell him he sucks, the words only driving him harder toward success, reverberating in his mind when he scooped the wild pitch, coming up to throw a rocket to second – and in a clearing cloud of dust, still managed to catch the runner. I do have heart! I do have what it takes! I do want it! As tears filled his eyes, he realized that his father's words were his driving force. It was his job to prove his father wrong - all the time knowing - his father knew it too. Mom was merely a mediator between the warring factions, always encouraging but not nearly the force of Dad. At the end of a bad game, she would smile and console him with…*Yeah, but you're still a nice guy.* Some help she was.

    Steve rolled off his bed and started to throw the ball in a sharp staccato rhythm against the cinder block wall of his dorm. His sorrow turned to restless raw anger as he blindly performed the drill that validated his barehanded quickness. Where was his brother anyway? He couldn't get through on the phone. He even tried the girlfriend's cell phone. What he saw in that ditz he didn't know. She'd get him into trouble somehow, that he was sure of. He tried the number for his brother again, throwing the ball as his dialed. The phone at Bob's apartment gave a monotone message that it had been disconnected.

As his anger increased, so did the pounding of the ball. A knock at the door interrupted him. "Yeah," he yelled, "What do you want?"

"Can you please stop throwing the ball against the wall. I can't study." The voice was weak, hesitant and unfamiliar.

Steve jumped off the bed and angrily threw open the door, grabbing the neck of the freckled faced kid and in a second pining him against the wall. "You don't want to screw with me – understand, frosh? It hasn't been a good day!"

The young boy struggled to speak, the toes of his sneakers barely finding the ground. "Please," his voice sounded girlish under Steve's crushing hand, "put me down. I don't want any trouble. It doesn't bother me that much."

He lowered the kid to the floor and released his grip. The liquid that had filled Steve's eyes trickled down his cheeks, and he carelessly brushed at it. He eyed the boy as if he were no more than an annoying fly. If anything, he should feel pity for the kid with his skinny stick figure body and eighth grade looks. He was probably one of those pathetic English majors, all pasty face and library like. Still, he needed to establish his authority in the dorm. "I should bitch slap you, you little prick. Don't mess with me again! Hear me?"

"Yeah," the boy replied, thankfully rubbing his neck. "I won't." He smoothed his shirt and picked his book off the floor. As the boy turned away, Steve noticed the title he was carrying under his arm.

"Hey! Wait a minute," he called out. The boy stopped and hesitated, wondering if he should run.

"I see you're taking calculus. Are you any good at it?"

"Yeah, I'm pretty good...I guess," the frosh answered still frozen in his tracks.

Steve smiled, putting his arm around him and leading the kid back to his room as if they were suddenly best friends. "I'll tell you what – what's your name, anyway?"

"Andrew...Andrew Seizman."

"Well…that's your first problem. No wonder you don't have a date on Saturday night!" He gave the kid a disapproving once over. "That - and that plaid thing you got goin' on there. You gotta' stop lettin' mommy buy your clothes!"

"Mom doesn't dress me." Andrew stammered, looking down at his shirt.

"Yeah, but don't worry, I have a solution. You help me and I'll help you. You don't have many friends here do ya?" Before the boy could answer, Steve continued, "I'm sure you don't or you wouldn't be in your room doing calculus. How about we make a little deal? You see, I have to go away this week, a family emergency. I'll be back on Friday night and I have a calc test the following Monday. You help me understand this crap so I can pass the test, and I might take you to a few parties."

The young man eyed Steve's thickly chiseled arms, knowing they were larger than his own thighs. He always envied athletes, simple things like friends, parties and girls seemed to come so easy. "O.K…I guess I can help you." He wasn't sure why he agreed, except that he was afraid to say no.

"You see, Drew… yeah, that works better," Steve nodded approvingly at the name change, "if this works out, I can hook you up with some fine lookin' women. But in return, I have to pass calculus or I don't play spring ball. If I don't play ball, well I get real mean. Got it?"

"Ah…I have a question though," Andrew started, "what happens if I tutor you and you still fail?"

"Then I bitch slap the hell out of ya and hang you in the girls bathroom by your underwear."

Andrew hesitated a moment, "That sounds fair…I guess."

"It's a deal then, and Drew, I mean it man, lose the K-mart shirts. You aren't in Kansas anymore."

"But, I'm from right here - not Kansas," Drew answered with naïve sincerity.

"Really?" Steve's mind started to see a further use for the young man. "So tell me Frosh, did mommy and daddy give you a car to go with those clothes?"

"Your brother really lives here?" Drew squinted from the early morning sunlight that broke over the dilapidated buildings. "I mean, there's a lot of broken glass."

Steve frowned, "Don't worry, I'll make your trip worth while - a real dump, isn't it? I call it *The Projects*. I just hope I can remember which apartment is his. It's been awhile."

"You gonna be all right walkin' around this place?" Drew eyed the junk cars and littered trash in front of the apartments.

Steve was humored by the kid's comment, "You gonna' protect me? Club 'em with your calculus book?" Steve chuckled out loud as he slid from the seat of the car, "Thanks for bringin' me, man, I'll be back before the weekend." He closed the door behind him, and watched Drew drive away.

He walked around the complex in search of his brother's beat up Subaru. It was the car that wouldn't die. Dad had always referred to it as the 'duct tape car'. It seemed to handle the mud and snow as well as a truck, but the body looked like it had gone through a meteor shower. At least it would be easy to spot. Steve found the car. The apartment door adjacent to it had been left wide open all night.

He entered without so much as a knock, wondering what he would find. His feet took the narrow stairs two steps at a time nearly tripping over an empty case of beer on the landing. "Damn!" He mumbled, stopping to rub his ankle. Several bottles tingled as they rolled, stopping at a sleeping body sprawled out across the floor. His eyes fell over the clothes, left over food, bottles and debris around the room, as he counted three sleeping bodies, two on the floor, one on the couch.

He walked past them all and threw open the bedroom door exploding into his brother's room. "Get up, moron!" he shouted, shaking the shrouded lump lying on the bare mattress. "I thought you were gettin' the phone turned back on! We got an emergency and I can't reach you!"

Bob groaned and rolled over to face him. He opened his eyes but the room was a blur except for the moving mouth in front of him. "What! What time is it?" He sat up and put his head in his hands. His brain was still pounding from last night's party. The music had blared until dawn and his roommate had brought friends back to the apartment to sleep it off.

The girl next to him rolled over, pulling all the covers over her head – exposing her bare feet at the bottom of the mattress.

Bob fell back on the bed still holding onto his temples. "How the hell did you get here?"

Steve pushed a box of pizza off the radiator so he could sit down. A fly lazily swirled above it. Trash was carelessly thrown all over the room. "I've been trying to reach you all night. Jesus…don't you have a phone anymore? How do you live like this?"

"It's being repaired." Bob was convinced that his little brother didn't need to know everything. "This better be good, so what do ya want?"

There was a brief hesitation then Steve's voice cracked in waves of raspy, breathless sobs that broke through his composure.

"Did something happen to Mom or Toby?" Bob's eyes widened and he walked over to the window. In all his life he had never heard his brother cry. He had always been the perfect image of pure testosterone.

"Dad…it's Dad…He had an accident yesterday…he's dead. Mrs. Alston called me last night. He fell off his horse or something. We've got to go home."

"But Mom," Bob continued, "Mom's all right then?"

"Mom's all right. She's at Alston's now. They wouldn't let me talk to her, said she was medicated and resting."

Bob breathed a sigh of relief. He wanted his brother to turn back into the jerk he was. He was easier to deal with that way. This scene was far too intense for him. "We'll go home," Bob said, "just give me some time to get things together."

"I'll wait outside," Steve answered, wiping his face with his hands, still trying to control his emotions, "I need some air." With that, he left the bedroom and made his way out the apartment to the Subaru.

Bob turned to the girl pretending to be a sleep. He knew she was listening to every word. He pulled the covers off her head.

"I've got to go," he started, "my Mom needs me right now. I don't know when I'll be back. It kinda' changes everything."

She ran her fingers through her short, blond hair and rubbed the smeared makeup under her eyes. She had a row of five eyebrow rings over her left eye that led to five more surrounding the contour of her ear.

"If you go with him, you're out of my life, jerk." She stated matter-of-factly. You think you can walk out on me and this apartment anytime you want?"

"It's not workin' out here anyway," he replied, as he tossed things into his backpack, "I didn't get very much for the computer stuff. I'll have just enough to make my portion of the rent this month. Then what am I goin' to do? I've got nothin' left to sell."

She yelled at him, "Here's a clue for ya! Try getting' a job like the rest of us!"

He brushed past her toward the bathroom, "Aren't we a snit this morning," he chided, brushing a lock of black hair out of his face with his fingers.

She followed him into the bathroom while he brushed his teeth, and whispered behind him, "I know where to get some money." He saw her in the mirror, her slender figure blocking the doorway, speaking with hesitation as she pulled on her jeans. She lowered her voice more, and her eyes darted in the direction of the living room. "I've a got a friend who needs some help…you know…getting rid of some stuff – you know..."

Bob pushed by her, grabbing his sweatshirt off the doorknob as he answered. "I'm not into that. So don't even ask."

"Why not? What's plan B? You already lost the phone, and you're ten days late on the rent again. O.K, so you finally got rent money – this month. My friend says your take on this job is fifteen hundred dollars."

She plopped down cross-legged on the mattress and strapped her heavy shoes to her feet, "You can pay a lot of bills with fifteen hundred dollars."

"I'm goin' home and I don't know when or if I'll be back." His mind was on his mother. She was the one person who was always there for him. Now he needed to be there for her.

The girl jumped up, her heavy shoes pounded on the floor. "Go ahead then, leave if it's what you want. But I'm doing it! And when I have the money, I'm done with you! You hear me? You can crawl back to your mommy and tell her why you weren't man enough to make it on your own!"

Bob ignored her words and grabbed his drawing pads and charcoals, cramming them into his backpack.

A second later the pounding of angry feet cascaded violently down the stairs. The front door slammed out the exclamation point of her anger.

Bob walked into the next room and threw money down on his roommate's bed. "This is my half of the rent. I'm outa' here. The phone bill is your problem. They were all your friend's calls anyway." The disheveled lump in the bed, groaned and cursed, then turned over drifting back to a narcotic sleep.

Bob looked around the near empty room. There was nothing else that he wanted from here. All the furniture had been trash picked and most of his clothes came from Goodwill or local thrifts. His turntables, stereo and computer had been sold to make his rent or buy food or gas. He walked down the stairs and out to his beat up car. His brother sat on the dented hood, waiting. One last look and Bob Winters said a silent goodbye to his once imagined life of freedom. He was finally going back home.

Bob tossed his belongings into the back seat, and yelled at his brother, "Get off my car!"

"Damn, it smells in here. How can you stand it? How can you stand this car?" Steve hooked his seatbelt and eyed the interior of the trash filled car.

"You can walk home, ya know." Bob pulled away from the curb and started toward the highway. He poked a tape into the cassette player and turned the music up to the loudest setting. His head rocked with the beat as he started to light a cigarette. "You got money for gas?"

Steve opened his book and handed ten dollars to his brother. "I thought you'd ask. Listen, I've got a big calculus test when I return next Monday. I've got to be ready, I have to pass or I won't make eligibility. Do you mind? I'd like to take a look at this while we drive."

"Listen to me, moron, it's my car and you got all week to study."

Steve angrily slammed the book and gazed out the window. He knew he wasn't going to get any studying done anyway, he just didn't want to have to talk to his brother. "You haven't changed a bit," he mumbled. He fought back the flood of emotion as he thought about his father. But after awhile the memories made his demeanor soften. "I'm glad you're goin' home. I almost thought that you wouldn't, ya know, come to Dad's funeral an' all."

"Don't kid yourself. I'm only doing it for Mom."

Steve glared at his brother, twisting sideways in the seat to face him. "You don't even care that Dad's dead, do you? You're probably happy about it! Now you can move back home and live rent-free. That's all you care about!"

Bob shot him a look and let the cigarette hang from his lips as he spoke. "I don't give a crap what you think, golden boy. I'm going home because Mom needs me. Dad couldn't wait 'till I was out of that house and he got his wish... he made it impossible for me to live there!"

"You're a dickhead, you know that? Look at you, with your big earrings and tattoos and homeboy clothes. You look like a drug addict...you look...messed up. You were the one with all the brains and it's the C student in the family who's goin' to college. I have to work my butt off to get C's. You should be here, not me, but no, you had to have an attitude. You had to get in Dad's face and give him grief. You had to be a rebel. You screwed yourself, so don't get all shitty with me because your life sucks!"

Bob chided him in a calm sarcastic tone. The hidden under layer of his resentment pierced the surface of his rebel appearance. "Do you think any school would have given you a second look if you couldn't play baseball? And that's the only reason you're here. No way...I stopped tryin' to live up to Dad's expectations a long time ago...it couldn't be done. I wasn't good enough no matter what I did or how much I tried - so screw it."

Steve shot back at him, his tone escalating, "So you like ghetto living, do ya? You like making five dollars an hour to lick someone's boots! Do you think it was easy being an athlete in that house? Dad gave up on you and concentrated on me! Every time I had a bad game, I had to hear the rehash and be reminded of every mistake I made for two weeks after. I had to make up for your lazy do nothing ass. He could be a jerk, but he did a lot of things for me too and he was usually right in the long run. His pushin' is probably the reason I'm in college right now."

"And the reason I'm not," Bob interrupted, "he didn't do jack for me. I don't need him, never did. I'm going home for Mom, so get that straight. We've got a long way home, so why not just shut up and let me drive."

The angry silence between them was replaced with throbbing music and the passing of endless sound barriers. Steve's gaze finally left the window, their sibling argument a forgotten explosion in history, like many before.

"Hey, do you remember when Mom and Dad went away overnight and I had that beer party my junior year? He walked into the garage and smelled where someone had spilled a little on the floor, and that's after I cleaned it up with bleach, it was like he knew something was up and he was lookin' for it."

A smile crept to Bob's lips. "Yeah, except Dad blamed me for that party, even though I didn't have anything to do with it. I told you they'd find out. I warned you. I thought Mom was going to have a heart attack. I've never heard her scream at anyone like that, like a witch with that high voice that grates right down your spinal cord. And Dad...after she pried his fingers off from around your neck, they grounded you for what - just about forever? How many people *were* in the house that night?"

"About seventy-five, and...well, yeah...a couple of months, but shit, the freakin' farm work I had to do was worse than being grounded." He mimicked his mother's higher pitched voice. "You need a fence put up? Steve's available. He'll do it for nothing and he'll start at 5:00am tomorrow." Steve laughed, "I think every neighbor cashed in on my punishment! But worse than that she ratted out just about every kid in Indian Mills. I thought I wasn't gonna have a friend left after that. I thought I was gonna go into school on that Monday and have my butt kicked by all the seniors. It would have been better if Dad just hit me, then it would have all been over, but Mom, jez...she holds a grudge and takes her time getting even."

They both started chuckling. It had been a long time since they laughed together and it seemed odd to both of them that those particular memories would pull them together.

"Yeah," Bob added, "and the more pissed off she got, the more Dad backed off and just watched like he was saying - see? These are the two buttholes you always standby and protect! They're YOUR sons, the boys who do no wrong! But you're right; you couldn't pull anything over on Dad. Mom was easy. She wanted to believe you were a good person. She wanted to believe that you would do the right thing, but Dad, it was like he could read your mind."

"No!" Steve laughed, "it was like he had done it all when he was a kid and he was just waitin' for us to screw up."

Traffic started to slow and Bob turned the car off the highway and into the town of Marlton. "Damn circle," he complained, "always a freakin' mess." They turned into the quaint town and headed toward Indian Mills. Only the locals used the road that paralleled the major highway, but still, it was more heavily traveled than Bob had remembered. The once scenic farmland, a landmark of this route, was nearly gone. It seemed to have been wiped away like a picture on a chalkboard. He hadn't been down this way since high school, and was appalled at the changes in two years time.

The open rows of planted fields that once seemed infinite on the landscape were permanently disfigured by ugly track homes on postage stamp lots. Occasionally, an old farmhouse was left in the middle of them, standing elegant, like a lone jewel surrounded by low class fakes. The sight disgusted and angered him as he drove the old route home. He recognized very little on it.

"Slow down," Steve said, "we're coming up on the new ball field everyone's been talking about. I've been wantin' to check it out."

"Good," Bob mumbled, "cause I've gotta' take a leak." He pulled the Subaru into the gravel parking lot of the recreational field. An entire crop field had been cleared to make way for the elaborate sports complex. It was an impressive display of lighted playing surfaces. All the sports, soccer, tennis, football and baseball were well represented with ample parking, sod infields and bleachers. A group of girls taking batting practice occupied a nearby softball field. Bob frowned and let out a heavy sigh, "another farm."

"What?" Steve was already focused on the young women playing softball.

Bob rolled his eyes, "I'm not gonna be long, Romeo."

"No problem, man, I think I'll check this out while you're in the john. Besides, I have to get my mind off things," Steve strode over to the girls.

As Bob made his way toward the restrooms, he felt a complete sense of loss that had little to do with his father. The emptiness nagged at him, resonating a deep and foreboding anger that began to swell within him like a hidden monster. There was something about this place. His eyes moved over the man made park, and a sense of longing overwhelmed him. It was progress, the evolution of change that he couldn't control, or so he tried to convince himself. Yet the urge to be alone, to follow the walking trails that beckoned at him was undeniable. As if this place were calling him, enticing him to explore and discover its secrets. He brushed the feeling off. It had to be nothing.

Steve approached the girls, and noticed a petite blond up to bat. Her hair was in a ponytail and she tugged at her baseball hat. She swung at the ball with all her collective might and missed.

"You're dippin' your back shoulder," he called nonchalantly, leaning against the backstop. "It's like choppin' wood, shoulders even, eye on the ball."

The girl smiled at him, but said nothing.

The red headed catcher recognized the young man's voice immediately, "Oh, great!" She tossed the ball back to the pitcher, "The Whore Master has returned."

The women broke into laughter, but Steve took it as the ultimate compliment and a wide grin spread across his face.

"What's up with you, Red?" he teased. "I'm just tryin' to help a fellow baseball player." He leaned against the pole of the backstop. He didn't know any of these girls by name, but he was sure they all recognized him. He could tell by the way they moved their hair over their shoulders and adjusted their posture. It was the perks of being a local jock.

"Why don't you do your pimpin' someplace else?" The red head chided him.

The pitcher threw again. This time it was outside and the catcher collapsed on the ball, keeping it in front of her.

"Good block, Red, but you could use a little work on your lateral movement."

She shot back without looking up, "And you could use a little work on your pickup lines."

He watched the young woman return to the crouch position behind the plate. He couldn't let her win in this little game of words. "Yeah, that's right," he whispered, "there's nothin' like a woman on her knees."

The catcher put her index finger against the inside of her thigh. It was a call for a pitch out. Usually it was in anticipation of the runner stealing, but she had other plans today. As soon as the ball made contact with her glove, she rose, spun and hurled it at Steve's head. He rolled behind the backstop just in time, feeling the air rush past him.

The women all exploded into laughter as Steve stuck his head out from behind the fence, "Jez, Red...you have a pretty decent throw."

Bob was walking back to the car when he saw the whole interaction play out. He stopped the ball with his foot and brought it over to the field. He tossed it casually back to the catcher. She pulled off her mask letting her curly red hair spill over her shoulders, and smiled at the man who had just joined them. Bob hardly looked at her, his eyes lowered apologetically, "Excuse my brother, he has a strange way with women."

Steve winked at the blonde.

As the two girls watched the young men walk back toward the parking lot, the blonde leaned in and whispered softly to her teammate, "Confident, isn't he, although he is kinda' cute. I think I may need to take some additional batting practice."

The catcher pursed her lips in disapproval, "The hell with him, wasn't that Bob? His brother?"

The blonde returned an invitation of a glance at Steve as the car pulled away, "Yeah, guess his brother's back. You stay away from him, Melissa. I hear the brother's trouble. And what's going on with those earrings of his?"

"They're called studs and unlike you, I go for a little more than a tight butt and a big…a big…bat!" Melissa started to giggle.

The blonde replied, "Yeah? Well I don't see you goin' for much of anything."

Melissa pulled her catcher's mask back over her helmet and resumed her position behind the plate. "Up to now there hasn't been much around here worth havin'," she mumbled.

Tate walked around the back of Mary's house and examined the broken window. His men searched for footprints and dusted for fingerprints. He went inside to face the waiting occupants. Glancing at the chaotic remains of the room, he directed his questions to Mary. "Do you know what's missing?" He had his pad and pen out ready to take notes.

"Nothing of real value," Mary uttered, still distraught and groggy from her ordeal. A break-in seemed small and meaningless in comparison to the horrible death of her husband that still churned inside her head. Still it was one more thing to add to her trauma, to throw her off balance.

"No jewelry, money, art, silver?"

"No one steals flat plate, our money exists only on paper, and the only jewelry of any value is on my finger." There was brief silence then she tempered her words, "My computer is still here and all our electronics. They didn't take anything as far as I can tell." She shuffled through some debris near the desk, pulling out her portable computer and placing it back on the table. She sighed heavily at the clothes, cushions and contents of drawers that were strewn around the room. The stereo components were tossed and broken on the floor, dressers were overturned in every room, but nothing appeared to be taken.

The detective acted concerned and paced slowly around the house watching the other officers dust for prints. "Someone was looking for something specific, or they were surprised during the burglary and just didn't get anything."

Mary interrupted him, "Look around you. This is a quiet place, no neighbors for acres. The most excitement we get out here is an occasional loose cow. It doesn't make any sense." She sat down and rubbed her temples as if to ease some imagined headache. This was one more problem she didn't need right now. The intense fatigue was returning and she wanted to lie down- to pretend it was all a dream.

Bob came over and put his arm around her. "Don't worry Mom, we'll get a security system or something and you'll feel safer." Bob's features resembled his mothers. His dark hair and tanned skin combined with his large brown eyes revealed handsome good looks that were marred only by his numerous body piercing. The worst of which was his bizarre earrings. They stretched his earlobes like those seen in some foreign culture on the cover of National Geographic. It was another way out trend of skateboarders and ravers in the inner city. It was a look at home with freakishly wide pants, sloped shoulders, of little ambition and drug use, pure in-your-face anti-establishment. He did everything in defiance of his father. Mary wrote this off as the growing pains of youth, and justified it to Mark by pointing out the long hair hippie look of their generation. But Mark had been brutal about Bob's image and how it reflected on the family. His relentless disapproval of Bob's lifestyle and friends had grown from legitimate concerns, but it had driven the boy out on his own and to some minimum wage job for survival. Their house had been a war zone when he lived at home and was the core of every argument Mark and Mary had.

Bob had moved out the day after high school graduation, leaving only a pile of trash in the middle of his bedroom floor. Mary suspected that he had sold most of his belongings to support himself. She had helped sign him up for college, but he dropped out after a few weeks. A rumor had surfaced that he had lost his job, but he never indicated so in his conversations with her. She suspected casual drug use and wanted to talk to him about it, but never saw any physical signs or evidence, so the conversation went mute.

He didn't need one more lecture. She was not going to push him away like Mark.

Still her suspicion of his lifestyle made her conscious of his behavior. She could only hope to guide him at this age, and it was her hope that he would seek out a more stable life as he matured. She consoled her fears by noting that Bob was always the first one there in a time of family crisis or concern. He had a deep understanding and intuition about people way beyond his years. And beneath the brazen exterior of his strange teenage culture, he was a close friend, and a gentle person. She and her son were united by their feelings of isolation, and she felt the pain he had grown cold to accept. She was certain that the values she and Mark had instilled in him would surface when he was ready to become a man. She hugged him, "I feel better having you home."

"Mrs. Winters," the detective sat down across from her, "exactly what kind of work did your husband do?"

"He was a heavy equipment operator for the Union. He ran all kinds of equipment."

Steve entered the room like a hurricane. His physical presence commanded attention. "Nothing missing in my room. But then, most of my stuff is at school." His compact, densely muscular figure and sandy blond hair were a sharp contrast to Bob's thin, darker and more subdued stature. He strode over and gave his mother a hug sitting on the other side of her. Together the boys sat like pillars on either side of her.

"Do you want me to get you anything, Mom?" His eyes were red and swollen. He and his father were very close. Although they argued intensely and often, it seemed that they were two of a kind in mannerisms, drive and temperament.

She shook her head and squeezed both of her son's hands, "I'm O.K."

"I'll need the name of his supervisor," the detective continued, undeterred.

"That would be the hall," she added, "He would report to whoever was running a particular job, but ultimately he answered to the Union Hall where he is sent from." She rose from her chair to get her address book and gave the officer the information.

"Was your husband doing any non-union activities, or did he mention any problems or arguments with anyone?"

She frowned at his remark. "My husband never worked non-union. He was no scab. And as far as arguments, they came and went with various people. They weren't important to him." She put the address book away and turned to face him. "He was a man that said what he meant. There wasn't any misunderstanding about what he expected from people, even if the discussions were...well, loud."

"Another thing. Have you had a vet out to examine the horse?" He was tapping the pen against the pad. "If so, we'll need a full report to try to piece together the incident. His injuries may help to unravel this. Don't put the horse down until we have a report."

A wave of anger swept over her. It was something that hadn't even crossed her mind. She answered curtly, "What makes you think I'm going to put the animal down? It wasn't the horse that killed him. Someone did this deliberately. Mark had that horse for six years and never had a bit of trouble with him."

"Mrs. Winters," the detective started, "your husband died from a massive crush injury to his chest." He straightened his back as if to add the power of additional height to the conversation. "Yes, there was a puncture wound, still that alone could have been repaired had he gotten to a hospital in time. We'll know more from the coroners report, but you work in a hospital, you know that it was the horse that ultimately killed him."

She stared blankly at his easy, scientific explanation, then answered in a cold professional tone, "Listen Detective, I've worked in the ER for seventeen years and I've never seen anything like that before. I can't get the image of his face out of my mind. "Let me ask you something," She started to walk him to the door as she spoke, a physical indication that she was ending the discussion. "How did he get a blow to the forehead, but there was no dirt in or around that wound? How can that happen? I keep seeing it, over and over again – there was no dirt. That didn't happen from a fall or from being dragged! Butch may have crushed him in the panic, but something else provoked the incident and WHOEVER made sure they finished it." She held the door open ushering the men out, then let it slam after them. She turned away and mumbled, "dickheads…"

The two boys exchanged glances with a smile reveling in their mother's choice of words.

John MacIntosh was called Apple for short. He was a small stocky man whose ties always appeared too short for his build. He was a local boy and Tate relied on his community contacts and knowledge of the area. Apple looked at his watch, then spoke in a low voice to his partner, "So what do you think? Is it still the easiest answer? Hunting accident?"

Tate tapped his pen on his pad, "It could be several things," he started. "Number one; the husband dies in a hunting accident and the break in is coincidental. Number two; the husband is deliberately killed and the break in is for a specific purpose of finding whatever is worth killing for. Number three; someone arranged the break in to throw us off track."

Apple picked up a cigarette butt near the driveway, and put it into a plastic bag, "What do you mean 'throw us off'. Do you think it was the wife?"

"There is too much coincidence here and the wife had motive and opportunity at the trial grounds. After all, farms aren't cheap to keep; there might be a big settlement here. And let's check out 'skater boys alibi'. He's pretty scary, and looks like he has some father issues. The other one's been at school, so his attendance should be easy to verify. Then we'll check out the job site and his co-workers and club members. I doubt there's a union connection, still even if it's a dead end we might get some insight into his friends and some information we can use. You can't rule anything out right now. The coroner's report will tell us more. For now, we assume it's an accident." He turned to his partner, "If nothing else – at least we're off the disappearing sheep case for awhile."

Apple grinned, "Pressure startin' to get to ya?"

The two men laughed.

No one spoke as Mary and her sons started the task of cleaning up. Each item held a renewed power that sucked the three of them into their personal recollections like a private black hole.

Mary's head was pounding again and the detective's words whirled around her aching brain. She glanced over at Steve who was staring at a family portrait, the tears flowing off his face and dripping onto his tee shirt as if he had no knowledge of their presence. Bob had a far more stoic appearance. He slowly returned the picture of himself and his Dad to its rightful place on the shelf. It was the picture of them both posing in front of his first car

She stared down at the family photo. *It was the horse that killed your husband, Mrs. Winters*, she heard the detective say over and over again in her head. She picked up a frozen image of her and Mark riding. Pictures of the boys holding baseball bats over their shoulders with a proud father standing behind them. There were so many recollections with each captured moment, smiling parents with sons wearing tuxedos and young women on their arms, Christmas, New Years, camping and birthdays, all gone… all just memories of the past. She ran her finger over the image of Mark kneeling with a ribbon in his hand. Toby seated happily in front of him. It would be for the last time. Her mind shot question after question to herself. What would Mark do if it this had happened to her? Could she really trust that animal again with anyone? What if the animal were to end up belonging to a child? Could she live with that on her conscience? The grief and anger and utter exhaustion from the last thirty-six hours pushed her steadily toward her breaking point. Hot tears rolled down her cheeks and blurred her vision. She made up her mind and knew what needed to be done.

It only took a second to find the key behind the freezer. She walked out to the garage, kicked a bucket out of the way and pulled the blanket off the tall black gun safe. She fumbled with the door pulling out the ten-gauge shotgun and reaching for the slugs. Her trembling hand pushed two into the chamber. The back door slammed as she headed for the barn.

Both boys jumped at the ring of the phone, but Bob grabbed it first. It was a recording from the local library. The mechanical monotone voice spoke, *The reference material you have requested is available at the reference desk until Oct..."* Bob rolled his eyes and turned to hang up the receiver. A glimpse in the direction of the kitchen window brought his attention to the figure walking with purpose toward the barn. "Hey, what's Mom doing with the ..." The realization came so fast that the sentence went unfinished. He ran out the door, stumbling down the access road toward the barn yelling, "Mom! Don't do it! Mom!" He was out of breath by the time he turned the corner of the first paddock. "Mom! Dad loved that horse, Mom! Don't do it! Dad loved that horse, Mom!"

A single shot rang out and he heard the horse snort in terror, the sound echoed throughout the large metal building.

He reached the barn door gasping for breath. Butch was still standing, but his mother was not. She was on her knees crying, the gun at rest in front of her on the ground.

"Mom it's O.K," he whispered, moving the shotgun away from her. He wrapped his arms around his mother. "It's gonna be O.K, Mom. Butch didn't do it on purpose. Dad loved him. He wouldn't want you to put him down." He felt her pain pulling at his soul and it brought tears to his eyes. He hadn't allowed himself to feel anything since he heard the news of his father's death. The years of angry words between them had cultivated a disrespect that had made him tough. But to watch his mother tormented like this was more than he could stand. He had to help her get through this. She always believed in him.

"I couldn't do it...I just couldn't do it...it would be like killing the last part of him," she moaned.

Bob's eyes drifted upward and found the gapping hole now cascading a single stream of light through the metal roof. It was something he would have to learn how to fix if he planned to live at home.

Melissa Peterson dusted the dirt from her hands as she threw the large bag of catcher's gear on the floor of the garage. She unlaced her cleats and walked into the kitchen where she washed her hands and then set the table. Uncle Joe and Ethan had always eaten in front of the TV before she came to live with them. They seemed content to buy a McDonald's happy meal and call it dinner. But she wouldn't have any of that. It was the very least she could do for Uncle Joe. He was a good person. When his troubled grandson, Ethan, got thrown out on the street, Joe took him in and put him to work on the farm. Uncle Joe's motto was always that farm work could solve anything, and it had certainly worked for Ethan. He was actually gaining respect in the community for his wide variety of skills, especially when it came to horses.

These two men were the only family she had left. After her mother died, Joe had offered his home to her without a second of hesitation. It was supposed to be just until the school year was over and her Dad could take her in. But looking back, she was sure Uncle Joe knew that was never going to happen. She pulled out the raw meatloaf she had made the night before and put it into the oven with a couple of baked potatoes. Dinner would be ready in an hour.

She mounted the creaky stairs to her bedroom. Her room didn't look like a young woman's bedroom. There were no pink curtains or smiling stuffed animals. No frilly bed ruffles or perfume bottles. It looked like the bunkhouse for a transient farm worker. One tall chest of drawers, one single bed with a plain brown blanket, and one old desk sitting by the window. The room had dark plank floors, and the only hint of color was a worn out braided rug in the center. It was clean and neat. She closed her door and pulled a suitcase out from under her bed. She crossed her legs in front of her and unlocked the side latches. It held her treasures, the items that meant something. She refused to unpack them because living with Uncle Joe was supposed to be a temporary arrangement. Now it looked as if it be her home until she finished college. Still it didn't feel right. It didn't feel like home. She picked up a picture of her mother and ran her fingers lovingly across the face of the image. This was the way she wanted to remember her, laughing and gentle, before the cancer racked her body and took her life. She had learned a lot during the bad days, how to cook, balance a checkbook, and how to push morphine through an IV. She straightened the faded 4H ribbons and carefully handled the trophies from her barrel racing wins, as if she could relive every event, every brief moment of youthful glory, by touching a bit of the past. Sometimes she needed to remind herself of the sadness, to appreciate how far she's come.

 She opened a journal and thumbed through the entries. She would never forget that day, that one incident in her life that altered everyday since. She bent back the page and read the entry again, seeing the horror of the day unfold in all its vivid detail.

 June 2nd^t: I thought when my parents divorced; it was the worse day of my life. I thought that when Mom died, it was the worse day of my life. I thought when Dad said he and his new wife just couldn't take me in - that was the worse day of my life. But I was wrong. Today was the worst. I was walking down the east wing to science class when I heard two girls behind me say: she's wearing the same pants again,- and then they laughed. Sometimes I feel like everyone is laughing at me. No one knows anything about my life and I don't want them to know. Sometimes, I feel that they would just use my pain as a weapon to bludgeon me with. So I keep quiet and stay to myself. I walked past a bunch of jocks standing in the hallway. There was no way around them and they blocked my way to get to class. One boy cleared his throat as I walked by, and that's when it happened- he spit on me- right there in the hallway! All the jocks started laughing. I wanted to die! What did I ever do to them? I ran into the girl's room to get away. I didn't want them to see me cry. I wanted to run away from school, run away from this town, and just go somewhere and never come back. But a boy came right into the girl's room after me. He said he saw what happened and those guys were a bunch of idiots. He showed me a broken water pistol and said that the kid didn't spit on me, that he was doing that all morning – acting like he was going to spit, but squirting girls with the pistol. All the time he was trying to calm me down, I was sobbing like a crazy person - out of control. I felt stupid, but I still couldn't stop crying. I know I wasn't making any sense, but I spilled my guts to this boy. I told him that I didn't want to live anymore; I wanted to leave and never come back. Life wasn't worth this kind of pain. When I finally stopped ranting and looked up at him, I realized he knew what I felt like. It was in his eyes- a kind of deep sorrow, an emptiness that I just can't explain. He then put his hands on my shoulders and said that he had been there - that dying, leaving school, or running away - it was like letting them win. That I had to get to a place in my life where I didn't care what people thought anymore – but don't let them win. Never let them get their way. He said that's what they want. He stayed with me in the girl's room until after the sixth period bell. When he finally left, he said that guy wouldn't be bothering me ever again.

June 5th. I needed the weekend to think things through. I got all my crying done and I'm so dehydrated that I don't have any tears left. I'm just angry now. That boy was right. I wasn't going to let them win. I came into school today with *an attitude. I told myself that I just have to get through one more year of high school and then I'm on my own. I saw those two girls hanging out by my locker. They stood back and gave me the once over with their eyes. I glared at the both of them, and asked if they had something they wanted to say to my face, instead of behind my back. They just said no and walked away whispering. They're a couple of princesses.*

I looked for that boy today. I wanted to let him know I was all right. But all I could find out is that he was expelled from school for breaking a kids hand in the science wing on Friday. Bob Winters is a strange kind of white knight. But I need to find a way to thank him, to do for him what he did for me.

Melissa closed the book as a tear rolled down her cheek. It was a painful reminder of the girl she used to be – a doormat at the entrance of life. One young man, at one important moment, had made her realize that she couldn't let life stomp on her without an argument. He hadn't even recognized her today, but then, she wasn't that meek little red-eyed, blubbering wallflower anymore. And now that he's back - maybe, she could find a way to thank him for stepping up and caring that day.

Chapter Four

"The *Mistress of Death* returning your call," Apple said, as he offered up the phone from beneath his stack of paperwork.

Tate grabbed it, then leaned back in his chair placing his feet up on the desk. "So Angie...what's the verdict?"

"Dr. Simone to you, Nathaniel," replied the throaty female voice on the other end of the line. Her Louisiana dialect was deep, lusty and deliberate. A grin crept across Tate's face as he imagined her red lips parting soft creases in her black satin skin.

Angolina was spellbinding, by far the most beautiful black woman he had ever encountered. She carefully accentuated her robust figure with tailored clothes that measured the seduction of the male species. She had a way of taunting him as she spoke, using her red lips as her weapon, never fully closing them as she formed her words, but always keeping them slightly parted, like an invitation to an affair. She was pure sensuality and it seemed to him that her attraction was as potent as witchcraft. She was a distraction that he tried to avoid but could not deny. The pull of this woman's spirit was too strong. It confused him and yet exhilarated him.

"Well Nathaniel, from the description of the accident and the evidence at the crime scene, coupled with what I've seen in the autopsy, looks like you got a homicide. This guy was hit over the head after he was dead. Guess the perp wanted to make sure he was a goner."

"How can you know it wasn't part of the horse accident?" Tate asked, almost smelling the lilac scent that accompanied her presence.

"You doubtin' me, darlin'?" Her voice was pleasantly sarcastic. "Well here's how. Minimal amount of blood flow from the head wound, no swelling, his heart had already stopped. The projectile that entered under the clavicle near the heart, well, there is none. It looks like the perp retrieved the object from the body and used a rather crude instrument when he did it. There's a lot of tissue damage around the point of entry and no gun powder residue."

Tate adjusted himself in his chair. "Wait a minute. How do you know that he wasn't just stabbed while he was down on the ground?"

"Guess I got to get all technical with you, sweetie." The words rolled off her tongue and he could imagine those parting lips. "It's what we call vascular physics. Now pay attention. I can say with certainty that the projectile was first… normal spray type pattern from the severed brachial artery. Then came the fifteen-hundred pound body slam to the dirt, multiple ribs, sternum and vertebra fractures…all the rest of the internal damage that goes with pulling an animal that size down on top of you. Kinda' like squashin' a big bug. Then we have the dragging injury to the back of the head, and the final blunt trauma to the frontal bone. The retrieval of the murder weapon was a relatively bloodless scooping motion in the wound after the heart had stopped, same with the final head wound."

Tate tried to counter with reason. "C'mon Angie, the man had a horse land on him and was dragged sixty-three feet for Christ's sake. Who knows what his head hit on the way."

"Hate to blow your theory darlin', but Mr. Winter's body's tellin' a different story. The projectile was probably an arrow, crossbow or compound. Based on the angle of the wound, he was shot from ground level and at relatively close range. The victim's hands indicate that he was pullin' on the reins with enough force to cut through his skin but no defensive injuries on the arms. The dragging injury to the head, the crush injury to the chest, the compound fractures to the leg… all consistent with your interpretation of the riding accident and the crime scene. But the whack on the head post mortem and retrieval of the projectile – well ya can't get more deliberate than that."

"What kind of weapon should we be lookin' for in conjunction with the head wound?"

"I'd say a rough axe shape with irregular edges, maybe even a jagged rock." There was a brief silence and he could feel her smile parting her face as she continued, "So are you done getting' stupid on me, darlin'? I've sent tissue samples from the chest to the lab to see if they can come up with anything microscopic. So Nate...I think we should celebrate. We've got us a real homicide in farm town."

Mary took a leave of absence from work. The staff would have to do without her for a few weeks. The department would barely survive, but she couldn't make it her problem. She had enough of her own. The hospital had cut back staff to almost critical levels in an attempt to cut costs. Radiology generated the largest revenue in the hospital budget, and between outpatient and inpatient tests, the equipment was run twenty-four hours a day. To make up for the loss of manpower, staff technologists were expected to work double shifts to cover the hours. It never made any real sense to those working in the trenches. The suits in the administrative offices cut back on the people who took care of the patients, but then would tell the public that care wasn't sacrificed. It made for good P.R., but just wasn't the truth. People could only work so fast and hard, until you crossed the line to just plain sloppy.

She watched a tremor pass through her hands and recognized that she was struggling with depression every moment of the day. There were questions looming over her every thought as she forced herself forward with bland reactions and meaningless gestures. On some level she needed to remove the visual reminders from her life, like Mark's clothes and shoes. On another, she needed to nurture the pain, each item at a time, just to make certain she was still alive without him. The daily reminders of losing Mark and the highs and lows of their life together tortured her with every remembered moment, every object that had ever graced his hand.

She glanced out the window to see if the car was still parked down and across the street - as if awaiting the movement of its prey. It was beginning to be a habit with her. She knew the police were watching and her daily routine was under constant scrutiny. In all of this, one highlight helped diminish all her sorrow and despair. She had her son back, and a second chance to help him get his life in order. It was a bizarre opportunity to have Bob home, to jumpstart his life. She had to focus on him in order to pull herself forward.

She forced herself to continue packing Mark's clothes. She found the old green leisure suit he had worn twenty-two years ago hidden in the very back of the closet. She smiled lovingly, remembering the first time he wore it. For a moment she saw him, young and handsome, leaning against his new custom van with the fancy airbrush paint job. That van was something. It was fully equipped as a camper and they had spent many a night parked in the old apple orchard confirming their love for one another.

Their relationship had happened quickly, but they were ready for a life together. She knew he was the one on the second date. He knew she was the one on the first. They were married six months later and delivered Bob one year after that. She had no regrets about her choices even though they were young. It was funny how kids and mortgages and the day-to-day grind of life seemed to drain the wanton desire out of a marriage and replace it with a comfortable familiarity that was complete and real. And now that the boys were grown and out of the house, they had rediscovered themselves as a couple, and it had been good…just like in the beginning.

Training their dogs and being in the outdoors had given them a unity and an outlet from their routine. It brought them together even through the turmoil of raising two headstrong young men. They enjoyed each other's company more than ever and the years had been good to them both. Their petty arguments over the course of their children's lives and upbringing seemed to fuel their passion, instead of diminish it. Mark was a good man. He adored his family.

She stared at the suit. How many times had she thrown it out only to have Mark retrieve it from the trash and hide it in the back of the closet. She guessed that he was either holding onto the past, or waiting for the return of a time he loved - a simpler time. She held the suit up to her face and breathed in the soft lingering odor of Brut. She cried into the material and wondered if the aftershave ever had a half-life.

The line for the viewing extended around the corner of the building and down the street. Tate sat in his car and watched the solemn procession of acquaintances wait quietly in line, only to hurry back to their cars when their mission was complete. It fascinated him how uncomfortable people were with death. It wasn't that they didn't want to pay respects to those who had passed; it was the frontal assault of facing the inevitable – as if denial could make it very distant from reality. He pondered this thought with a Wawa coffee in his hand, more for the warmth it gave than for the flavor. It had been years since he was on a stakeout and he was exhilarated by this new puzzle of a murder. He had never seen so many people attend a closed casket before. He figured that the gaping head wound the victim had sustained influenced that decision. Still, hundreds of people lined up to pay their last respects to the family. It was an indication of Mark Winter's popularity as a person and member of the community. Tate watched as Apple worked behind the building writing down the license plate numbers of the attendees for future interview purposes. Murders were rare in this small town, and no detail was going to be overlooked.

His attention turned from the line to a figure coming out the side door of the funeral home. He recognized the person as Mary. He watched as she removed her jacket and pushed a tissue to her eyes, her friend, Susan, followed behind her. It was a cold night and he could see their breath in the air as they spoke.

Mary was dressed in a tailored black dress that was conservative in cut and style, but seductive by virtue of its fit. She looked quite different from the night of the accident or the day of the break-in. Her athletic build didn't resemble a woman in her forties, and she carried herself with a certainty that disturbed him. Her black hair was curled and fell in soft dark waves to her shoulders, and he could imagine her being as comfortable with a glass of champagne as with a can of beer. This was a woman of contradiction and now his first and foremost suspect. Maybe she was the type to take a lover, but was she the type to kill or arrange to have her husband killed?

Susan gave her a hug on the steps and was obviously trying to comfort her friend. She handed Mary another tissue and the two of them leaned against the wall of the building, talking. Mary lifted her head toward the sky and closed her eyes. When she opened them, her gaze trailed to Tate's car and her eyes pierced through him with an intensity that made him straighten in his seat. She looked away with disgust and a moment later the two women went back inside. Tate consoled himself with his belief that nothing was very complicated when it came to murder. It always came down to sex or money, and he was determined to find out what killed Mark Winters.

Sometimes you need to let go of the world and succumb to the soothing rhythm of motion, the soft beat of hooves, the smell of damp earth, the sun on your face…the sensation of flying.

Mary rode Shortstop out the back of the barn and down a narrow trail into the woods. Butch neighed from his stall in an echo of protest. He didn't like to be left behind.

The leaves whirled and floated down in front of them like soft rain, the shadows dancing in time with the rustling of the breeze and the crescendo of the wind. She knew the woods spoke a language unto itself. The dry autumn chatter of the tall oaks and the siren's whisper of the short awkward pines seemed to lure her to its solitude and protection. It pulled at her soul and begged her to come back with an urgency she couldn't understand.

Mary Evans had been an adopted baby. The doctors had suspected that she was of Native American ethnicity but all she would ever know of her past was that she was a Jane Doe abandoned at a hospital in Oklahoma. Her adoptive parents took her from Oklahoma, moved to New York and then to the town of Indian Mills when she was very small. As a couple, the Evans' gave her all the love and support she could ever want, but they couldn't make her fit in with the rest of the children. Childhood had been difficult. It was obvious to her schoolmates that she was an afterthought to a childless older couple, and her teenage classmates used that knowledge like a sword. Her dark bronze skin and deep black hair didn't fit with the aging couple of Irish heritage and fine European traits.

She loved Marion and Tom Evans. Her mother had a way of turning petty childhood disputes into major lessons in life. She heard her mother's words resound in her head, *anger and sadness are good things, child. They serve an important purpose. These feelings build up inside of you and force you to make changes that affect your happiness. Use them to recognize the changes you need to make.*

At the time it seemed like gibberish...but now it was perfectly clear. She wondered what words her mother would have used today. She longed for the smell of peach pie and the soft fleshy hug of unwavering acceptance. She wished her own boys could have known the two people who opened their lives to her, but both had passed before Bob was born. The Evans had given her the ultimate gift, offering a full life filled with opportunity and education - and all this to an orphan child, who was left by the roadside - discarded by her own blood.

She breathed in the cold pungent air. She had felt this connection with the woods since her youth when she used to pretend among the quiet of the pines. She would fight hostile enemies, climbing into makeshift forts hammered into the highest trees. She could look out for what seemed like miles. When adolescence became lonely, she found herself sitting for hours in the tree house, built from left over plywood and two by fours. There she could imagine herself someday as beautiful and smart, and revel in how gracious she would be to the ones who shunned her.

Riding helped her put everything in perspective and lifted the weight of her fatigue. It reminded her of a time when she could run and hide from problems and return renewed, with a perspective like her mother's, certain that all this emotion would pass and the future could be changed by simply wishing for it. She survived her outcast childhood by holding on to that promise and never looking back.

Nature had a lesson to teach her and it was as clear now as then. This was a place where death always gave way to new life. Where the decomposing tree helped fertilize the growing seedlings next to it. Where the autumn leaves were a patchwork quilt of mulch and protection from the winter cold of the barren tree. It was a place that absorbed and celebrated it's dead by reducing them to the elements essential to the renewal of life. Animals didn't fear or mourn. When it was time to die they accepted their passing as a willing duty to nature, and found a quiet place to let it take them. It was a message that was humbling to those that listened; especially those connected to the land. She felt this connection resonate within her. It underscored her heritage - and she knew it must be true, as the rules of nature made her feel small and insignificant in relation to its power.

The trail opened to a large field of tall gangly grass with a glistening reservoir in the middle. The breeze took Shortstops mane and tail, gracefully toying with it like silken thread in a child's hand. He turned his head slightly as if knowing he had reached his destination. She dismounted, reached into the brown mesh bird bag and placed a gray homing pigeon safely in the brush. Then they took the long route back to the barn to get Toby. She knew he would be waiting in the same spot as always, sitting patiently anticipating her return and ready to play.

He sat at the end of the barn, ears forward and alert, knowing full well the exercise before him. Once released, the dog ran ahead through the woods understanding the purpose of his existence and the rewards of pleasing his master. His muscular body stretched with each lengthy stride. The narrow trails led to the open field and Toby scoured the edge of the high brown grass and came to a rigid halt at the edge of the brush. It had taken Toby far less time to find the bird than it had taken to hide it. She dismounted and unsnapped her blank gun from her holster. Toby eyed her movements from the side, but stood very still. Every muscle of his body was tight with anticipation.

Her foot swept the brush and the gray pigeon flew upward into the blue sky. She fired her blank gun and knelt down stroking him affectionately. They watched the bird float effortlessly in the air above them, moving in larger and larger widening circles, finally heading home in the direction of the coop. Toby loved his practice bird work, and treated these exercises as if they were an elaborate game of hide and seek. It was as primary a task as retrieving a stick, throwing a frisbee, or chasing a ball would be to a normal house pet. Only this was what the dog was born to do, not just some meaningless exercise created for man's amusement. The pigeons worked well for this purpose and would simply fly back home to the safety of the coop after a session.

In the distance, Bob's voice echoed through the woods and Toby's ears perked and flopped forward attentively as he listened to the sound of his name. He looked up at her and turned his head slightly, as if asking to leave.

"Go ahead, boy, go home." The dog lunged forward and bolted down the path disappearing into the trees. When Bob was home, they were an inseparable pair. The boy did have a way with animals.

Her dog work done, she remounted and rode deeper into the woods enjoying the gusts of wind that waved the last colors of autumn like clothes out on the line; wishing the trail would never end. The sun stretched long shadows across the sandy earth and the smell of dampness was welcome to her senses. They turned by the old abandoned car, a rusted skeleton that was the summer home of groundhogs and bees. The windows were all broken and the seats torn out, and now trees were growing through the gaping holes in the floorboards. A left turn would have taken them toward the state forest. It was easy to get lost in the Pine Barrens. The old abandoned car was as good as a sign and she turned right towards the town. They traveled behind some of the neighbor's farms, eventually coming out to a cracked asphalt road. There were very few cars during the day and the surrounding farms boasted grazing horses and livestock who raised their heads from the deep green carpet as they passed.

 She saw Old Joe out in the field and he waved her over to talk. He was trying to coax a large black stallion into a bridle. The stallion was young and sleek with proud conformation, its body shimmered like black silk, and its forelock hung like twisted rope, dancing lazily over its eyes.

 "Ya beast!" Joe held the bridle in his hands. It was obvious that with each approach the old man made, the magnificent animal took off prancing and playing almost mocking him. It was a game that the horse was winning, but it seemed to Mary that Old Joe wasn't really trying that hard.

 He was happy for the distraction. "Sorry about your man." He squinted up at her. The lines of age at the corners of his eyes seemed to travel down to his chin with each facial expression. He spit some tobacco onto the ground and lifted his hat to scratch his hairless head. His hat sported the phrase; *Bite Me.* It brought a smile to Mary's lips as she watched the man tug at his sagging work pants.

 No one was really sure how old, "Old Joe Peterson" really was. He was born at home some eighty or better years ago and always said he didn't have a birth record. His words were short and pointed, but he was a man who said what he thought and did what he said. His gruff exterior was offensive to many, but Mary knew this was as sincere as it got with Old Joe, and she accepted his greeting with understanding.

"Damn beasts," he nodded toward the animal who was now tossing his head and kicking up his heels with playful delight, "you gonna put the big walker down?"

"Don't know yet, Joe." She leaned forward and rested her arms on the saddle. She had already made up her mind to give Butch a second chance and label it a freak accident. What she hadn't decided was if she was going to ride him herself or send him to a professional trainer to evaluate. She continued with hardly a break, "I'm not convinced that the horse was the only problem, so the investigation is still going on."

"Yeah, I know. Some fellers stopped here yesterday askin' a bunch of questions about what I knew about ya. Then another two fellers stopped this morning. When I told'em I already spoke to the police, they said they were FBI, FDA...damn if I don't remember...EPA, DEP ...bunch of assholes if you ask me. Anything to screw us farmers." He spat again, this time angrily, clearly agitated with his insolent memory loss. He leaned his short stocky figure against the fence scraping something off the bottom of his boot and onto the lowest plank. "I didn't tell'em nothin'. None of their damn business, if you ask me."

"Thanks, I appreciate that." She knew he had nothing to tell them anyway, except for what car she drove and what animals she kept. Their relationship was based on farm unity and was no more personal than an occasional wave from the road. It occurred to her that this was the most Joe had ever said to her in one conversation. "Us folk have to stick together, Joe." She tried to smile, but the paranoia over being watched created a hollow feeling that swelled inside of her as the weight of worry clouded her mind. Why would the FBI or whoever else be interested unless there was more to this than she could understand? She decided to change the subject, figuring Old Joe was probably confused. "So...how you doing with him?" Her eyes were back on the stallion, "gonna geld him?"

"Oh, he's a crazy bastard, he is." Joe took off his hat and scratched his head again. "Even my grandson can't stay on him. Like a buckin' bronc." He looked up at her, the lines on his face connected again. "Got spirit though. Some dumb lawyer bought him for his kid. Do you believe that? More money than brains, I reckon. He's a beauty, but my god...for a kid? Anyway, the first time the kid gets thrown, he tells the trainer to shoot 'em." He leaned in to whisper as if anyone were close enough to hear, "Now the trainer knows better, so I picked him up for a song at auction. I'll get him broke. Then I'll sell him for what he's worth. I figure around twenty grand." A smile curled the ends of his mouth up. "Feelin' lucky?" His face went serious as he realized the insensitivity of his remark in the wake of her husband's accident. "Sorry...I didn't mean that...er...with your husband and all."

Mary chose to ignore the comment. "So Ethan can't tame him for you?" Old Joe's grandson was well known for his way with horses, and stories of his adventures were beginning to take on legendary proportions. It was once suspected that he rode through the town at night terrorizing the local kids.

Joe patted Shortstop on the neck. "Ethan's havin' his trouble with 'em. The kid likes a challenge though. You got a nice old horse here, but you look too big on him. You need something a little taller, a little prouder - a little more feisty." He spat on the ground again as if punctuating his sentence.

She laughed trying to put the old man back at ease again, "You know me, Joe, don't care if I look too big on him. I'm a one-horse woman. You can keep feisty here."

He smiled, and started to cough. "Heard a gun shot at your place the other day. Glad to hear ya didn't put 'em down. If you need anything..." He turned away from her letting his voice trail as he started back toward the barn.

She marveled at the way he could end a conversation. "Hey, Joe," she called to him, "Thanks."
Joe didn't turn around, but put up his hand as if to wave as he walked away.

She started back through the woods thinking about her future and what it could possibly hold. She loved this little town and loved this life. She couldn't imagine living in a different place.

Indian Mills was a small friendly town where people minded their own business until there was trouble - then banded together like family. Primarily rural, it was dotted by small developments filled with young growing families. It would appear to an outsider to be safe and accepting, but under the surface the town was divided into three distinct factions.

The young families wanted better schools and facilities for their kids, the elderly were focused on keeping taxes down so they could maintain their lifestyle, and then there were the farmers who existed in a class of their own. They saw the plague of housing developments that had overrun neighboring townships with enormous taxes, summertime rationing of water supplies, side by side living, and the total destruction of farmland. That fate had escaped Indian Mills for now. Much of the remaining woods and farm ground in the area could not be developed under the laws that protected the New Jersey Pinelands. But it was a constant battle to keep it that way and developers had far more money and political connections than they did.

This was never more evident then when a rumor emerged that the livestock fencing laws were on the township agenda to be changed. It brought the emergence of this powerful faction of the farm community forward. The township meeting was greeted with what resembled the mob scene from Frankenstein, as hundreds of angry farmers filled the hot auditorium for a standing room only session. The only thing missing were the torches.

The community leaders saw the impending threat of political assassination, wisely decided to table the notion and move on to other business. The new fencing proposal died a quiet and swift death in the rural town.

That was Indian Mills. It was a place where teachers still called home to discuss homework and behavior problems. It was a place where farmland and pineland leaders fought for protection of wildlife and preservation of open space so the community would remain affordable for farmers, retirees and young families. It was a place where developers fought to own land. And...those that didn't like their politics were obliged to pay three times the taxes in neighboring communities - if they could afford to buy a house there to begin with.

Mary turned up the trail and headed back toward the barn, noticing the car still across and slightly down the street. It was a plain looking car, but out of place on the side of the road. The police must not have seen her ride through the barn and into the woods. It stood to reason that the metal Red Rose barn blocked their view and consequently the trail out the back. She found a brief freedom in her ride, but had also suffered some new concerns. Being under constant watch returned her state of anxiety.

Bob waved from the drive, Toby at his side. Perhaps she could talk him into spending some time with her this afternoon. She had to get away, to take her mind off her problems and focus on his. As she approached the barn, her eyes fell upon a disheveled pile of gray feathers, a violent indication of the returning pigeon's final end.

"Damn hawk," she said angrily, squinting toward the sky. She felt a pang of guilt at having released the bird into the sights of a silent waiting predator. Though she had no control over nature's course, she felt a responsibility to protect her animals. She tried to console herself with the knowledge of human ineffectiveness in controlling the balance between predator and prey.

Chapter Five

"Pull!" The orange disc flew off the hill of the Semi Wild Club and exploded into the air, shattering pieces in all directions. "Pull!" she called again, the recoil from the gun dug into her shoulder, but she was satisfied with the shot. She pulled off her ear protection and smiled down at Bob, who was controlling the launcher. "I'm glad you came with me. Why don't you take a turn?" She opened the shotgun and reloaded it for him. "I can see why men like to play war. It's therapeutic, you know, blowing things up."

Bob appeared skeptical. He took the gun carefully. "I haven't held a gun in my hands since I became a vegetarian...five...no seven years ago."

"Come on," she teased, "you aren't killing anything. And, just so you know this - you're not really a vegetarian. I've never actually seen you *eat* a vegetable. I call you a pastaterian." She helped him steady the gun on his shoulder. It was good to see him smile.

"The trick is to follow the skeet in one fluid motion, eye down the barrel, barrel following the target." She placed her foot over the pedal of the launcher, "Tell me when."

"Pull!" he said quietly. The skeet flew into the air. It sailed lazily by and landed on the ground intact. Bob whispered with the gun still up on his shoulder. "Mom, a car is sitting behind the trees down at the turn in the road. I think they have binoculars or something, because I saw some glint. They're definitely watching us."

"Can we pretend we didn't notice them?" She saw them too, but it was a different car than the one at the house. Bob looked puzzled and with that, Mary realized their time together was over. She placed the remaining box of skeet into the back of the pickup.

Bob unloaded the gun and started to help her. "Mom, what's going on? Do they really think you killed Dad?"

Together, they lifted the heavy launcher, and put it next to the box of skeet, sliding it noisily into the bed of the truck.

Mary responded as she brushed dirt from her hands, "I guess I'm under suspicion. Everyone is accounted for but me."

He opened the door of the truck, "This is crazy."

The loud rumble of the diesel engine was the only sound between them as they slowly rolled down the hill past the grouping of trees that hid the car.

"Wait a minute!" She stopped the vehicle abruptly and threw the truck into park. "I'm sick of this!" She jumped out of the truck and walked bravely up to the car. Detective Tate opened the door and stepped out. Apple followed.

Her eyes flashed with anger. "Do you think you could be a little more discreet about following me around? I can see you parked outside my house, following me on every errand – even my husband's funeral." Her eyes settled on the old gray 79 Oldsmobile. "And your surveillance vehicle here is a piece of crap! Could you get any more obvious? Why don't you just pick me up in a black and white and haul my butt everywhere I need to go!"

Tate had heard enough. He put his hand up. "You need to calm down, ma'am." He was amused by her female version of anger. It was good to put pressure on a suspect. She was more apt to make a mistake that way.

Mary took a deep breath. "You guys are pricks. I didn't kill my husband. Why don't you do your job and find out who did!"

Tate decided to press a little further. "You're pretty good with that thing," he nodded toward the area where they had been shooting, "You know, it's been said that hunters are just state sanctioned killers." He leaned against the car as if to taunt her.

Her anger became clear, concise and to the point. "Spoken like a know nothin' city boy - and I guess that makes police…what - paid assassins?"

He pushed himself away from the car, "I want to see a permit for the gun, Mrs. Winters."

She turned and waved to her son in the truck. Bob had the window down. "Pull the paperwork for the good officer," she called sarcastically.

"Any other guns in your house?" He had pulled out his pad and pencil again.

"You already asked me that. Don't you write this stuff down? I heard you visited Petersons twice this week and asked the same questions both times. Here, why don't you give me the pad and I'll spell it out in small one syllable words for you…" She reached her hand out mockingly, but Tate ignored her.

He took the permit from Bob and wrote something on the pad. "We're watching you, ma'am. So get used to us being around." He extended the permit and Mary snapped it back from his hand and turned abruptly toward the truck.

She overheard Tate mumble to his partner as the men started to get into their car. "Did you go back to Petersons?"

Mary glanced back in time to see Apples baffled look of a response.

Tate started the car and began to follow his suspect out the dirt road. His car struggled with the mud spinning beneath the wheels of the Olds. His partner reached over and turned on the radio. "So where to next?"

"First, tell me the truth," Tate started, "is my car really a piece of crap?" He was cautious to avoid the large dips in the dirt and gravel road.

"A real shaggin' wagon," Apple replied confidently, tuning the radio.

"But, it's a classic!" Tate sighed, and returned to his partner's question. "I guess we take a ride to Joe Petersons and get a description of our mysterious doubles."

Apple found a country western station. "Aren't you worried that whoever else is involved may be putting her life in danger? She seems to be pretty clueless as to what they're after. She isn't trying to run. She may even be completely innocent."

Tate glanced over with a sarcastic grin. "I doubt it. Did you see the way she handles a gun? Did you ever know a woman who could handle a gun?"

"Sure I do. So what! That's part of what they do. You know people pay money to hunt and that money goes towards conservation. This isn't the city. Out here you need to thin the herd or be prepared to watch 'em starve to death come winter."

"Jesus...you sound like one of them." Tate didn't want to hear it. He never understood the concept and he didn't like the idea of anyone having a gun except the police. "She has aggressive tendencies. And the last thing I'm worried about is protecting her. She can take care of herself. Meantime, we'll check out Peterson's story, then decide what to do."

Bob blurted over the noise of the diesel engine. "What the hell was Dad into? What are you gonna do, Mom?" He looked back over his shoulder at the car behind them, slipping slowly through the mud.

Her knuckles gripped the steering column and her face was flushed with anger, "I have no clue what he was into. I'm beginning to feel like I didn't really know him at all. If he was in danger why didn't he tell me about it?" Her rage and lack of sleep was overriding the last remaining thread of judgment. Her ranting continued, "He went to work everyday, came home on time every night, there wasn't anything unusual." She shook her head and continued to spill the thoughts running through her mind. "It doesn't matter, what I have to do now is look ahead and prepare for the worst. Be ready for anything. Did you see those guys? They didn't know anyone else had gone to Peterson's. That means, I'm being watched by more than just them. If it had been the FBI, like Old Joe said, then they would know, wouldn't they?"

"I'll stay and help take care of things, but I've got to give Steve a ride back to school tonight. Are you going to be O.K until I get back tomorrow? Why don't you go stay with Kevin and Susan?"

Her eyes remained adhered to the road. "Apparently, I have plenty of people keeping an eye on me. I'll be fine."

"No, Mom, go stay with someone. I don't want you to be by yourself."

"I'll go...I'll go...stop nagging me. Take Toby with you to keep you company on the ride back from school and I'll call Susan. And, be careful what you say on the phone, write on the computer, everything, be aware. Low tech is better and harder to trace. Whoever these guys are, they may be listening in. Now, I have to think..."

Bob felt suddenly cut off by his mother's words. She had dismissed him as if he wasn't part of the family. And why shouldn't she. He had made her life a living hell when Dad was alive, testing the boundaries of every rule in the house. Mom had tried to keep peace between them but would end up withdrawing in silence, waiting for the explosion to end, so that the pieces could be glued back together. That was her true talent, a negotiator - a peacekeeper. He studied her as she drove. She looked distraught and shaken. He wanted to help her, but didn't know how. She was the only person in the world who understood and accepted him. The woman he had always seen as strong and independent, now looked vulnerable and confused, unsure of everything and angry with everybody. For the first time in his twenty years he was afraid for her and could sense her fear.

The trees rolled by him and he thought about his dad. His interaction with his father existed in arguments and resentment that seemed to compound with every confrontation. It was a pattern of behavior that they both carefully cultivated. He had wanted his father to respect him as an equal, a man who could make his own decisions. But when those decisions were not what his father would have chosen, the gap between them worsened and would forever be an abyss. His father couldn't accept that he would never be Steve. He was going to be his own man, not some template that his father wanted him fit. Dad had never shown him any respect.

But this...this just didn't fit his father's personality or his lifestyle. Despite their arguments, Dad believed right and wrong to be as simple as black and white. There was never any intrigue or mystery about the man himself. He lived his life devoted to his family and friends. He had a good reputation at work and in the community. He would be sick knowing the kind of havoc his death would have caused. There had to be something they were missing.

Once home, Mary fed Butch, cleaned his stall and re-checked his wounds. She bent down to look at his leg, but then straightened up and pointed a wary finger in his face. "I'm watching, you." Her voice was low and threatening and Butch knew the tone. She ran her hand slowly down his leg. The swelling was down, but he still had a limp, so she decided to limit his activity a few more days by keeping him confined to a stall. She straightened up and stroked him down the neck. He kept his left eye closed and looked weary and broken, not like the spirited animal that had once been her husband's horse. She stood in front of him and rubbed his neck. While her fingers gently kneaded through the coarse brown coat, he closed his other eye and gradually let the weight of his head lay heavy on her shoulder.

She stroked him and spoke soothingly, "I know boy, I feel the same way...kinda' bitchy, kinda' alone, like you're not in control anymore. I don't like it either." She rubbed around his ears and he turned his head slightly so that she would find the spot he liked. Her shoulder began to ache from the weight of his head. His melancholy behavior had her concerned. It wasn't like him. She supposed that he missed Mark on some level.

Butch was purchased during a mid-west drought. A farmer had brought up ten horses for sale and they were all skeletal, docile and cheap. Out of the lot, Butch was the largest and strongest. Mark negotiated a fair price and was pleased with his purchase. The previous owner had named him Skippy, but that would never do for a field trial horse. Mark renamed him Butch. He had a large strong neck and well shaped hindquarters. He possessed the fluid smooth liquid gait that was the trademark of the Tennessee walking horse. He was aristocratic in demeanor and well behaved under saddle. However, after a few months of proper nutrition, a personality flaw began to emerge. Butch was pushy and dominant with his equine counterparts and if annoyed, would nip an unsuspecting human bystander- usually as they bent over. This certainly was not a typical trait of the breed, but a quirk in this particular horse.

Mark surmised his fight for food during the drought had made him a self-proclaimed alpha horse. Butch stood guard over the hayrack so Shortstop could not approach and eat. The same was true for shelter. Mary would find her little horse standing out in the driving rain and wind while Butch stood warm in the walk-in shed. Putting out two piles of hay and providing two open shelters easily cured those issues. However, one day when Butch bit her while picking out his hoof, she decided to correct this problem. She was ready the second time he went for her. With the hard bristle brush steady in her hand, she whirled around and nailed him right in the nose. She didn't like hitting any animal, but respect had to start with correction, and biting would not be tolerated in her barn. He never went after her again in all the years she handled him. Still, she chose to give him a gentle reminder before bending over to pick his hooves. It intrigued her why Butch never once challenged Mark the way he challenged all others who handled him.

She turned on the radio and started to stock her saddlebag. She wanted to be prepared for anything. With a glance out the door, she acknowledged the car's silent presence. It wasn't Tate's Oldsmobile. She was careful to stay away from the open ends of the barn as she packed. She threw in a pair of wire cutters, hoof pick, duct tape, and wire. She clipped a halter and a bundled lead rope to a clasp and attached both to the rings on the back of her saddle. Most were supplies used for extended trail riding, but she added some packages of dried fruit and nuts, small bottles of water, plastic snack bags of horse feed, and pen and paper. She threw in a plastic folded poncho and a trash bag, a small flashlight with extra batteries and a box of matches. She kept convincing herself that she wouldn't need to escape and that all this was just a silly precaution. Still, the knowledge that she had a covert plan to escape her surveillance made her feel more in control. There was one more problem she needed to consider. She didn't have a waterproof sleeping bag, so she would have to use an old camouflage bag that belonged to one of her sons. She would wrap it up in an old brown plastic tarp and clip it tight to the rear of the saddle.

She walked back up to the house to grab the sleeping bag. While in the privacy of the garage, she put on her long oilskin coat, shoved heavy gloves into the pockets, and tightly rolled the sleeping bag length wise under the coat. She pulled on her Browning boots and slipped her sneakers under the coat for the walk back to the house. She wanted everything in one place if she had to leave fast, and that one place was the barn where her escape could not be detected.

"But, I can skip this semester, and pick up again next," Steve shut the bedroom door and argued with his brother, "if Mom needs me, then what's one semester?"

"Mom would kill you if you skipped college to stay home and baby sit her. Now don't be a pain in the butt and finish packing," Bob replied.

Steve zippered his backpack, and threw it with a thud onto the floor, plopping down on the bed exasperated. "Look, you and I know she didn't kill Dad. What're they thinking? He drove us both crazy. He drove you right out of the house. So why aren't we being watched?"

"The reason, dumbass, is our whereabouts are accounted for. You were at school and I was at a party with lots of people. Mom was at the scene and no one saw her until after the accident. The family members are always the biggest suspects. Jeezz...Steve, don't you ever watch anything besides sports? If you did, then you would figure this stuff out. Try reading a few mysteries or watch some detective programs sometime."

Steve cursed at his brother. "Hey, butthole, if you know so much why aren't you in school instead of me?"

"Because you're the Winter's prodigy. I'm just the rebel...remember?" He started to walk out of the room. "Now, I'm going to warm up the car. Be ready."

Steve smirked, "Dickhead."

Bob shot back, "Pussy."

"You are what you eat."

"Excuse me, then you're a dick."

Both boys experienced a quick sharp pain that started at their ear and ran down their neck, bringing them to their collective knees. Neither saw their mother come into the room behind them. The earlobe grab was a technique made famous by their grandmother, and it had been passed down to Mary to become the most debilitating tool in her arsenal. "Not in my home, boys!" Her voice was stern and reprimanding.

"Yes, Mom, anything you want, Mom." They both cried in unison. Her release left them both rubbing their ears.

The boys worked together packing the car. They came into the kitchen to find their mother cleaning up the dinner dishes. Guerrilla warfare now forgotten, she smiled at the two of them. She always made sure they got a few home cooked meals before leaving.

"I'm gonna miss you, Mom. You sure you're gonna be O.K?" Steve dropped his last bag on the floor and held out his arms to his mother.

She hugged him tightly, "I'm going to be fine. Bob's home, he'll help me. You need to go on with your life and get your future in order. Your father would be proud of you - I sure am. I'll call you tomorrow. Now...work hard!" She pecked him on the cheek and walked them both out to the car, kissing him again before he got in.

She pecked Bob on the cheek, "Be careful there's a storm moving in tonight." She stared up at the angry sky with its waves of rippling blackness and icy gusts of arctic air, then the Subaru pulled out of the driveway.

She noted the contrast between the two brothers; one blonde, outgoing and popular, the other dark, mysterious, introspective and intuitive. In a way she always felt sad for Bob. She watched him relive her outcast childhood and could do nothing to make it better. No one seemed to pay any attention to him, except to give him a hard time...or ask if he was the one who played baseball. He had a college level reading ability in eighth grade, and with that, he couldn't even keep a minimum wage job. It was such a waste of a talented mind. But in her heart she knew he wasn't cut out for some typical desk job. He was creative and funny, a free thinker of sorts, able to solve problems in a way that wasn't logical by the majority. He had to find his way like she did. He was such a good guy, and Mark died not even knowing him. All that fighting was such a waste of time.

She locked the door behind her as she entered the house and called Susan about staying over. It was already dark and a bone chilling cold hung in the air and seemed to cut through every thread of her clothing. Things would freeze up solid tonight. She had changed the water in Butch's stall, but the outside water tub would need the new film of ice broken before she left. Shortstop could usually push his nose through, but the wind was already tearing at the trees and a drizzle was starting to peck at the earth. The water would freeze solid by morning.

Mary pulled on an old sweatshirt, zipped up her Carhart vest and headed out to the barn. She left the car warming up in the driveway, bellowing puffs of heat from the exhaust. The cold front had moved in quickly and with it a heavy pelting ice began to fall like needles around her. It stung at her face. The cold wind whipped about her clothes and lashed her hair against her face. She wished that she hadn't taken the oilskin coat out to the barn. It was the warmest piece of clothing she owned.

Butch was still munching on his hay, but snorted hard when she opened the door and walked down the center isle. She reached over the chest high stall and patted him on the head then moved past him to the open end of the barn. Shortstop had wandered into the shed to escape the sudden onslaught of the driving rain. She threw some more hay on the floor and went out toward the tub. The large gray water container was shared between two paddocks, and was close in proximity to the barn. She picked up the pitchfork that rested against the post and with the heavy handled end hacked at the thin layer of ice that had formed on the top of the water. She used the prongs of the fork to fish out and throw the broken transparent chunks onto the ground. The water faucet creaked and exploded into the tub as she let it run at full force to increase the level of the water. She returned the pitchfork to its resting place and walked back to take one last look at Butch's leg before she left. As she leaned over the side of the stall to get a better look, the sound of the heavy rain battered the metal roof in a pounding refrain. The sound always made Butch edgy. He paced uneasily in his stall, still favoring the leg.

There was a brief glimpse of movement behind her. She lifted her head and started to turn when suddenly, something struck her hard across the back of the skull and catapulted her onto the clay floor. She was dazed by the impact. Her vision went gray and distorted and she couldn't hear anything except a buzzing like static on the radio. A dark figure stood over her with a shovel yelling something that she didn't understand. She couldn't see the figure's face, only a silhouette looming over her with a weapon raised high, ready to strike.

"Where is it?" he yelled over and over again into her face, his voice in competition with the pounding noise of the rain and the buzzing in her head.

"I don't know what you're talking about! I don't understand!" Her vision and hearing was starting to clear. She tried to back away, crawling on her hands toward the gate of Butch's stall.

"You're gonna' tell me where he found the hawk, or you're not gonna tell anybody!" The shovel came down in one sharp movement on her lower right leg. She screamed as pain took over every nerve in her body, but her cries were muffled by the ravaging waves of rain and ice on the roof. She couldn't breathe from the pain that seared up her leg and through her whole body.

"Tell me now!" the voice boomed in her ears.

In one quick motion, she rolled under the stall's iron gate. She felt like she was in a dream, like she was moving in slow motion. Her leg seemed to drag behind her with a clawing, agonizing pain. The man opened the gate, and swung the shovel at the horse. Butch reared, then turned his hind feet in an attempt to kick the man. Mary managed to pull herself over the side of the stall and fell hard into the walk-in part of the shed. She scrambled onto her feet, and ran screaming from the barn into the driving rain.

The man jumped the stall and came for her. She could almost feel his hands on her as she struggled to reach the water tub, grabbed the pitchfork and wielded it toward her lunging attacker. In her panicked frenzy, she slipped and fell, driving the handle of the weapon hard into the ground.

In a heartbeat the tongs of the pitchfork seared noisily through her attacker's throat, his own body weight impaling him on its spears. He landed heavily on top of her, gargling and struggling to free himself. The prongs had ravaged and lay open the skin on his neck and blood sprayed wildly as one carotid was severed by the trauma.

She slowly freed herself and rolled him over onto his back, keeping pressure on the pitchfork. He kept trying to speak and to breathe, but it was useless.

There was no sympathy in Mary's eyes as she watched him bleed out on the ground. A rage and triumph began to fill her soul and overtake her mind. Fear turned to victory. She leaned over him and went through his pockets. The man started to twitch and shake uncontrollably, gasping for air, his arms flailing wildly. In his coat she found a poor imitation of a badge, and a handgun. She shoved the badge into her pocket and threw the gun into the water tub. She limped back toward the barn and her eyes settled on the shovel. She returned to the twitching body, and slowly raised it over her head. It came down in one angry merciless strike.

There was no remorse, no sense of right or wrong. She thought only in terms of survival against whatever force was propelling her life. A panic spread through her aching limbs as she realized that her actions would confirm the detective's suspicions. She was capable of killing a man in cold blood. He was as good as dead, why did she use the shovel? She could have simply called the police and proved that this man was involved in her husband's murder. Now she had confirmed what police suspected, and why? What made her do this?

She looked around nervously knowing she had to leave. Panic had turned to triumph and was now turning to fear. Fear from the police, and if Old Joe was right, fear of the man's partner, who probably wasn't far behind. Old Joe's words reverberated in her thoughts. *Two of 'em stopped by asking questions.*

It would be her or them...and it had to be her. She couldn't count on the police to understand or protect her. She went back in the barn and wrapped her leg with a rag, saddled Shortstop, and pulled on her oilskin coat and hat. Her hands were trembling and bloody. She had to think this through. She breathed rapidly as the checklist went through her mind, and out of distrust and blind panic, she kept walking back to make sure her attacker was truly dead. His head was marred by a huge gash and his eyes were open.

As she walked Shortstop to the back door of the barn, she glanced at the blackboard on the wall. She needed to leave something for Bob so he knew she was all right. She lifted the yellow chalk and scratched hastily emphasizing the word with a thick sweep of her hand. As she placed the chalk back in the trough, she noticed that it was stained with blood. Her eyes searched for a way to stay in contact with her son. Limping out to the pigeon pen, she stuffed two of the oldest homing pigeons into a brown bird bag and clipped it on her saddle. She hoped it would work.

A short time later, horse and rider moved quietly down the dark trail into the woods. Shortstop shook his head wildly in the rain, but they had to get as far as they could by morning. She guided him through and down the trail, the heavy layer of wet leaves as soft as carpet under his hooves.

The woods at night can be a black force of unyielding power. It's driven into rage by the desperate screams of rain and wind, leaving the trees to twist on its demand. Her eyes acclimated to the blackness and soon the distinct sound of water slapping metal heralded the next landmark in the dark. The abandoned car emerged like a large dark animal crouching between the trees.

Shortstop froze and snorted, but she urged him quickly past. Freezing water crawled off her wide brim hat and down her neck and back. She chose the path to the right and made her way toward the pavement and Old Joe's place, making sure to walk the horse down the grassy shoulder towards the south. Then she turned her horse up on the pavement and headed north, hoping to mislead anyone who would try follow her tracks. The rain that washed across the road in streams would surely take with it any mud left from the hooves. It might buy her some time, since the storm would slow them tonight.

They moved in a tedious slow walk, fighting the will of the wind. Sometimes it drove right into their faces in unnatural bursts like an invisible wall of power. Her leg was pounding, and she knew from the warmth that pulsated over it that it was bleeding badly into her boot. Luckily, the rain would wash that away too. She kept Shortstop on the road and only left the pavement when they saw an oncoming car.

Kevin and Susan would look for her eventually and find the barn lights on and the running car in the driveway. Then the police would be patrolling for her. She decided the safest place would be the Stiles farm tonight. At the rate they were moving, they should be there in the middle of the night and could even make better time if the storm lightened up. She had to cross one highway, but in this weather pedestrians were non-existent and cars were few.

Her hands were numb from the cold and the wet. Her gloves were not waterproof. She couldn't feel the reins between her fingers, and kept switching her hands, shoving one, then the other into her pockets. Shortstop pulled toward trees that might offer protection, but Mary kept him on the road in the full force of the storm. He kept his head low fighting the weather, his strong husky body pushing forward at her will. Movement seemed slow and treacherous, the water running in huge sheets of glass off the asphalt surface, but finally they reached the long winding drive of the Stiles farm.

The Stiles farmhouse wasn't visible from the road. It was merely a long drive and a small ranch style house nestled among some trees. Its beauty was in its total isolation. It had acres of prime pasture, two barns and one old horse. She took Shortstop off the road into a thick hedgerow of trees that split the Stiles grounds from their neighbors and they followed the fence line all the way to the back of the property. She spoke softly to Shortstop as she dismounted, slid out the fence rail from the eye post and walked him into the pasture. She put the rail back into place and led him up to the large blue trailer parked behind the barn. The rain was now mixed with snow and her face felt as if it were on fire from the unrelenting force of wind and cold.

Agnes Stiles had an old two-horse slant trailer with white lettering on the side. Mary opened the rear of the trailer and the wind caught the door, swinging it back with bang. She coaxed Shortstop into the trailer, unhooked his bridle and unclipped the halter from the ring of her saddle. At least they would be out of the storm. She closed the door behind him and fought the wind as she limped painfully to the barn. She returned a few minutes later with a sliver of hay, tossing it into the rack in front of Shortstop. Then she took the rope out of her saddlebag and secured the trailer doors shut from the inside.

She shook the water from her coat and hat. The sheer mass of Shortstops body warmed the inside of the trailer and started to form steam on the windows. Mary let herself slide down onto the floor listening to the soft sound of her horse pulling hay off the rack, and the steady pounding and rocking of the rain and wind against the trailer. It would be hours before dawn. A warm tear rolled down her cheek as she thought about the scene someone would be finding back at the house. What was becoming of her? What was she doing?

Chapter Six

When Tate arrived at the Winter's barn, Bob was sitting on a stool with his head in his hands. Kevin stood next to him talking to a uniformed officer. Tate motioned the officer aside. The pounding rain against the metal roof made the conversation inaudible to everyone else. "What happened here?"

The clean shaven officer leaned in to be heard. "The tall guy over there, Alston, got concerned when the woman didn't show up at his place. So he came looking for her. He found the car running in the driveway, searched the house, then out here. Saw the blood on the floor," he motioned to the black pattern that made several passes across the clay floor, "and discovered the victim. In the meantime, the kid came home after dropping his kid brother off at college."

"Where's the woman?"

"Gone. She's on horseback. Went out the back of the barn and into the woods." He motioned toward the back door of the barn. There were flashing lights bouncing along the path in search of hoof prints.

Tate turned his attention to the end of the barn where the lights were pouring over the crime scene. "The coroner?"

"Yep. She heard it on the police band and got here about the same time as us."

The barn was cold and damp and Bob blew into his hands for warmth as he stared helplessly at the floor. The caged halogen lights overhead gave a soft orange glow to the stalls. He felt like he was going to be sick. His color was pale and his forehead clammy. The beads of perspiration dotted and then rolled down his face.

Kevin pulled a red and black bandana out of his coat pocket and handed it to the boy, "You can come stay with us you know."

Bob looked up at Kevin and spoke making sure Tate was out of range. "Mom's all right. She got away. I need to stay here in case she needs me." He took the bandana from Kevin, unfolded it, and then quickly stuffed it in his pocket, suddenly consumed by the urge to vomit. He ran out the side door bending in half as his body heaved from the memory of the bizarre sight near the water tub. The rain drove against him in the dark, but its cold served to revive him. He took a deep breath and returned to the stool.

A police photographer was snapping pictures of the blood on the floor and the stall boards. The officers yelled commands to one another. The crime scene outside was blinding and unorganized. Tate squinted, trying to look through the spotlights and the driving rain. The officers had put up a temporary tarp, but the wind had rendered it useless and they spent all their effort trying to hold it in place.

Tate was clearly annoyed that he and Apple were the last to arrive. A large black woman with red lipstick looked up from the body.

Angolina smiled with a mouthful of straight white teeth and motioned toward him pulling her yellow vinyl collar against the wind. "Hello Nathaniel, seems you've been busy the last couple weeks."

He hated to be called Nathaniel. It eventually led to his nickname, Nate, and when combined with his last name it sounded like a cartoon - Nate Tate. She was obnoxious enough over the phone, and impossible in person. He cringed a little and answered tartly, "And I guess you're not. When did you start making house calls on your own? Slow night?"

She continued, "Finally got some excitement in cow town here, and you want me to sit at home? Her eyes drifted into the barn and then back to Tate. "This poor kid gets back from taking his brother to school, and finds this little present in the backyard. Nice surprise huh?" She directed her attention to the corpse lying in front of her and extended her perfectly manicured hands toward the body like she was offering a prize on a game show. "Your boy here took a pitch fork to the neck, within the last...I'd say four hours or so. Hard to tell exactly when in this cold, tends to slow processes down, ya' know. Have to get'em to the lab to make sure. Nasty looking wounds. Probably took a little while to die too, couldn't talk or hardly breathe, but your girl, well...she didn't want to take any chances and decided to help things along with that shovel over there. I think she was pissed." She took a deep breath, never fully closing her lips. "Looks like the struggle started in the barn and finished out here. I like her - go girl, don't take no crap off these men!"

Tate leaned down and took a closer look at the body. "The kid's in the barn, Angie, keep your voice down. You guys have a weird sense of humor, you know that? Do we have any ID on this guy?" He took on his formal police tone, trying not to stare at her while she spoke.

"First off, I'm ALL woman, honey! And...yes...well your guys pulled a gun from the water tub over there, no ID."

"You realize this woman is the number one suspect in her husband's murder? And funny – he had a head wound too. Still like her?"

"Ahh, he probably deserved it anyway, Nattie. Probably asked what's for dinner one too many times." Her grin went from ear to ear. She knew he hated his name.

He could smell the lilac wafting in the dampness, "You women all stick together."

Tate stood up and walked back to the boy in the barn. He was glad to get out of the storm and shook the water from his coat staying clear of the bloodstains. He leaned over Butch's stall, noticing the fresh bleeding gash on the horse's side and let himself in to take a closer look.

Tate wasn't comfortable with animals. He spoke low and moved so cautiously that the horse became suspicious and protective. Butch countered his approach by turning his hindquarters to the face of his visitor. It was the ultimate equine insult. Every time Tate would try to get around him, Butch would move his rear end in front of him, countering the position with his buttocks.

Apple saw this dance and offered a suggestion. "You're being assed," he said confidently, "walk up to the horse like you know what you're doing - you're making him nervous and he's positioning himself like that for protection. He's threatening you."

Tate was embarrassed by his obvious lack of know how. "He isn't even lookin' at me. How does he know to do that? Why don't you come in here, Billy Bob, and take a look at this yourself." He shot back.

"Believe me, he *is* looking at you. Horses have pretty much three-sixty vision. He's watching every move you make." Apple moved toward the stall and pointed at the puddle of blood as he recreated the events out loud. "Looks like the struggle started here, she was probably hit here. That would explain the blood on the stall board. Then hit again - here. Managed to roll under the stall door, the perp attacked the horse; she got herself over the stall and into the walk-in. That would explain all the blood on the boards and the bloody handprint here. Then the struggle moved to the outside, and the pitchfork well…finished the discussion. Looks like it might be self-defense, if you ask me. And now she's afraid enough to be on the run."

Tate had given up on the horse and turned his back to him. "And the shovel? Does that seem like self-defense to you, too?"

Angie's voice broke in from the end of the barn. "Seems like it to me, honey! I know I like to finish a job right!"

Tate deliberately paid no attention to her. "Dust for prints?"

"Already done," another uniformed officer replied, writing as he spoke.

Tate called to the boy still sitting on the stool. "Was the horse in this stall with the blood stains when you came in?"

Bob nodded.

"Your Mom tell you anything that might be associated with events here? Something that would give us a direction?"

"No."

"Know where she would've gone?"

"No."

Tate looked around the barn. "Anything missing?"

"No." Bob was determined not to offer any help.

"If she tries to contact you we'll need to know. You'll let us know, right?" Tate sensed his distrust. "Listen kid, that's the only way we can help her."

Bob didn't respond.

Tate frowned and didn't seem to notice that Butch had repositioned himself with renewed interest in his intruder.

His eyes traveled to the writing on the chalkboard. "What does that mean, on the board?"

"Nothing." Bob answered.

"It must mean something or she wouldn't have wrote it there."

Bob turned around on the stool and glanced at the blackboard as if he saw it for the first time, then turned back to him. It was the word hawk with a heavily lined circle around it. He said the first thing that came into his head. "There's been a hawk around here. It goes after the pigeons, probably gets one or two a month. Guess she wanted to remind me that it was still around."

Tate leaned across the stall gate pondering the explanation, "Seems pretty ridiculous that something like that would be important to her when she was fleeing for her life." He stared at the word, letting his eyes follow the splattering of blood in the isle way. It didn't make sense, if her attacker had a gun, why didn't he use it if he wanted to kill her? What was he after? He leaned over the stall gate to get a closer look at the drops of blood that led out the back of the barn.

Butch decided that this intruder was far too close to his pile of hay. His ears flattened and he tossed his head in a spiral motion. No further warning was needed. He barred his teeth and pinched his unsuspecting visitor on the left buttock, sending him hard against the metal gate and tumbling into the isle.

Tate jumped and yelled. "Goddamn horse, he's a menace. What the…am I gonna need a tetanus now or something? Jesus! He's dangerous!"

Tate turned and yelled at his partner and the photographer, "Stop your laughin' and get a picture of the chalk board and the layout of the barn." He rubbed his rump awkwardly as he hobbled away.

Apple spoke softly to the photographer, "Guess the sheep case is lookin' pretty good right now…" They both started to snicker.

Angie leaned into the conversation and whispered, "The *what* case?"

Apple tried to refrain from a chuckle, "Lawn sheep are being reported missing all over the county. It's the biggest crime spree this town has ever seen."

"Those ugly fake fuzzy things stuck in the ground?" She looked skeptical but amused.

"Yep. They're the ones."

Angie smiled as she packed up her equipment, reveling in the idea that Tate had been relocated to this little town to work in purgatory too. She figured he must have ticked someone off, and then convinced himself that small town living agreed with him. It would stand to reason. A young city detective with a future suddenly sent to an almost crimeless town to handle such harrowing cases as neighbor disputes, teenage disturbances, and the worst, missing lawn sheep. She could identify with him. This little hick town was a place that couldn't attract someone career driven, so it was passed over by her colleagues, like she was passed over by every other place she applied – she ended up here by default.

The county position was supposed to last for only a few years, until she padded her resume and found something better. Instead, she had settled into nightly TV dinners and armchair critiques of forensic crime shows. Finally, this Mary Winters person had given her and Tate a test of their skills. Somehow, she knew there would be more to come. After all, she had a strange sense about these things.

The dawn began to break at the Stiles farm. Mary had dozed off inside the trailer, but the soft melodic sound of Agnes talking to Muffins awoke her. She peered out the trailer window and watched her friend do her morning feeding. She spoke to Muffins like he was a child.

"Now, you be a good boy today." She pushed the manure cart outside the barn and the massive thoroughbred followed her every move like a giant puppy on its master's heels.

Agnes was well into her fifties, a tall, slender woman with an elegant walk and a dancer's body. She used to show and teach dressage and Mary envied her ability to always look graceful, on her feet and on her horse. It wasn't easy supporting a farm without two steady incomes. So, Harry and Agnes both worked to maintain a twenty-two acre farm for one old horse. They had given up boarding years ago. Boarders just couldn't live up to Agnes' standards when it came to horse care.

Muffins was immaculately groomed and seemed to stay that way. His stall was cleaner than Steve and Bob's rooms, and he lived out his retirement in clover bliss. She knew that her friend would permit her to use the house, but didn't want to get either of them involved with the police. Although they each had different ways of keeping their horses, they got along well and would help look after each other's animals from time to time. Mary peered out the little window of the trailer, careful not to be seen, and watched as Harry and Agnes chatted by their cars, then with a quick kiss, they drove down the lane and off to work.

Mary opened the back of the trailer and led Shortstop to the barn. The rain made the pasture smell fresh and renewed, the storm a mere memory that left only downed leaves as its afterthought. The early morning sun pushed through the streaks of dark clouds and the night would soon be gone.

Muffins raised his head in brief interest and resumed his grazing, undeterred from his job. She led Shortstop into Muffins spotless and deeply bedded stall. Agnes always left the barn open so her horse could enter during the day. She had prepared it carefully, leaving hay and water in case he had tired of the afternoon sun. Shortstop would get some much-needed rest before they had to move at dusk.

After getting Shortstop settled, she jotted a note on a piece of paper, wrapped it in a snack bag and peeled a thin piece of duct tape from the roll she packed, carefully wrapping the tiny package to one of the homing pigeon's legs. She threw the bird into the air and watched as it circled once, and headed for home.

Her fingers fumbled under the large flowerpot by the door and slipped the key from underneath. The door creaked as she entered into the garage. Setting her watch for a four o'clock alarm, she removed her boots and used the same key to unlock the interior door to the house. She needed to take a look at her leg, dry her things and get some rest. She needed to think and develop a plan. Whatever the rest of the journey held for her, it probably wouldn't include access to a house. She had to keep her friends out of it as much as possible and buy some time until she could figure things out.

She undressed in the bathroom. The rag around her leg was caked with dried blood. Agnes kept a wide variety of medical supplies, and she found some antibiotic ointment in the bathroom closet. She tried to clean the large gash that scored across the front and side of her shin. Her lower leg was distorted from the swelling and shades of blue from the impact. Diagonal and ragged was a gaping wound that lay open and in need of stitches. It began to bleed again as she cleaned it, and the pain of weight bearing made her wonder if she had a hairline fracture as well. She cursed under her breath as she poured peroxide over it and coated it with the antibiotic ointment. Then using a series of adhesive strips, she tried to close the wound by placing the bandaids crosswise across the gash, pulling the gaping sides as tightly together as the strips would allow. She placed sterile pads on top and then re-wrapped it tightly with gauze and finished with an elastic bandage to control the bleeding. She found some Tylenol for the pain and lay down on the sofa with her leg up on pillows. She was too worried to sleep, but closed her eyes while the dryer in the utility room rhythmically spun her clothes dry. She planned her next move, playing different scenarios out in her mind.

Bob stretched out on the couch with Toby. He had made himself eggs for breakfast and with the plate resting on his chest, was mopping up the yolk with a piece of toast. The TV was blaring some fifties sitcom, but he wasn't paying attention. He kept turning over in his mind the events of the last few days and what must have taken place in the barn the night before. The scene he had witnessed still made him dizzy and he glanced out the window in the direction of the yellow tape, broken and wagging from the end of the barn. The look on the man's face wouldn't leave his thoughts. He kept seeing it over and over again like it was burned into his eyelids. The blank open eyes and gaping mouth, but it was the pitchfork that was more than he could stand. It had ripped the throat open and the man's hand had frozen into position as if he were trying to pull the weapon away. He had seen many such stunts in horror movies, but to see it in person, first hand, was disturbing and sickening.

The flashing lights alerted all the local neighbors and Bob could imagine that phones were ringing off the hook with speculation. You couldn't hide much in a small town. It was another reason he hated this place. The murder was already on the news this morning and so was a picture of his mom - reported as missing and probably injured.

He stared at the blank space on the wall where the photgraph had once been. It was the picture of her next to her horse and smiling at the camera. Detective Tate had asked to use it for the investigation, and Bob had reluctantly agreed, knowing there was no real choice in the matter.

He tried to focus on the note left on the black board. It was suppose to mean something to him. He tried to recall every phone conversation where that word had come up between them, but could recall nothing more than the story he had told Tate.

He threw on a jacket and went out to check on Butch. He scooped up the manure and tossed it heavily into the wagon, changed Butch's water and gave him more hay. Toby sat patiently in front of the pigeon pen and his presence reminded him to feed the birds while he was there. He swung open the door and placed the seed dish inside. He barely ever looked at the pigeons. They were perched side-by-side and stared back at him, clucking and fidgeting in rows before him. As he placed the water container on the floor of the coop, a brown bird with duct tape dragging from its leg jumped down to eat. His clumsy hand chased the bird around and with a flutter of wings he managed to grab it, and gently pull the tape from the pigeons leg. He read the small piece of paper:

Something to do with "a hawk" – Be careful who you trust.
This is as low tech as it gets-
We'll figure this out. Mom.

The smell of coffee lingered in the heavy air of the conference room. Tate had spread a map of the county across the large wood table. His pad and pencil rested on top with a scribbled list of interviews in his notebook.

He pulled out the picture from his briefcase and set it in front of Apple. "An injured woman on a horse can't be that hard to find. Someone had to spot her." He picked up his coffee and walked to the microwave.

"You forget where you're at. She's one of them, you know. They're not going to rat out one of their own."

Tate poked at the buttons on the microwave. "So what did you come up with at the job site? Any leads?"

"Nothing that I would flag. He didn't talk much about his wife. As far as they know he didn't have other women, just went on about his dogs and field trialing. Nothing unusual."

"You, know?" Tate started, "I don't get this whole sport. They follow the dogs around on horses and watch them hunt." He was intently watching his coffee revolve in the microwave.

"Well it was explained to me in these terms," Apple replied. "It's kinda' like a test of whose dog is better. Not only do folks show in the show ring, but their performance in the field counts for something as well. And when you win so many times, the dog's considered a field champion. It's more complex than that of course, but at least I understand the reasoning. It makes the dog more valuable for breeding purposes - I guess knowing the pups came from good champion stock. It's a test of performance." Apple's attention turned back to the map, he figured his words were pretty much lost on his colleague. There was brief silence as he refocused, then continued, "Now, here's what I would do if I was injured and being pursued." He leaned across the table with a wax pencil in his hand. "We know she's hurt. She might try to get medical attention. I'm going to go over to the hospital today and talk to some of her co-workers. As far as the horse goes, I'd hide it during the day. Any reported break-ins in the area might be her doing," he looked up at Tate who was now blowing the heat off his coffee. Apple continued undeterred, "Of course, if people are helping her, then it will be impossible to find her. Question is what direction is she going?"

Tate contemplated his partner's input, "So you're suggesting that we search every home within, what…about five to seven miles from her house?"

His partner grinned and a mocking sparkle came to his eye. "Good start, but I wouldn't stop there."

Tate had pulled out the chair and sat down in front of him.

Apple continued," Joe Peterson said that she owned a Missouri." He picked up the picture and studied the animal. "I did some checkin', not many of those around in New Jersey. They were bred to do a job. They were used to transport rangers from fire tower to fire tower in the Ozarks."

"Spare me the livestock lesson, Billy Bob!" Tate was clearly losing his patience with this subject.

"What I'm saying is they're engineered for long distance rides, has to do with their trotting gait. One of these horses can do anywhere up to fifty miles a day with hardly breaking a sweat. Provided he's in good shape," he hesitated as if in thought. "My guess is that with her being injured and moving in the dark, her travel time has been cut down considerably...but if she wants to move and knows the territory, she can cover a lot of ground without much down time."

"And exactly where would you hide a horse and not be noticed?"

"Well that's the best part. You're in horse country out here. Hide it on any farm in the township. With the exception of the larger farm operations that employ help, most small farms in the area have working owners. So, there's no one home to notice one more horse in the paddock during the day. Some of the large farms, like Matson's Lucky Circle are perfect for hidin' out, even keep a number of retirees in the back paddocks. And being a resident here, I bet she knows who would and who wouldn't notice an extra horse. Meanwhile she can rest, eat and move on."

Tate's finger moved across the map, directing attention to the road that paralleled Petersons, "The hoof prints we found started south until she went up on the pavement. She may be in Wharton State Forrest by now. If she curled around this way, maybe even Lebanon." His index finger swept toward the south of the map. "A lot of farms out there back up the perimeter of the state ground. You don't think she'd hold up somewhere in the woods?"

"I don't think so. You can't stay in the woods very long before you need supplies. Now, we're gonna' have to do a wide sweep. The rain last night pretty much washed the roads. We haven't found any prints leaving the road to the south or the north. My suspicion is that she turned around on the road and will stay where she can get out of the weather, steal some food and let that wound heal, buy herself some time. I think she'll stay where she knows the territory. Thanks to you, she thinks we're the enemy now, so she won't be comin' to talk to us anytime soon."

Tate added, "Peterson identified the dead guy as one of the men who stopped by his place, so we just need to find her before the second man does. Any name yet?"

Apple shifted in his seat, "Yeah, he fits a missing person. The wife is coming in this morning to verify. We think it's a guy named Jerry Rabinowitz. He worked in a lab connected with the University Museum. We're still workin' on it, but right now there doesn't appear to be any concrete connection."

"So in the meantime, the plan is to find the horse and wait until the woman's seen."

"That's right. It's gettin' too cold out there to be in the middle of the woods…anyway, that's what I'd do." Apple looked closely at the picture, studying its detail. "We just need to find a stocky chestnut gelding with a rear left white sock. Find him, and we'll find her."

Tate leaned forward in his chair. "Why do I get the feeling that it's going to be like trying to find a spotted dog at a Dalmatian festival."

Apple frowned and threw up his hands. "It's the best plan I can come up with until someone calls in and says they've seen her. Then we'll use the dogs to pin her down."

Tate sucked the last drop from the bottom of his coffee cup. "All right. It's a place to start, until something else comes up. Assemble some men, and let's start in this quadrant." He took the wax pencil from his partner's hand and circled the area on the map. "Let's see how good a tracker you are, Billy Bob."

Bob threw his cigarettes into his book bag and started to drive over to Kevin's house. He didn't know what he was going to say, but had to get word out among friends that his Mom was all right and in the area. He needed to get food and supplies to her somehow.

Kevin opened the door and smiled wearily. He had been up most of the night with the police and although it was now late afternoon, he looked unshaven and exhausted. "Bob, come on in."

"Don't think I want to, Mr. Alston. Can you take a walk with me?" Bob looked tired and nervous. He kept his eyes on the ground as he spoke.

Kevin glanced toward the car where Toby sat at attention in the driver's seat patiently waiting for his master.

"Yeah, sure." He grabbed his coat, slipped on his boots, and walked out onto the driveway.

"Heard from Mom. She's on the run. I figure she didn't take enough supplies to camp long in the woods. Don't know how hurt she is, but apparently she can ride."

"Good. Then she's O.K. for now." Kevin saw the distress on the young man's face. "Pretty gruesome sight last night. Are you doing all right? Are you sure you don't want to stay with us awhile?"

Bob politely shook his head, "I've never seen anything like it...and thanks, but no. Toby and I are fine. Besides I got Butch to tend to."

"Look, your mom's a tough woman. She's probably safer on the run. Do they even know who the guy was?"

"The police called me this morning. They said that he didn't have a police record. They asked me if I knew him, Rabinowitz." Bob shrugged his shoulders, "I never heard of him. In her message, she said somthin' about a hawk, just like on the blackboard. That's what the guy was after...something about a hawk. Does that mean anything to you?" The frustration echoed in Bob's voice, "I don't know...I don't understand what we're lookin' for."

Kevin looked puzzled. He wrapped his arms around himself and shivered. "No, honestly, the only hawks I know are the ones you see around the Semi Wild Club. Place has got a few of 'em. The last time I talked with your dad was the weekend of the club workday. Plenty of hawks around then."

Bob looked disappointed. He reached into his bag and pulled out a cigarette. His hands shook as he lit it. "What's a club workday?"

"It happens a couple of times a year. The club sets a day aside asking members...or I should say, more like begging members, to come out and help do maintenance on the grounds...you know, wildlife maintenance. Widen trails that trees have fallen into, repair the small bridges over ditches, smooth out the road to the clubhouse - anything that needs doing. Anyway, that's what it is. Your dad was clearing some dead trees at the back of the old cemetery. They always put him on the backhoe because...well...it was something that he was good at. He made it look easy." Kevin looked down at the driveway, kicking a small stone with his foot, "In fact, I was giving him a hard time because the stump he was pulling was so large that it seemed to take him all afternoon. I had a bet goin' with him that he couldn't get it out of that damn hill. But you know your dad; it became a challenge. At the end of the day he had pushed the stump back into the upright position and left it be. Guess he gave up. I told him he was losing his touch – gettin' soft. That's the last time I spoke to him." He hesitated for a moment and his watery eyes came back to Bob's. "Listen, why don't you come in and have some dinner. Susan made some pasta and I'm sure you haven't eaten with all this going on."

Before Bob could respond, Jack's blue Explorer rolled into the driveway and parked next to the beat up Subaru. The two men turned and watched as Jack opened the door and stepped onto the driveway. He was dressed in jeans, but wore a shirt and tie under his heavy wool coat. He walked toward them extending his hand to Bob.

Bob tried to smile, but the weight of the last few days was evident on his face.

"Any word about your mom? We're all worried about her."

Bob nodded, "Yeah. Between us, I've heard from her, but don't know where she is. She might be trying to get to you if she's hurt bad enough. I bet she'll try to get to your place."

Jack concurred, "Heard all about last night and I've set up my barn and left the key out. I wasn't able to make the viewing or funeral, so I guess I'm not on the police list yet."

Kevin interrupted, "Good thing, too. I hear they've been interviewing everyone who came that night as well as folks involved in the Semi Wild. They asked for a complete club list from me so they'll be gettin' to you eventually."

"Well from what I've heard the club members aren't giving out very much information."

Bob felt out of place in between the two men. He turned to Kevin. "Thanks for the dinner invitation, Mr. Alston. I appreciate it, but I have to stop at the feed store before it closes and check the animals. The least I can do is have Butch back to normal when Mom returns." He realized his statement seemed childlike under the circumstances, as if time could be reversed and the event of last night was some casual misunderstanding.

Kevin smiled with approval. He wasn't going to stop a boy from becoming a man. "Keep me posted. By the way…how's your mom getting info to you? You know police can track cell phones."

"You wouldn't believe me if I told you," Bob called over his shoulder as he started to walk toward the car.

"And be careful around that damn horse." Kevin shuffled from side to side in the cold, "I'll think about what you said, if I come up with anything, I'll let you know…and if you need me, for anything, just call."

The two men watched as the Subaru pulled out of the driveway. Susan walked out of the house, and the screen door banged behind her. She tried to wave balancing two cups of steaming coffee in her hands. She handed one cup to each man.

"Is this a secret meeting or are women allowed?" She smiled sweetly at both of them, brushing her thin blond hair from her face.

Jack's face turned focused and serious. "No, you should hear this too."

Kevin took a deep sip of the coffee and watched Jack's expression as he spoke.

"We have a big problem, that's why I'm here. I just got word from one of the primary trustees of the Semi Wild Club that he's looking to sell his shares and retire to Florida."

Susan interjected. "So, we need another trustee?"

"The problem is that if he doesn't sell them to someone connected to the club – and soon, then he's going to sell the shares to a developer – it's quicker, easier and more profitable."

Susan's brow wrinkled as she spoke. "Can he do that? And even if he does sell to a builder, how about the rest of the people on the board – surely he wouldn't be the majority."

"This guy wants out fast, and wants his money now so he can move. One person on the board who wants to dissolve the club could start buying out everyone elses shares, and before you know it, we're another strip of ugly track homes."

"How much time is he giving us to come up with the money?"

"Ninety days..."

"How much we talkin' about?"

"More than any of us have."

Kevin angrily dumped his coffee onto the ground. "Damn – where are we goin' to get that kind of money in ninety days?"

Jack interrupted, "The guy is already being romanced by every local builders. I just don't have that kind of money since the divorce."

Kevin's gaze met Jack's, "We have to figure something out and we don't have a lot of time."

Jack responded bluntly, "Part of the problem is there's no understanding of what we do here as a private club, so don't expect help from the town when they don't have equal access to the land, and let's face it – ground is valuable out here."

"Where are we going to field trial, or train if we lose this club? Is there anyway we can buy the ground? Is there anyone in the club who could even front the money while we come up with a long term solution?"

"I can have my lawyer look into some options, but how - or the better question is who can afford to help us?"

Kevin walked into the house and left Jack and Susan planning alternative strategies. He pulled a beer out of the refrigerator and sat down in his recliner. His livelihood, his whole existence was at stake with this news. Sporting dog owners from all over the country, sent the finest specimens of their breed to his program to work and mold. Sometimes he could make them champions, sometimes just great foot hunting dogs. It was a big business and a good life…a life he loved.

He would rise at the first slit of dawn and his dogs stood waiting, anxious to work and do what breeding had born out in their spirit. Finding birds was the reward; it was what handler and dog lived for.

As he sat in his oversized recliner, he felt the lifeblood pulse from him. This was the only thing he was good at. He thought about the future of the sport he loved- a sport that had been a tradition in his family for generations. His eyes flowed over the discolored trophies and silver plaques that crowded his bookshelves. Black and white pictures of famous dogs decorated with ribbons, surrounded by proud handlers. His grandfather had taught his father and had passed to him a love and respect for the bird dog life and the outdoors. He had been a part of a long tradition of winners, but it was more than that. He had campaigned champions from all over the country who were the foundation dogs for great breeding programs, dogs that had sold for up to fifty-thousand dollars; dogs whose earnings could bring their master three times that amount in stud fees and purses- while doing what came naturally. And then there were dogs who never saw a trial, but were equally as valued by their masters and brought them the satisfaction and joy of a good private hunt.

His kennel was among the best on the east coast. His eyes filled with sadness. He felt drained and defeated. What would he do if he couldn't do this anymore? Where would he go?

Chapter Seven

There was a flurry of activity in and out of the local feed store. Bob rolled up to the red painted barn, noting the contrast of vehicles that surrounded it. Sitting in front were rusted, dented pickups interspersed with shiny livestock rigs. What had once been a simple horse barn was now converted into a place of business. It was the best place to shop for information on farm sales, fair market hay, or livestock purchases – as well as local gossip and advice. Bob opened the creaky screen door just in time to overhear some discussion about the murder at the Winters Morning Farm.

"Yeah, she got him before he got her…"

"Pitch fork…ya don't say."

He acted undeterred by the conversation and let the door bang behind him as if to warn them he had arrived.

The room went quiet and it was all he could do to pretend not to notice. He stepped up to the counter feeling everyone's eyes on him. He put his money down and looked the shopkeeper in the eye.

"Need a fifty pound bag of Blue Seal Natural 29 and 5 bags of wood chips." He tried to act self-assured, like this was a duty routine to him, but he could feel the weight of scrutiny, sizing him up and rating him on the 'worthy' scale.

The shopkeeper grinned as he spoke, blowing a clean hole in Bob's facade, "You mean Blue Seal Natural **26** for your bird dog, don't ya, son?"

Well, so much for fitting in, Bob thought, as he pushed the money in the man's direction with a nod.

A red headed girl winked at him from over the fly sprays, and he returned a blush and a smile. She looked oddly familiar. Old Joe pushed past her and tugged at his reading glasses, putting down the box of horse wormer. He was the first to break the silence, and Bob could sense that his actions were a direct effort to break the tension in the room.

"This new crap says that I shouldn't have to worm for twelve weeks. I usually worm every eight. Do you guys trust this stuff?"

The man behind the counter replied by curling his lip and shaking his head as if scolding a child. "I wouldn't," he said flatly, "it's twice as expensive and I would still worm my horses every eight. I only keep it in stock because the racehorse folks ask for it by name. It probably works, but I don't trust the new fangled stuff much. Never had any trouble with old stuff."

Joe grinned. He liked the honesty of the folks out here. He turned to the young man standing beside him and extended his hand in friendship as if seeing him for the first time, "How you gettin' on by yourself out there, boy?"

"Doin' all right I guess, Mr. Peterson." Bob reciprocated, gripping the man's hand as tightly as it was offered.

Joe squinted a little at the quarter size holes in the young man's earlobes and focused on the tattoo running down his neck. He couldn't stop looking at the ring on the boys lip. Finally, Joe couldn't help himself, "Ya look like a little gay boy with those things in your ears ya know."

Bob smiled and shrugged, he leaned forward as if to take a closer look at the old man's ears. "Ya know, Joe, you would look really good with an earring…after all, you already have the baggy pants thing down."

The room burst into laughter and Old Joe pulled his pants up with a wide grin. "You're O.K., boy," he said, slapping Bob on the back, "I was just telling these folks that once you let those damn FBI fellas on your property, the EPA will be breathin' down your throat for some drop of oil you spilt from your tractor ten years ago! And the next thing you know, your property is a hazardous waste site and you got nothin'."

The room started to whisper in agreement and people returned to their browsing.

Bob saw this as the perfect opportunity to spread a little information. "Thanks for the heads up the other day, Mr. Peterson. You know, after you talked to Mom about the other cops at your place, she prepared for the worst, and the worst happened."

"Have you heard somthin'?" There was sincerity in the Old Joe's eyes that caught Bob off guard.

"She's on the move, although I don't know exactly where she is. What I do know is, thanks to you, she knows that more than the police are looking for her- and if she's found...well you know what happened in the barn."

The shopkeeper peered out the window at the Subaru, and interrupted. "Hey kid, I can put the dog food in your car, but you don't have enough room in that beat up little tin can for the wood chips. Come back with your dually later this week and I'll load you up good. For now you can only fit one." His eyes flashed a mischievous gleam as his words took on a prodding humor, "Damn boy, if you're gonna' be a farmer - drive the part! Drive the real truck!"

Bob knew he was right. His little car sure wasn't a farm vehicle. It looked impotent and pathetic, dwarfed by the massive horse pulling, trailer dragging, power vehicles beside it. Even the beat up old utility trucks spoke to their daily farm duties like retired old generals.

The man continued, "And if you run into any trouble with those animals, well I can usually help most folks out...don't be afraid to ask. Your parents were good customers, O.K.?"

Bob thanked him and said goodbye. He noticed that folks in the store were discussing something in low tones. He didn't recognize more than a few of them, but one by one, they all came up and said nice things to him about his parents. Someone put a cherry pie on the seat of his car.

It took him longer to get Toby's dog food than he thought. But it was good to know that people cared about how he was doing and what was happening with his mom.

He had no idea that his parents were this well liked. He didn't feel as out of place as he used to among these people. In fact, they seemed to have an easy way about them that he never noticed before...or maybe they just saw him different now. Complete strangers had looked him in the eyes, offered help or a kind word. He clung to the hope that maybe he had helped his mother, somehow.

He turned his car down the lamp lined main street of town. A few years ago he couldn't wait until he got away from here. Now the quiet of these streets seemed to soothe him. He supposed that he had enough excitement and intrigue during his apartment days. But it wasn't just that. He swelled with a kind of importance he never experienced before. He had a job, a purpose. Running the farm was a responsibility that he would never have chosen on his own, but since the choice was made for him, he was determined to do it right. He owed both his parents that much.

He had been foolish to think that living on his own and splitting the rent with other roommates would be utopia, a gateway to freedom, an escape from his father's constant condemnation - but that wasn't the reality. He fought all the time with the other guys. There were strangers in and out of the apartment day and night. There was never enough hot water, or food...and then there was the mess. They lived like pigs...no...pigs lived better. He had to admit it was nice being home - long hot showers, clean sheets and plenty of food. And then there was Toby, who checked on him several times a night and sometimes crawled into bed right next to him. Life at home without Dad was comforting, quiet and routine. He was beginning to understand the sense of satisfaction that small town life provided, an unwavering routine. There was a kind of comfort and relief that he couldn't describe in all its familiarity. Whatever he was feeling, he needed to repay the emotional debt he owed his mother in her time of crisis.

The lights in front of the library gleamed as he passed, and the monotone voice from the week before reverberated in his head. He remembered the phone call that probably saved Butch's life.

He turned the car into the library parking lot. He might as well stop in and pick up the books she ordered. In the back of his mind, he had to believe that she would just suddenly come home and this whole business would be over.

He strolled up to the desk and approached a pudgy woman with puffy looking skin and stiff hair. A painted pink lipstick smile stretched across her face.

"Excuse me," he started, "I got one of those calls. Ya know, the one that says reference material has arrived. I need to pick it up for my mom."

Deep smile creases formed at the corner of her eyes as she pulled out a file from under the desk. "What's her name, honey?"

"Mary Evans Winters."

She flipped through the cards, "Got something for a Mark Winters, not a Mary."

His eyes widened, "Dad actually came to the library?"

"Why yes honey, I guess he did."

"To read something? Dad...are you sure?"

Her smile broke into an embarrassing loud laugh that gulped at the air and ended with a snort. "I'm sure your Dad can read!" She was still laughing when she set the stack of books in front of him. She placed them into a plastic sack and pulled the string handle closed. The bag mocked the quiet intellectual fortitude of the institution, portraying an owl on the front wearing glasses and a graduation robe.

"There you go, honey," She took his library card and looked at it puzzled. "Haven't seen this in a while." She pulled a new card out from a box and typed something into the computer. "We got new ones now. Now have them back in three weeks. The date's on the slip." She handed him the new card with a wink and a smile.

Bob took the books and tossed them into the back of his car. Something was up. He had never known Dad to go to the library – ever.

Elva Matson had one of the most respected horse farms in New Jersey. The Lucky Circle Farm sat back off the road in all its white gleaming glory. It was a vision at the end of a shadowy drive that meandered between perfectly spaced elms. The old farmhouse was large and square, with an old lookout on top. A long wrap-around porch framed the structure with small, but ornate Victorian accents that countered the stark new coat of paint.

Elva and Harold Matson had created a regal and elegant reminder of agriculture's lost history of prosperity. But the people who knew the Matsons weren't fooled. Beneath their carefully manufactured reputations stood a well-oiled business where a simple farm could no longer survive.

On the surface, Elva enjoyed playing the pushy farmer's wife, but in truth, she held a dual degree in equine management and business from Rutgers. Her astute business and financial sense combined with Harold's fearless cowboy nature and farm equipment know how, had transformed a rundown fire trap into one of the most efficient full service facilities in the state.

Their land extended farther than could be seen from the house. The very back paddocks of the farm kept over forty retired horses. Elva had started the trend years ago and found it to be the most lucrative and least demanding part of her business. She took in the lame older horses that could no longer be ridden, and yet out of attachment and devotion, the owners just couldn't put down or sell. For a large onetime fee, these animals had lush pasture, standard vet and hoof care, clean walk-in sheds, plenty of horse company, and a life of leisure for the rest of their lives. They were put out to pasture in very literal terms. It was the best retirement home a horse could have.

The performance, show and racehorses belonged to the largest and newest barn on the property. It housed endless rows of thickly bedded stalls with overhead misters for cooling comfort in the heat of summer. Elva called it the high rent district. Those horses were worked, groomed and trained on a daily basis by her staff in her lighted indoor riding ring. They were worth a great deal of money and the most intensive care came with an equally high price.

The second barn catered to normal maintenance horses, those that required daily turnout and casual attention. And finally, the smallest barn housed problem animals. It was designed with the help of a veterinarian and used for foaling, occasional illness and adverse horse personalities that had to be isolated from the others.

For the simple trail and pleasure riders there were part and full board options, as well as acres of trails that backed up to the edge of the state ground. Elva liked the teenagers willing to work off their board and managed them with an iron hand, setting up schedules and defining duties like a drill sergeant. The clients liked it too. If your horse was promoted by Matson's Lucky Circle Farm, you had a good chance of winning - or Elva would tell you flat out what you were lacking. Sometimes she would let experienced students use one of her seasoned horses, just to give them a taste of the winner's circle. It was good business as they would later buy a better horse, and continue to board and train with her.

But what gained her respect in the equine community was her outright, blatant brand of honesty. Elva was always straight with her pupils about their expectations in the ring, and what their horse was capable of accomplishing. Her farm had a waiting list of horses and owners, and few argued with her ways.

Elva put the needs of the farm and her students in front of all else. It helped her mask the one thing her life lacked - children of her own. Well into her fifties now, her children were now her students, and her only heir, and steady farm hand, her nephew, Frank.

Tate expected resistance from her based on her reputation. Her large stocky figure took up most the doorway, and when she crossed her chubby arms in front of her chest he knew his chances of enlisting her cooperation vanished.

"Ma'am," He started, "we will need to inspect the horses on your premises to find this woman. We need your permission to look around."

"You got a warrant?" The corners of her mouth turned down and stopped at her neck.

"No Ma'am. We're hoping that you will cooperate with us in finding Mrs. Winters."

"You thought wrong, Detective."

"Ma'am, you know the penalty for aiding a fugitive?" His voice turned unpleasant as he became more forceful.

"Oh...Now she's a fugitive is she? Seems to me she's a victim. Well, I don't give a damn, because I'm not helping you. No warrant - no entry." Her arms changed position from her chest to her hips.

"Ma'am, I can have a court order by the end of the day and you can bet I'll be here first thing in the morning with my men. Now we can do this voluntarily, or we can do this involuntarily."

Her appearance did not change. "See you in the morning, Detective." With that, her heavy hand let the door slam in his face.

Detective Tate walked back to his car and slammed the car door shut behind him, then opened it and slammed it again as if to work off his anger. "Damn it! What's with these people?"

His partner chuckled. "You handled that well. Make Elva your enemy and no farm in the county will cooperate with a search. It's bad enough she's the reason we can't find a vet willing to help us. She's already put the word out – I told you they protect their own."

Elva pulled back the lace curtain and watched out the window. "Bunch of dumbasses." She let the curtain fall from her hand..."Frank?" she called sweetly, her voice turning to maple syrup and her eyes sparkling with mischief.

A young boy about nineteen came up behind her and followed her into the kitchen.

She lovingly addressed him, "I have some errands for you to run. Go to the hardware store and pick up the following items." She scratched out a list on a pad. "After you pick it all up, call the help and tell them we have a special job today. Then bring all the horses in for feeding. Got it?"

The young man looked at the list and brushed an obstinate lock of brown hair off his freckled forehead. "What if they don't have that much?"

"Then go to another store until you find it."

"All seventy two horses? Even the retirees?"

"Frank," she said lovingly, "you're like a son to me, but sometimes the porch light's on and nobody's home. Now just go get the stuff. Watch and learn from your Auntie. You'll be runnin' this place some day."

Frank was her sister's boy. He was a little slow in the mind, but he was kind to the horses and a hard worker. Elva would make sure he made a good living as their lead hand, and in return, she got a son for her legacy.

Mary dozed in a fitful sleep. Her leg hurt wildly and woke her early. She cringed as she poured more peroxide into the wound and changed the bandages again. She disposed of them in the trashcan by the garage, carefully pushing them beneath the other garbage.

The day had turned sunny and pleasantly cool. The storm had taken what was left of the fall leaves and a thin layer of ice appeared on the puddles of the driveway. It would be solid ice again by tonight. She took her things from the dryer and helped herself to some soup in the pantry. She cleaned up everything she used, looking around for anything out of place that would give her presence away. She put a pop-top can of chicken noodle soup in her saddlebag and took some slices of bread Agnes had on top of the refrigerator. Questions raced through her mind and taunted her conscience as she prepared to leave. Where would she go? Who could she involve? Who could she trust? What were they after? She took one last look around the house and locked up as she left.

The Stiles farm would know no trace of her presence. Agnes would assume the mess in the stall was from Muffins, although she might wonder why he chose to be inside on such a lovely day. Mary would wait in the woods until it was dark enough to be swallowed up in the shadows.

The stars began to show themselves and the moon rose over the tops of the trees backlighting the dark branches that stretched awkwardly toward the heaven. Shortstop's breath rose slowly from his nostrils circling like white puffs of smoke. They slowly moved through the woods staying clear of the trails but close enough to the road to hear the noise of the occasional cars.

There were many back trails that snaked through the pines from farm to farm. Some were merely fire lines cut by the last controlled burn, others just dead-ended with no warning. It was easy to lose your landmarks at night and get turned around in the darkness. Using the distant road as a guide she could move silently, but the going was slow and thick. At least she had the light of the moon, peeking through the twisted branches of the muttering pines.

They carefully picked their way through the woods. The moist leaves beneath Shortstop's hooves made no sound as they worked a narrow path of their own, the branches and dwarf brush scraping against them. Moving through the storm had its problems, but at least the driving elements they fought kept her from exploring her childhood fears of darkness and the night creatures of the woods. It was beautiful and safe during the day, but became an ominous domain of demons at night. The very place that offered refuge to her aching teenage soul, could create spine tingling fear in the dark. Shortstop snorted at the occasional movement of deer, the chatter of birds and the harsh cry of some terrified night creature. Shadows rose and lunged away from them in the night, her eyes adjusting enough to catch the white tail as it bobbed into the darkness.

She assured herself that if they kept moving at a steady pace, they would be near Matson's farm by morning. The retirement horses in the back paddocks only received AM feedings. She would sleep in the woods somewhere and let Shortstop rest with his equine elders. If she could get to Jack's house, then she would be close enough to the Semi Wild to get a better look at the place where it all happened. At least it was a plan, and once at Jack's place, she would be able to heal her leg. Whoever killed Mark knew he would be there that day.

The night started to pass in a series of distant crossroads and water filled ditches. The branches that hung in front of them started to freeze, and crystallized water reflected the bright moonlight like wands of frosted glass. Geese cackled overhead in their invisible night migration, and the sound echoed in the sleepy darkness.

In the distance headlights of a slow moving car were approaching. A spotlight from the window slowly filled the woods along the road with a moving stripe of thick brilliant light. She knew they weren't spotting deer.

"This way, boy!" She turned Shortstop into the thick of the twisted scrub pines. Branches and hanging tentacles of foliage that were beautiful and brilliant a moment before, now scrapped against them like barbwire, as she pushed the animal quickly into the expansive darkness of the woods.

The police car slowly passed and the lights swept beyond them. She stayed a distance from the road and continued to move forward. The ground ahead started to rise and a wire fence offered a flimsy barrier to what gave way to a series of bogs and dikes, shimmering in the moonlight like a second quiet sky. It was a breathtaking sight in the pines, but tonight it was only the next obstacle to safety. She came to a stop and contemplated the best way around. A series of bogs repeated themselves to the right until they fell out of view under the moonlight. If she tried to go around, she would surely be lost in the woods. If she ventured closer to the road, the lights would expose her. She decided the best route was to cut the wire and go directly through the cranberry bog. If they stayed off the rim of the dike, they could continue to move virtually unnoticed. There didn't seem to be much choice. She glanced at her watch. The distant car lights and occasional spotlights seemed to come by in ten to fifteen minute intervals.

The bogs were flooded and cranberries floated on the top of the water in undulating collections of floating pellets. She clipped the wire with the cutters, rolled it back, and led Shortstop in behind her. Once in, she bent the cut ends of the fence and hooked them back together. She felt uncomfortable destroying property, but acknowledged with a flash of misplaced humor, that the man in the barn had been dealt with using far less internal turmoil. She remounted and steered Shortstop down into the watery bog. He balked, the water's silver surface lay before them like a shallow teacup filled with dark rippling brew. She encouraged him to advance down into the water, but he stood still, frozen by this new experience. He had crossed many streams and deep puddles during their rides, but usually following other horses with confidence. Alone, he was unsure of the cold and murky depths of the water. Her gaze caught the sweeping light in the distance. She dismounted and the cold water of the bog spilled over the top of her boots and up to her thighs. She spoke softly, encouraging him to move forward, tugging on his bit until he was up to his belly in water. Once she started to lead the way, he followed willingly.

Shortstop moved one leg at a time feeling carefully for the bottom, but encouraged by his mistress. The berries swirled and moved around their legs, the water, warmer than the air, gave off a thin rising mist. They pushed on, and the water in her boots made her legs feel heavy and clumsy. Their breath filled the air and Mary moved slowly, careful not to make a sound in the water. She wished she had taken her boots off and gone barefoot.

They came to the end of the bog before reaching another fence and another patch of woods to offer protection. Shortstop splashed as he hurriedly left the water, struggling from the bog up onto the last dike. She heard a car slow down as she started to cut the wire. A white, hot light came sweeping toward them and she turned Shortstop so his eyes wouldn't give them away. There was nowhere to hide. The car stopped on the road and she feverishly fumbled to cut through the last section, her cold stiff hands slipping on the handle of the wire cutter. She heard yelling and confusion as another light shot her way. She coaxed Shortstop through the fence and they were quickly absorbed by the darkness of the woods.

"Damn it, we had her. Call the dog unit! And Get Tate on the phone!" The officer yelled.

Mary was breathing heavily and her heart was pounding. She kept Shortstop in a steady lope, ignoring the branches and brush that whipped across them, slashing against their skin and punishing their movement, until they finally stumbled out onto the shoulder of the highway. It was a busy four-lane stretch of road, and the lights dashed by them in continuous streaks of momentum. Once she was across she would be in the State Forest. It wasn't what she wanted. This was unfamiliar territory and she didn't have a compass or even an idea where the perimeter would be found in relation to where she was entering. It was a vast tangle of sandy roads and twisted trees that all looked alike. But she also knew there was no choice right now. She waited for a large break in the traffic. Then she cracked her reins and leaned forward waiting for the bolt. Shortstop lunged as if running for freedom and kept going, past the state forest signs and down one of the narrow side roads. Without the main road as a guide she would never find her away around.

A panic and terror began to creep into her marrow as she questioned every decision she made. Time was passing, but she had no acknowledgment of her pace or progress. Right or left, stay on the sandy road, or in the woods. She was torn and frozen by indecision. The moonlight seemed to expose her, to throw a spotlight on her for anyone to find, but through her panic and fear, her eyes struggling with the right path and the right direction - exposed something else…more hoof prints and many of them. They were partially frozen from last night's storm in the wide strip of sandy white road.

She spoke softly to herself, as if the sound of her own words could diminish her fear and restore some order to her racing thoughts. She was certain that horses and four wheelers had come through here earlier, maybe this morning. She strained to see the tracks as they followed the pattern in the white ribbon of the road. It had been a beautiful fall day for a trail ride. Elva and other local farms around the state ground perimeter sometimes organized group rides from their farms. The hoof prints were set deep in the mud of the morning. Mary stayed on the shoulder of the road and followed the prints for miles. It would take a while to discern which prints were fresh. She looked up at the sky. The white moon illuminated the sandy road before her, while the sway of the pines issued whispers of warning in the dark.

The state forest trails wound through the pines in an endless tangle of routes. There were small riverbeds to cross and lakes that were barriers. She tried to suppress the chill that crawled down her spine; it was down right spooky out here in its human silence. Cars could no longer be heard, only the distant drone of the highway left far behind. An animal screamed out in the night and she could only imagine the horror of its final ending. She shook it off and asked herself what was worse, what lay ahead or the evil behind. Someone's farm trails eventually would meet up, she would have to take her chances as to where. She thought she heard the faint sound of dogs barking and yapping, but their echo gave no clue of where they were coming from – only that the sound was rapidly increasing.

Mary kept moving through the night. She followed the dried hoof prints as long as she could see their impression. She was far ahead of the men with their dogs that grunted and barked in the distance. They were being walked on leashes - that she was sure of. Had they been released and the men on horseback or four wheelers, they would have caught up to her by now. Her leg felt damp and stiff and cold, but there was no time to tend to it and no time to rest. It ached with a deep and unrelenting pain that stretched from her hip down into her toes. She would have to lose them before she could rest.

The large number of prints began to thin and she noticed that several veered off down a grass path and into the blackness of the woods. Maybe it was a short cut to one of the farms that lined the perimeter. Maybe it was just a dead end.

She turned Shortstop off the road and followed the narrow path. The moonlight was smothered by the thickness of the trees and it became difficult to see. The path was no larger than a deer trail. The earlier group of horses couldn't have moved through such a narrow stretch. She was following the trail of probably only one or two horses. The sound of the dogs echoed louder in the night and she knew they had to be gaining.

The path came out behind a wire fence that opened to a large paddock of cows. The trail went farther, but the narrow path connected her to exactly what she needed to throw off the dogs scent. There were several paddocks with probably hundreds of Holsteins meandering about the field, capturing the moonlight with their random patches of white. She dismounted and opened the chain on the rear gate, careful to re-lock it behind her and Shortstop. She rode her horse around the pasture and eventually to the next gate where she repeated the same procedure. The cows became excited and began to move and romp restlessly around their visitors, their massive forms loping awkwardly around the pasture, mixing her scent with the choppy mud and manure.

She cut through three large paddocks when she noticed the water filled drainage ditch that ran along the fence line. She hoped that the heavy scent of the manure and the cows would throw off the dogs. Using the drainage ditch as a guide, she followed the road to another large black tangle of woods and turned Shortstop toward it. It was getting too close to dawn to try to reach Elva's now. She wasn't sure which direction to go and would have to hold up somewhere close.

It was just another area of woods until the dawn silhouetted acres of tall spiny brush whose twisted branches sprawled like skeletons planted in rows. It was acres of time worn blueberries, grossly over grown and abandoned for years. The rows stood like soldiers in the early cold of the breaking light. She might have some luck after all. Where there were blueberries, there were old blueberry packing houses and sheds. She snaked through the narrow rows cowering down and putting her head against Shortstops neck. They went from one overgrown field to another until finally she had to dismount. The rows were collapsing on top of them. Some branches still had berries, but they were small and hard, like beebes.

She led the way, partially bent over, encouraging Shortstop through the brush. The arching bushes opened to patches of oaks and cedar trees and then a series of sandy deer trails and further on to a broken down shack barely visible from overgrown vines and brush. She approached it with caution. It was time worn and sun bleached, leaning to one side. Boards were missing on the outside and some of the building had caved in during the last snow. An old metal kitchen chair sat precariously on the partially collapsed roof, a sign that a hunter had laid claim to it as his stand.

It would do. The back of it was open to the woods. She led him into the three-sided shed and slipped off his bridle. She pulled the halter over his head and tied him to a beam, then offered him a little feed from her saddlebag. "This will have to do until tonight, boy," she whispered softly, pouring the feed into her hat and holding it out to him. When he was done, she unrolled the tarp and sleeping bag, layering them on the ground. She poured the water bottle into her hat and coaxed Shortstop to drink. He reluctantly sniffed at it, drawing the liquid into his mouth like a siphon. She left a small amount in the bottle for herself. She sat down and pulled off her boots, squeezing the water from her wet socks.

The early morning sun stretched across the small patch of open ground and shone inside the building. She no longer heard the dogs in the distance and a sense of safety was found in this place of total isolation. She glanced over at Shortstop. His rear leg was bent and his head was low, already at rest in the makeshift shelter. There was no sound from the woods other than the call of birds and the soft rustling of the pines; only the day beginning. She dug a small hole with a scooping motion of her hands. The loose white sand was easy to move and she cupped out a place to build a small fire. Gathering some leaves and small sticks, she put them into the hole and retrieved the matches, wire cutters and the can of soup she had taken from the Stiles.

The fire she built was small, but big enough to put the can of soup in the middle until it was near boiling. She gripped it with the wire cutters and sipped, careful not to press her lips on the edges of the can. She had laid her boots and socks in full view of the rising sun and placed her bare feet near the smoldering fire. The soup tasted good and was a welcome relief against the remaining chill of the morning. When she was finished, she removed her jeans, still wet from the bogs, and placed them in the sun to dry.

Mary dusted the sand from her feet, and filled in the little fire. She wrapped herself in the sleeping bag, and her body warmth combined with a full stomach and the gentle heat of the sun, began to relax her. Lying on her back, she let the cold October air fill her nostrils, letting her eyes drift to the sky and the spiny branches that tossed rhythmically in and out of her weary view. The shimmering rays reflected on every swaying blade of tall grass. Squirrels jumped from tree to tree oblivious to the stranger resting beneath them.

If they could only reach Elva's by the next morning, Shortstop could rest most of tomorrow. She hoped that the owner of the lone kitchen chair only used his stand on the weekends. She turned on her side and dozed softly, waking at the slightest movement around her.

Chapter Eight

It was in the first full light of dawn when the men and dogs left the sandy road of the state ground and took the narrow path toward the woods.

"Are you sure these dogs know what they're doing?" One officer asked as he followed behind.

"They're picking up scent in this direction," the man growled back, his large body lunging forward as the dogs pulled him off the road.

"But the prints are all goin' in this direction." The officer pointed along the sandy road that disappeared farther in the shadows.

"If my dogs say this way, then this way it is."

They proceeded through the woods and stopped at the back of the murky cow pasture. The smell of manure and wet earth filled their senses as the sun began to warm the soil. The handler made his dogs sit while he surveyed the situation. He took a rag out of his pocket and wiped the moisture from his sweaty forehead stuffing it back into his plaid shirt pocket. The morning chores were well underway, and the cows chased and kicked their feet up in joy as they ran after the rumbling tractors heavy with large rolls of hay.

The men stood there breathing hard. They eyed the horse prints that went to the rear gate then disappeared in the choppy mud and manure of the wet fertile pasture.

"This is as far as my dogs go," the handler said as he pulled out his portable phone.

"What? We got to find her, can't you let the dogs go?"

"Nope. They'll only lose the scent in the manure and probably get kicked to boot. I don't risk my dogs." He turned and flipped open his cell phone.

"You told Tate you could find anybody."

"You said a woods search, not a farm search. This is where I stop. If you don't like it then get somebody else." He started to talk loudly into the phone, giving pick up directions. The dogs sat obediently and waited.

The officer called the dispatcher and was connected with Tate. "We're in a cow pasture at the north west perimeter of the state ground. The dog guy won't go on private property with the dogs. We're close. Can we start a farm to farm search?"

"Good work," Tate replied as he peered down at the township map on his kitchen table. "We've narrowed it down. We'll fan out from there. I've got business over at Elva's place this morning," he said confidently, "keep me posted."

Daybreak was heard with a pounding on Elva's front door. She swung it open with the same stone face that had left Tate the day before. Her gray hair was pulled back tight and her slate eyes scanned the flashing lights of the police cars lining her drive.

"Mrs. Matson, I am serving you with a search warrant for the premises." Tate had a slight smirk on his face as he slapped it into her hand.

She put her glasses on, in a slow deliberate motion as her husband read over her shoulder. He knew it was best to let his wife handle this.

"I have one for you too." She shoved her paperwork into Tate's hands. "It's a letter from my lawyer. If you or any of your officers here gets injured during this inspection I am not responsible for your stupidity. If you injure one of my animals, then you're personally responsible. And you're not to interfere in our operation here."

"My men aren't going to get hurt and they aren't going to cause any problem. By court order, I can inspect your property whether you like it or not."

"Just as long as we understand each other, De-tec-tive." She accentuated the *T* as if sharpening a blade. The exclamation point was the door slamming in his face.

He smiled at his victory and waved to his men. They had assembled seven officers to help find the horse and on a farm this large it might take awhile. If they located the animal, then the dog search the night before was an expense well taken. Tate was certain that she was around here somewhere – on one of these perimeter farms.

The officers slid open the barn door on the largest building and walked past endless rows of clean empty stalls. The barn smelled of wood chips, fly spray, shampoo and something else, a chemical that he just couldn't put his finger on. There was no sound except for the humming of the halogen lamps that hung in rows over their heads, and the soft raking sound of someone mucking manure out of the end stall. The men ignored the young man going about his chores and two of them put heavy hands on the metal door that opened to the first paddock of horses.

Tate turned his back to the doors to face his men as he held up the picture. "So men, just to be clear, we are looking for a chestnut horse with a rear left white sock…" The doors slowly opened and the men walked out into the sunlight.

"Sir, I think we have a problem," one of the officers stated.

Tate continued to talk, "Don't let the horses intimidate you, just walk up to them and look for the white sock." He was busy patting his pockets down for his pen.

"Tate…" Apple turned and beckoned him outside.

Tate walked from the barn into the open paddock. "What's the…" he stopped short in recognition. His eyes slowly moved from one paddock to the other, over dozens of horses, paints, blacks, chestnuts, browns and bays. He squinted and shaded his eyes trying to take in all he was seeing. There were so many horses all alert and staring at the intruders… and every horse had a left rear white sock.

Elva pulled back the curtains in the kitchen and started to chuckle, "Come look at this bunch of dumbasses, Harold."

Her husband walked up behind her and just shook his head at the sight. "Ya know, El, we're gonna be washing horses for the next week. Don't need to make the police our enemy either." His slender facial features gave way to a frown that tried not to turn into a grin. He knew his wife had this occasional need to even the score. It was one of the things her loved about her. "Now can I get some breakfast? Something tells me it's gonna be a long day."

She was still chuckling when she went to the stove, scrapped the eggs from the pan, and set the plate down in front of her man. "You gotta' admit," she started, "the look on those jackasses was worth the work. Make sure you stop by the feed store today, Harold, they'll get a kick out of this one."

Harold smiled back affectionately, and secretly thanked God that Elva was on his side.

The officers worked through the day trying to determine which horses had paint and which wore natural socks. They eliminated all the non-chestnut horses, but the going was rough as the animals did everything they could to avoid the unfamiliar visitors closing around them. To add to Tate's troubles, the Winter's veterinarian refused to assist him in the search. All the vets he contacted had declined, saying that making Elva their enemy wasn't worth the loss in business. So his team reluctantly had to go it alone with only a picture in their hand.

The retirement herd was the biggest challenge. Tate was convinced that they worked as one evil old unit. The large brown draft horse was clearly elected leader. The huge muscular beast stood well above the rest, proud and strong, his long blond raggedy mane and forelock only made him more intimidating. Tate decided that the horse had an air of authority that even he found disturbing. It made him uncomfortable, this posturing between him and a dumb animal. It was on this horse's movements that the others responded and followed. It was a silent language in which the draft horse cued the rest of his herd. It took all seven officers walking in a chain formation to get the herd corralled into a corner of one, fifty-acre paddock. And all this, so they could get a decent look at the feet. But if the animal was here, then their suspect was close, and it was worth the effort. The horses stood like statues watching the men approach; the draft horse at the front, watching and waiting, all eyes and ears focused on the uniformed visitors.

"This was your freakin' great idea, Apple," Tate reminded his partner as they approached one step at a time.

"I didn't think you could actually paint a horse for Christ's sake- at least not in this day and age," Apple replied as the men cautiously moved another step forward.

Tate took one step too close to the herd, crossing the invisible line that defined the herd's safety. The large draft horse threw his head in dominance and charged toward them, thundering brazenly through the meager string of men, mocking their pathetic line of defense - the rest of his followers close behind. The men cowered and scattered as the horses ran through them. Several threw themselves into the mud covering their heads with their hands. The herd stopped at the far opposite end of the field behind their leader as if extending another challenge. It was clearly a game of wills to them.

Tate was splattered with mud and had dropped his pad during their flight but was relieved he wasn't knocked to the ground. He faced the animals and his voice echoed across the field toward them. "O.K. you win!" He motioned the men toward the cars.

The large draft horse was the only one to respond to the leader of the uniformed herd. He pawed at the ground, tossed his head in triumph, and then returned a stony gaze to the men. Together the animals stood like a band of motionless brigade of guards, watching their enemies in hasty retreat.

Toby stuck his head in the pigeon pen with Bob, fascinated with his winged playmates. There was no note on any of the birds today and Bob was clearly worried. His mind had imagined his mother half dead somewhere in the woods unable to find help. He couldn't shake the image out of his mind. So when Ethan Peterson showed up with a ladder in his truck, he was happy to take his mind off his problems. He spent the day fixing the hole in the barn roof with some help from Old Joe's grandson.

Ethan was short and tough. What he lacked in height he made up in build and attitude. His muscles were etched deeply into his chest and arms. He had been a high school football player once, until he was thrown off the team for being arrested while intoxicated. The two young men had never acknowledged each other while in high school. They moved in different circles. But today, things seemed different, and Ethan spoke and treated him like they had been buddies for years. Bob figured Old Joe was punishing him for some new infraction. No kid voluntarily did farm work. Ethan knew a lot about repairs and the job went quickly. Eventually the young men stood in the barn and nodded approvingly at the lack of light, where a hole to the sky had once been.

Ethan unlocked Butch's stall and patted the horse on the neck. "So how's the old boy doin'?"

"Swelling's down and he's not limping as bad," Bob answered.

Ethan ran his hand down the horse's front leg. "Looks pretty good. You know if I were you, I'd let him out in the pasture and get him moving it again. Then in a couple of days, throw a saddle on his back and walk him around."

Bob watched him examine the horse with an ease and knowledge he envied. "What's the point of just walkin' him with a saddle on?"

"Gives him a little weight to carry on his leg, without a two hundred pound human on his back."

Butch let the young man push him aside, and Ethan ran his hand down the hairless stripe. The animal lashed his tail and flattened his ears. Ethan slapped the horse under the belly moving him away in a cool confident manner. He stepped out of the stall and locked it behind him. "The trick is not to let him push you around. Make him respect you – not by being mean, because then he'll never come to you, but command his attention and never let him intimidate you."

Bob smiled. "You know a lot, don't you?"

"Enough." Butch was leaning over the stall and Ethan rubbed the horse's face affectionately. "I could teach you, ya know, how to ride and handle him...when he gets a little stronger. He's a nice horse, but he's a leader. You have to show him that you're number one in the pecking order- not him."

Toby followed the men through the barn as they talked. He sniffed at the dried blood on the floor and watched patiently as his master climbed into the loft and threw down a bale of hay.

Ethan leaned against the stall, his eyes trailing the dark stains on the floor. "If your mom's hurt, wouldn't she need medical supplies?"

"Probably."

"She was seen by the cranberry bogs last night."

"How do ya know?" Bob climbed down the ladder interested in this new information.

"Joe has the police band on all the time. They had some guy with dogs trailing her and now they think she's held up somewhere between Bozarth's Dairy Farm and the Lucky Circle. At least that's what the police think. Joe's got a bet with the guys at the feed store that your mom will last five days out there before getting caught."

"Oh yeah? What's her odds?"

"We could make 'em better if we knew where she's headin'. I was thinkin' about takin' Satan for a ride tonight. Ya know, make sure I get seen. Kinda' help her odds. I could use a little money myself."

Bob chuckled, "You actually would name an animal that?"

Ethan shook his head, "Actually, his name's Satin, I've just added a bit of my opinion to the pronunciation. And you think Butch has an attitude?" Ethan scowled, "Satan throws you, then laughs. I swear he laughs! It's a game, ya know. Just when I think I have him broke, have his respect- and he's doing everything right – all of sudden, I'm flying through the air and landin' on my butt."

The young men laughed, but Bob was careful not to speculate on his mother's possible destinations. Still, this police band thing might be helpful in getting supplies to her.

"Can you let me know if you hear anything else?"

"Sure and you let me know how he makes out with the saddle, and I'll show you a few things."

Ethan picked up the extension ladder and walked toward his old beat up pickup with a nod goodbye.

Bob went out into the paddock and cleaned and filled the water tub, checking all the gates and making sure they were locked. He leaned against the stall for a while watching Butch pull at his hay, considering Ethan's suggestion. With every new mouthful the horse stared back at him with intense interest.

Finally Bob gathered his nerve, "O.K," he said, "lets do this, Butch." He lifted the halter from the hook and slid it over the horses' head. Then he led him outside in the pasture. One reassuring pat on the neck and he pulled the halter off.

The horse stood there for a moment allowing his eyes to search over the fenced paddocks, and then let out a deep throaty bellow. Bob walked back into the barn and watched as Butch walked stiffly into the middle of the field and grunted again. No animal returned the call. He began to walk, hesitant in his step, his ears forward and alert, listening for his partner. Slowly he began to accelerate his movement, each step became more staccato, propelling his body into a broken, pacing, run. Within minutes, Butch had frantically worked himself into a fractured awkward lope, desperately searching each paddock, bellowing his unanswered call.

Bob broke into a cold sweat, realizing that this move wasn't good for the injury, and more importantly, how was he going to stop it. As he watched the horse, Butch's stiff irregular motion became a smooth running walk. The animal's pain now forgotten and replaced by adrenalin spiked panic, his movement became fluid and natural and lofty.

He had never witnessed a horse in full flight before, let alone the grace of a Tennessee walker in high reaching natural stride. He had never appreciated in person the beauty of their movement, power, elegance and speed. The high stepping gait made Butch appear to be floating above the ground as the action of his fetlocks gave an effortless impression to his movement. Butch held his head high and proud, his mane and tail drifting like flags in the wind, as he followed the fence line of the property in search of his companion. It was a lesson in the athletic elegance of nature's power, and Bob was frozen in awe of the experience. But he had to put a stop to this before Butch injured himself further –he had never intended him to run. Bob's admiration turned to guilt when he realized that this normally dominant self-assured horse was in terror of being alone. His mind raced through ideas to stop the tirade when he remembered the conversation at the feed store. He and Toby jumped into the dual wheel truck and drove into town.

He pulled into the feed store and caught the largest of the shopkeepers as he was locking up for the day. "You said I could come to you if I needed help. Well I got a question for you," he called from the truck window, "that horse of dads is going crazy in the field without my mom's horse around. What should I do?"

The man scratched his chin. "Sure, I got something that might work for ya."

Bob watched as the man casually walked out behind the feed store and returned pulling a reluctant old goat behind him. He flung open the passenger side door and lifted the animal into the front seat of the truck. "Name's Martin. Wife named him. He's old, he's ornery, but he's company."

Before either passenger knew what was happening, Bob was eye to eye with the black and gray haired goat. It seemed as curious and dazed as Bob was. "But...but...how do I get him home?"

"Oh, he's O.K. Martin likes to ride in the car. Just don't make any sudden stops."

"And this will calm Butch down?"

"Yep." The conversation was over as the man shut the door and tossed the remaining wood chips he owed him in the back of the truck bed. As he walked away, he called back, "Now you look like a farmer, boy!"

Bob sat dumbfounded, looking at the goat, who was looking at Toby, and then at him. He backed the dually down the dirt drive and headed for home. He should have asked what goats eat, but it was too late now. He was in a hurry to return and he had to hope this worked.

As he turned down the road toward his house, Martin slipped off the seat and fell noisily on the floor. Bob tried to reach for him, but the dually swerved sharply as he went to grab the animal.

The squirt of a siren and a flash of lights demanded his attention and filled his rearview mirror. "Damn, see what you did?" He reprimanded Martin out loud, as if he would understand. He brought the dually slowly to the shoulder of the road.

A young, clean-shaven officer tugged at his hat and took notice of the earrings and the lip ring on the young man as he approached the vehicle. Bob recognized him immediately from the night in the barn. He rolled down the window to greet him.

"Can I see your license?" The officer stated flatly.

"What was I doin'?" Bob asked.

"Your driving is a little erratic. You haven't been drinking have you?" The officer peered into the driver's side, his eyes scanning for alcoholic beverages or so much of a whiff of alcohol.

Bob frowned. He was used to being treated like a criminal simply by virtue of the way he looked. He ignored the officer's invasion and leaned over to reach for the glove compartment, searching for the registration and insurance card. Martin didn't like Bob leaning across him. He jumped back up on the seat, scuffled with the dog and suddenly popped out eye to eye with the young policeman.

The startled officer jumped back from the window as his hand went instinctively to his holster. "Is this the proper way of transporting livestock?"

Bob was still fumbling around in the glove compartment, oblivious to their actions, "I just came from the feed store, I needed some company...." He started to realize how ridiculous he sounded, and returned to a sitting position pushing Martin back on his side of the truck. He handed the officer the paperwork, "I only live down the road, Martin and I..."

The officer put his hand up to stop him. He sounded exasperated as he spoke. "Just...go and don't let me catch you driving with a goat again." He turned and walked back to his car mumbling, "I can't believe I just said that...damn farm town..."

Bob breathed a sigh of relief and glanced over at Martin, who had lost interest in the officer and was now munching on some papers in the glove compartment. A crinkled sheet dangled lazily from his mouth, bobbing up and down as he chewed. Bob snatched the paper from the goat with one sweep of his hand, and threw it back into the glove compartment slamming the door with a bang. Martin stared at him. Bob burst into laughter and put his head on the steering wheel. It was a good thing his friends couldn't see this.

It was the sight of another animal helping himself to the pile of hay that brought Butch to an abrupt stop in the middle of the field. This action suddenly demanded his immediate attention. His ears flattened against his head and he approached the little goat with a slow walking authority. But when he went to nip his daring intruder, as a reminder of who was boss, the little goat lunged at the much larger animal his horns set and ready to strike.

Butch jumped back again and again, and soon it was clear that in order to eat, he was going to have to learn to share with this brazen little creature. Martin munched on hay and Bob moved some bales of straw in front of the water tub so the little goat could jump on them and drink. Martin acted as if he lived there all his life. He pranced into the shed after the horse, and was unaffected by Butch's cranky disposition. The horse eyed him curiously, but the company of another stopped his furious rage for the lost herd that was once his buddy, Shortstop.

Bob watched, amused by their interaction and began to clean Martin's slobber from the interior of the dually. He brushed the hair and fragments of half-eaten paper from the seat, considering how upset his dad would have been if he were still alive. His dually was his baby, and Bob was beginning to understand why. There was a kind of power behind driving the huge vehicle. He felt as if everyone turned to see the truck as it passed. He smiled as he wiped the rag across the seat. He was being ridiculous, of course. It had to be the sound of the machine itself that drew the attention. It was a horse hauling power machine with a rumbling diesel engine that spoke serious business as it did its work.

He picked up the piece of ripped paper he had pulled from the goat's mouth and un-crinkled its torn counterpart. The paper was dated several weeks before his father's death. Its letterhead was from the University Museum Laboratory. He studied the paper, another confusing piece of his father's puzzle. A number was printed on it, but there was no description of the item. It was signed and dated by a Dr. Roy Collins, Department of Anthropology.

His hand moved through the glove box passing over the owner's manual, flashlight and insurance papers. He pulled out a heavy lined envelope at the very bottom. He unsealed the package, and pulled out what he initially thought was a gold pocket watch. The cover portrayed an engraved hawk, flying above the trees, and he rubbed his fingers across it. He gently opened the claw of the cover and was surprised that the inside revealed a compass, instead of the watch he had imagined. On the inside of the cover was engraved:

Bob –

So you will always find your way back home.
Love Dad.

He stood, staring in frozen silence. It was devastating to read those words, his father's voice echoing lost chances from the dead. He turned the compass over in his hands and fought back the tears, eyes so filled with emotion that they seemed to burn into his skull. All those years of fighting, of thinking his father hated him and believing that he hated his father - when all the time it was a battle of wills, to prove no more than he was an individual. He collapsed on the seat of the truck and as his tear filled eyes wandered over the pasture, he realized he and his father were no better than the stubborn animals they cared for. They postured for dominance like Butch and Martin – their pathetic species having learned nothing through centuries of evolution. What had happened to his father that changed his mind? Why didn't he give this to him? Did he just run out of time?

Bob slid across the seat and adjusted the mirror, brushing the hot liquid from his eyes, looking himself in the face. So much had been left unsaid between his father and him. He looked the spacers in his ears and the ring in his lip. The piercings weren't a statement of his individuality, merely a weapon used to enrage his father. It seemed so mute now, all the pride and anger that surged between them. He locked the gold claw of the chain around his neck and the circular compass fell at the base of his throat. He forced himself to finish the mundane job of cleaning up the dually, digesting the meaning, knowing his father had meant much more than the simple line that was inscribed. His father was not an emotional man. It must have been hard to write what he felt…and more impossible to deliver. This one last gift …a peace offering of sorts. He owed his father to find out what happened and clear his mother.

He continued the cleanup of the vehicle, all the time struggling with the turbulent emotions that had spiked between he and his father. He tugged at a box of tissues in the driver's side door and it made a heavy movement that drew his attention. He reached in and pulled out a smooth semi circular object wrapped in tissue paper. The item was deliberately scribed and he turned it in his hands trying to find the most revealing light to examine its surface. It had two holes, one at each end, and -similar to the compass, carried an image of a hawk. But that was the only similarity. The hawk carved in the smooth cold stone was angry and vicious; it led talons first, extended like knives toward another image that Bob couldn't make out. He turned it upside down, and a similar but reversed image reappeared. It was masterful in detail.

Determined to know, he walked up to the house and logged onto the University website searching the faculty list until he found Dr. Roy Collins, Professor of Anthropology. His bio defined him as a professor and author on Native American history in New Jersey. Bob called the office number, and identified himself leaving his cell phone number.

He spilled the bag of library books onto the floor of the living room. Several were about legends and gods, another on early New Jersey archaeology, and others were historical speculation on their early lifestyle. All were specific to Native American tribes known to the region. Bob flipped through the heaviest, experiencing a part of the past that he had somehow missed in high school history.

The fact that these people once roamed New Jersey seemed so out of touch with any reality in today's world. As he read about their inevitable relocation and isolation, a slow kind of anger began to grow inside, fueled by his understanding of what it was like to be an outcast to society, shunned by the community, and ultimately pushed from even your own home.

They seemed to want no more than their own survival and never took more than what they needed. They were a people who understood they were mere visitors on the earth – and left it unscathed as they roamed. He slammed the book shut. It enraged him to read about the lies and deception that led to the destruction of their society. Why should this bother him now? It was only history, and change was always inevitable. His hand went to the compass at his neck and he re-opened the book and continued reading. He had to help his mother, and so far, this was the only lead he could follow. There had to be something in here that might help him understand. Dr. Collin's book on archeology had several chapters on the unearthing of a critical local find in a nearby town. On that site, the prehistoric human skeletons of fifty-four people were uncovered. The remains and their buried contents from this tribe were uncovered and catalogued for the scientific community. That site was less than ten miles away from the house, less than five miles from the Semi Wild Club. How could he not know that? How could human remains that ancient be untouched by the damp sandy soil of the area? He stared at the stone carving of the hawk, and wondered if the item was connected to Collin's site, connected to his father's murder, and ultimately connected to his mother's note about the *hawk*.

He was flying above the trees, while strange mounds of green brush and treetops swept beneath him at high-speed vision. Soaring above an unscarred landscape, effortless and powerful and all knowing, his soul filled with exhilaration and crystal clear purpose. He was invincible in this strange metamorphosis that pulsed through him and lifted his soul to euphoria. The sensation of the thrill wanted to scream from him as he wafted toward the ground sweeping over the fields, but the sound he made was only a long sorrowful call. He was in control of this flight and his existence - master of this domain. A sense of peace filled him as the wind passed beneath him harnessing its power of movement, the heat of the sun...pulsating on his face...and the smell...a smell so unpleasant...

The sharp intrusive ringing of the phone shook him into consciousness, forcing him to squeeze one open eye. Toby stared down at him panting. He grabbed the dog playfully, and wrestled him to the floor. As he reached for his phone, he wished for that dream back. That sense of power was so illusive and distant.

"Hello?"

"Is Mr. Bob Winters there?"

"This is him," he answered cautiously.

"This is Dr. Collins at the University."

"I want to know what business you had with my father," the young man said directly.

There was an uneasy silence, "Can we meet?"

Chapter Nine

Mary awoke while daylight was still strong and decided to vacate the shed. If a hunter were using the stand, he would be in and set before dusk. Her pants were dry, but her boot linings were still damp. She would have to count on the warmth of her feet to dry the insides. She thought about the day she bought them. She had cringed at the two hundred dollar price on the Browning boots - warm to minus seventy degrees the tag stated. She had tossed them aside, complaining to Mark, *if it's that cold, I'm gonna be by the fire in the clubhouse.* But Mark just laughed and purchased them anyway. There was no scrimping when it came to outdoor gear. It was always the best, Orvis, Filson, Browning and Cabelas. But mention to Mark about buying matching end tables? *I'm not spending that for somethin' to put a glass on.* His words made her smile. His forehead wrinkled when he became as stubborn as a mule. She thanked God that he had made her buy those boots that day. She could never have imagined this kind of test against the elements. Mark always took good care of her. Tears welled up in her eyes. It was time to leave. It was time to run again.

She hoisted her leg over Shortstop, rode a distance from the shed, then dismounted and crouched behind a cluster of scrub pines patiently waiting for complete darkness. She had no idea where she was and in which direction she should ride, but she knew that she couldn't go back to the road. The police had to be combing the area for her. She watched the position of the sun set. At least she knew which way was west.

It started as a faint rhythmical crunching sound in the distance. It wasn't long before she realized it was the sound of someone approaching through the dried brush of the woods. Shortstop turned in the direction of the sound and whinnied nervously giving her position away.

The steps abruptly stopped and an angry voice called out into the woods. "Who's there? And what're you doing on my property?"

Mary figured the man to be well into his sixties with a voice that was deep and threatening. Her eyes took in the shotgun over his shoulder and the spotlight dangling from his belt.

She stepped forward assertively, "Fish and Game Officer Horseback Division," flashing the fake badge that she had confiscated from her attacker in the barn. She started firing instructions and questions at the man. "Put the gun down sir, and let's see your permit. Got reports of poaching in this area," she continued with authority in hope that he would be too confused to question the badge, "and I'm sure that spotlight there is for walking out of here after dark...right? You wouldn't be doing any night huntin' now right?"

"I didn't do nothin'," he fumbled in his coat pocket and retrieved a crumpled up permit. His demeanor started to soften as the shift in power changed.

Mary continued, "And I don't see much orange on you either. That's another violation. Two hundred square inches!" She reached into her saddlebag and pulled out her tablet as if to make it official.

"This is private land," he started, "no one is suppose to be here. Don't you need permission to be trespassin'?" He unrolled an orange skullcap from his pocket, pulling it tightly over his bald head.

"You sound a little nervous, and no, I don't need any permission - other than a complaint." She had no idea, but was happy the man didn't know either.

He avoided eye contact, and it was clear to her that he was guilty of something. She examined the permit. If he were on his property, the neighbors probably wouldn't care. The deer population was out of control in the area and did more damage to vehicles and crops than most people cared to report. So like most the locals fed up with being told the rules on their own land, this man took a shoot, shovel or eat-it-for-dinner kind of attitude to keep nature in check.

His gaze came back to her, "Aren't you suppose to wear something to identify yourself?" He asked under his breath.

"Now if I did that, I wouldn't catch anybody, would I? Besides, you aren't the biggest problem I have right now, so I'm gonna let you slide tonight."

The man was clearly relieved. "You lookin' for the Winters woman too? Cops were over at Matson's today. They packed up and left not long ago. And last night there was some kind of commotion down at the Bozarth Dairy farm. They had officers and cars there. But it took all day to do Elva's. I guess they think she's nearby."

She ignored his attempt at pleasant conversation, but only nodded as if she already knew. "Keep the orange on and I better not hear any firing after dark, Mr. Handley." She wanted him to know she had his name.

A smile started to spread across the man's lips as she turned to her horse, and his eyes settled on her limp. "You're her aren't you…Jesus, you are…you're all over the local news."

"You don't know me." She mounted Shortstop and wanted to disappear into the woods as quickly as possible, embarrassed that her lie was found out.

"Yeah, you're the Winter's broad." He threw his hand out toward her startling her with the motion.

She looked down at the extended hand, calloused and spotted by the sun. She saw nothing but sincerity in the man's worn face and hesitantly reached out to shake it.

"Not often we get a celebrity out here. My wife and I've been livin' out here for years. Ain't nobody bothers us. Why don't you come to our place and let her get a meal in ya." He pointed to a narrow sandy trail that led through the forest. "We live about a mile that way…you can rest your horse."

Shortstop needed more water and it would be another hour until dark. At the very least the old man could show her exactly where she was and what pitfalls she might be able to avoid along the way. She nodded in reluctant agreement. "You know these woods pretty well? "

"Sure do, lived here all my life. Follow me then and we'll fix you up before you move on." The man trudged off with horse and rider right following behind.

The Handley's lived in a small run down home. Mary put Shortstop in a small broken shed where light came through the roof and grass grew on the sandy floor. The fence that used to keep in livestock was now half down broken wire strung from tree to tree.

"Had a mule once," he spoke as he put a bucket of water in front of Shortstop, "but up and died four years ago. We should all go that quick. She was a good worker too. She and I would pull the trees out of the woods. I'd cut it for the wood stove." He closed the shed door behind the horse, and Mary noticed a tear in his eye as he spoke about the animal. "Sorry I don't have any hay around," he added.

Mary limped behind him into the house. Her leg was agony with every movement. The pain seemed to be worsening. The front porch creaked as she entered the little house. She followed Ralph Handley's lead and hung her coat on the wood rack by the door, as if she had visited there for years. There was the smell of venison stew on the stove and a small thin woman stood over the kettle stirring it.

"Anna we got ourselves a guest," Ralph announced, "so put another bowl on the table."

The woman turned and smiled. "You lost?"

Ralph laughed. "This is the Winter's woman, Anna. Ya know, the one everybody's talkin' about."

"Well now, everyone's been looking for you, honey." Her skin had a parchment texture when she smiled that made her look older than her true years. Her eyes gravitated to Mary's leg. "You're hurt. I don't have much, but I got some peroxide and some Telfa. Before Mary could respond, the woman was in the back room bringing an armload of supplies and placing them on the kitchen table. "Here honey, fix yourself up."

The three of them sat down at the kitchen table while the smell of vegetables and venison simmered on the stove. It smelled wonderful. Mary had to lift her leg up onto the chair; the swelling had turned the pant leg of her jeans into a denim tourniquet. The couple watched as she took a pair of scissors and cut the pant leg up to her knee. They talked about what was being printed in the local newspaper, versus what was the truth.

Mary slammed her palm on the table as Anna poured the peroxide into the oozing wound. She dabbed at it with a paper towel. It fizzled angrily back at her.

Anna frowned, "That looks bad."

Mary said nothing as she opened each band-aid and stretched them like a bridge across the gaping yellow wound. She re-wrapped the leg with sterile pads and gauze. She would have to get to Jack's as soon as possible. This infection was going to tumble out of control and he was the only one who could help her. She turned to the old woman, "Do you have any antibiotics around here?"

Anna rose again and rummaged through the bathroom. She came back with some pharmacy containers. "These are old, but I don't throw anything out. Some of this so called generic stuff, I wish they would say what it's for on the label because I don't know what it does anymore."

Mary examined the containers and found one prescription of penicillin 250mg with four tablets in the bottle. She took all of them with a large glass of water.

With the injury taken care of, Anna soon put a bowl of steaming stew and a hard roll in front of her. As good as it smelled, she still had to force herself to eat. It was the infection starting to make her nauseous.

Anna and Ralph had an interesting but simple life. Ralph grew blueberries in the spring and worked on cranberry farms in the fall. They had two children, both grown and moved away. One was an engineer working on waste management sites all over New Jersey. The other was a wife and mother married to a pharmacist in north Jersey.

Mary was surprised that they had put two children through college, and yet still wanted to live in the middle of the woods.

"Yeah, both the kids wanted us to live with 'em," Ralph explained, "but the pines, it gets in your blood. You need the sound of the whispers to get to sleep at night. And I'll tell ya somethin' else. People out here – they mean what they say. Hell...when the kids want to get away and relax...they come back. You just can't leave it, not entirely anyway."

As they ate and talked, Mary realized that Ralph was a welcome wealth of information when it came to the Pine Barrens. The conversation started to lean toward the way to Elva's and the best way to survive in the pines.

"How do I know which way I'm going out here, Ralph? I mean, sometimes I wake up and I can't remember where I am and it all looks alike. Sometimes I get into a field of squatty pines that rake over you and seem to go for miles. I lose direction with no landmarks."

Ralph dipped his bread in his stew and closed his eyes as if he were in heaven. He swallowed, savoring every bite, then snapped back to reality as if digesting the question. "Easy. Just look at the pines, girl. The longest branches are always on the south side of the tree. Moss on the north. Once you determine that - you know where you are."

After dinner, Anna stood washing the dishes in the sink and Ralph unfolded a map and made several marks on it. "You're here. Elva's is here, highway 72 here, now if you cut through there, cross the highway, stay behind the development...."

Ralph helped to devise a plan. "You're only going to make it to Elva's tonight. But tomorrow night, ya need to head due west, cross the highway near the WaWa," his finger showed the way, "then head north towards Jackson's crossroads. You're pretty exposed at that point, so circle around to the high school and cross the farm from this direction."

Ralph leaned back in his chair and discussed the landmarks to look for along the way - and the history of the trails she was taking. "Ya know, a lot of them started as deer trails, then became In'gin trails. Some of those became paved roads and still others are unknown, but are used by only us Pineys." He pointed back to the map, ya' know, there's a dam a ways south made of teak. It was an old British ship that was pirated and dismantled during the revolutionary war. Those Pineys were smart. Broke down the wood and built a dam so the ships were never found. No lie. It'll probably last forever too. I think a lot of folks don't know the secrets of the woods out here. But everywhere you turn there's history and lots of secrets. And we like to keep it that way - secret that is..."

Mary marveled at his knowledge and finished her iced tea as she listened intensely to the old man. She wished she could disappear into the woods too, like Ralph and Anna. They seemed to have everything that was important, food right outside their door and just enough contact with civilization not to make you distrust it.

The couple walked her out to the shed about 10:00 pm. They had refilled her water bottles and put some muffins in her bag. She thanked them for their kindness, mounted Shortstop and disappeared into the woods. Elva's would be the next stop tonight if the series of landmarks Ralph gave her were solid. There, she could rest Shortstop and he would have plenty to eat and drink. He would have to be ready for the next leg of the journey. It would be a greater challenge because there would be more inhabited areas to cross, and in some areas, they would lose the protection of the woods altogether.

Darkness obscured the landscape except for the cold blue shadows of the moon and the woods that crouched before her like a waiting beast. Her eyes adjusted well. She headed west, searching for each item on Ralph's list as a guide. She turned off the path at the first white sandpit and followed a partially cut path to some blueberry fields. The sounds of the woods didn't seem to bother her anymore. She followed the edge of the fields until she found the path that was to the right of the pile of wood that used to be a blueberry-packing house, but had collapsed a few years back from a heavy snow. Ralph was right. He knew these woods. They picked their way down the overgrown path through the trees until slow moving cars mumbled far into the distance.

Like a white ghost rising from the ground, the square structure of the house and white lined fences of the back of Elva's farm emerged from the darkness. She suspected that searching Elva's had given the police a sense of safety that she was no longer in that immediate area. She crossed the little creek that drained Lucky Circle's fields and hid under the rickety old drainage bridge until she was certain it was safe. When she was sure that the area was deserted, she followed the fence line to the very rear of the property and the retirement herd where an extra horse would not be noticed.

Clouds had gathered in luminous streaks across the moon as the dark silhouettes moved silently across the expansive pasture. The herd grazed quietly watching the visitor pass. Mary knew the old and the unsound were kept in the very rear paddock, far away from the road and the high priced barns.

Elva kept the retirees as great a distance from the main road as the property would allow. Death was inevitable of course. Animals died from many of the same reasons and ailments that humans succumb to - even old age. The very rear paddock was surrounded by a narrow access road just wide enough for a truck with a wench for the discreet removal of a carcass.

It was perfect for Shortstop. She looked over the large rolling lush pasture that extended farther than the darkness would allow her to see. The only horse near the fence was one old gray mare, an obvious outcast from the safety of the herd. The rest grazed as a unit in what seemed like acres away, and acted uninterested by her presence. She unsaddled her horse and led him into the paddock through the rear gate. Turning toward the woods, she covered the saddle and bridle with the plastic rain gear she had packed, and hid it under some brush. She was careful to count the fence posts so she would remember where it was hidden. Shortstop put his head down eyeing the gray horse and grazing near the edge of the fence. The other horses watched him as they ate, and one horse limped forward assertively to challenge the newcomer. It was a huge draft horse. He was magnificent in stature. His mane floated in the cold evening breeze and reflected like cobwebs in the moonlight. Shortstop moved away with his head low, acknowledging his pecking order and staying far away from the herd.

Mary walked along the woods trying to find a place to hide herself during the upcoming day. The sky was turning a hint of opal when she spotted a deer stand about midway into the woods, high up in an oak tree. It seemed large in comparison to most deer stands, and overlooked a small reservoir, part of the field's drainage from the paddocks.

With her saddlebag over her shoulder and her bedroll under her arm, she slowly and painfully climbed into the stand. Her leg felt like it was dragging behind her. She watched the first quiet beam of light start to take the sky. She felt exhausted and sick. It would be important not to wake up disoriented, especially the way she was feeling. She laid out her bedroll on the generous stand and curled up with her knees to her chest and her head toward the south. She pulled the sleeping bag up to her neck and put her hands over her face to block the rising light of the sun.

She glanced one last time across the vast open field and noticed that Shortstop had teamed up with the old gray, two outcasts on the edge of the retirement herd. Mary covered her eyes with her hands and fell into a cautious sleep.

Chapter Ten

"I had to hear about it by e-mail - from my friends! Why didn't you call me, butthole, what the hell's a matter with you!" Steve yelled into the phone squeezing it with white-knuckle rage.

Bob could hear his brother's voice quaking on the line. "Jesus, Steve, it's three-thirty in the morning!" He rolled into a sitting position on the bed, the phone tight to his ear as he spoke. "Listen! I don't want to talk on the phone and you shouldn't be puttin' nothing in e-mail to anybody! You got it?" He tried to take control of the situation using his newly acquired authoritative tone that he learned from working with Ethan. "Now just cool your jets and I'll be up to talk to you- in person. Be waiting outside your dorm." He hung up without giving his brother a chance to reply. He had to be careful. He called for Toby and both of them got into the car.

Steve ripped the phone from its tenuous cord. It crashed against the wall of the dorm, its parts spilling from beneath its plastic skin and tingling across the linoleum floor. He was fed up with his brother's antics. He was tired of always picking up the pieces of his brother's screw-ups. Mom and Dad seemed to give Bob more freedom and choices...and always he would find a way of throwing it in their faces. This was just another example. How many days had gone by and his own brother never called to tell him about the man in the barn and the disappearance of his mother. He couldn't count on him for anything, let alone to keep a farm going and to help his mother when she was in trouble.

He pulled on his baseball jacket and went for a walk. He needed to cool off before his brother got there. The college was quiet in the early hours of morning. The sky was clear and cold and the moon was bright with only a veil of silvery clouds reflecting its glow. There were a few couples meandering around in the dark, talking and laughing. The occasional orange glow of a cigarette lit the darkness as couples whispered between one another.

He rested his head in his hands and thought about what his mother was doing tonight under this very same moon. Maybe she escaped to an obscure friend's home and had found safety there. He decided that he needed to believe that, since the alternative, her lying somewhere injured and starving was a thought that would drive him crazy. But what could he do to help her? He felt powerless.

As if that wasn't enough, he heard that Bob's old girlfriend was picked up for drug possession and breaking and entering. In his mind, it only confirmed his brother's connection to drugs. As much as they fought, they were still part of one another. He had made up his mind to confront him.

Steve was still sitting on the cold concrete steps, lost in his thoughts, when Drew returned from his date. "Hey," he started, "Carol and I really hit it off. We went to a movie and back to the sorority house, had a great time. Thanks for hookin' us up."

Steve nodded but said nothing. His mind was elsewhere.

Drew opened the door to go in, but changed his mind and took a seat along side of him. "What's up? Can't sleep? You did good on your last test, so I know that's not it."

Steve responded, his eyes faraway, "Drew," he started, "Do you have a brother?"

Drew noticed the serious demeanor of his friend, "Sure. Believe it or not I'm a twin, but you would never know it by lookin' at us."

"How's that?" Steve asked in an almost disinterested tone.

"He's a linebacker at Nebraska State."

Steve lifted his head and stared at him, "What? You shittin' me?"

"No. Angus, that's his nickname. We were twins. Mom said he almost killed me in the womb. He was always the big athlete and I was always the little sickly kid brother. Funny huh?" The two men looked out into the darkness.

"I got a brother," Steve replied. "He's a lot different from me, too. I hardly know him anymore." Steve realized he had more in common with this young man than he knew, "Let me ask you something. If you knew or thought your brother was doin' drugs, what would you do? How would you handle it?"

Drew sat in silence for a moment. "I think I would try to talk to him if I thought his life was in danger. You see, Angus and I never knew each other - not really anyway. The only thing we had in common was that we lived in the same house. I studied – he lived. It was like I was invisible to everybody growing up. It was always, how's your brother doin', what college is he goin' to, how'd he do in the last game?"

"That's too bad. I guess in some ways my brother felt that way. Maybe that was the whole problem between us."

"But all that changed when we got out of high school and I came here," Drew added, trying to cheer up his friend, "I gotta' tell you, that night you threatened me in the hallway? It was the best thing that happened to me."

"How do ya figure that?" Steve managed a grin, knowing that he had hooked his tutor up with some fine looking females. But Drew wasn't merely a sympathy case. Steve genuinely liked him. He was funny in a nerdy kind of way, and the guys on the team looked out for him. They always ran to him for help with their classes. It was a friendship built on mutual respect.

"I feel like I'm doing something important. You got me helping all your baseball buddies and they even invite me sometimes just to hang out. I like being on the team, even if it's just doing statistics. I feel like I'm part of something even though I never stepped out on the field."

"Well, if it weren't for you, not many of us would be on the field either. We wouldn't have much of a team come spring." Steve was pulled back into his thoughts about his brother. "Here's the thing with my brother," he started again,

"A few summers ago I got friendly with a kid at work. Ya know, we weren't best friends, but we told jokes while we packed blueberries into crates during summer break. One day, the kid just didn't come to work. I found out later that he died, mixed crack and alcohol, and was so messed up he couldn't turn his own head to vomit. So, he suffocated on his own vomit. How messed up is that? If I had known he was doing drugs, maybe I could have stopped him. It was like one day we were talking and laughing about what college we applied to, and the next he was gone – wiped from the face of the earth. I can't, I just can't let the same thing happen to my brother. I don't think I could live with myself."

The two young men talked for hours until the headlights of a car turned toward the dorm and Steve rose from the steps in anticipation. He had been sitting out there much longer than he thought.

Drew saw it was time to leave. "If you need...well, you know where I'm at." He opened the door to the dorm, "And Steve...I hope you're wrong about your brother."

Steve walked to the parking lot and angrily threw open the car door and jumped in. "Are you goin' to tell me what the hell is goin' on?"

Bob wasn't sure who would win if they ever got into a real fistfight but he had a feeling he might find out tonight. Although he was older and taller, Steve was more athletic. Still, Bob wanted to believe he could take him anyway just on the age thing. "I didn't tell you because Mom said not to talk on the phone and not to use e-mail. The house was being watched." He acknowledged what his brother had heard, and explained in more detail what happened in the barn and what the police suspected. "But, she sent me a message by pigeon, yeah...do you believe that? She's O.K. at least for now. She's on the run and I suspect she's hidin' out somewhere on different farms in the county or in the woods."

Steve looked devastated. "What are we gonna' do? We gotta' do something to help her!"

"Nothin', we can't do nothin' till we hear from her."

"I've got to come home. I've got to help her."

"No way. Mom will kick your ass for cuttin' class and kick mine for lettin' you. I have everything under control at the house, and I have a contact now with Mom. She'll let me know what she needs when she finds somewhere safe."

"And what about you?" Steve looked his brother squarely in the eyes. He was shaking with anger and acted as if he might strike him. "Are you really trying to help her, or are you just getting' high all the time. Oh yeah, in case you haven't heard, your old girlfriend just went to jail for seven years!"

Bob went quiet. This was news to him, but he wasn't going to let his brother know that. "I'm not seeing her anymore. And frankly, I have more to worry about right now than what you think of her."

Steve lunged at Bob grabbing him by the neck and pinning him against the window with a thud. Toby began to growl and bark in the back seat, but Steve yelled over the commotion, "you prick, I don't even know you anymore to trust you. Don't try to lie to me. She got arrested trying to distribute…and you were just lucky you weren't with her at the time. Well you know what? I'll report your ass to the police myself before I'll let you kill yourself usin' that stuff. Do you hear me? I'd rather see you in jail than see you dead…do you get it?"

Bob tried to push him away, but Steve had him tight by the throat. "You're my only brother…" his voice started to crack. "I'm not gonna' let you become another statistic." Steve shoved him one last time and released his grip.

"I'm not doin' that." Bob rubbed his throat, relieved that he could breathe again. For the first time he was afraid of his little brother. He knew he meant what he said and in a way, he was surprised at his concern. "I told her I wasn't in - it was all her gig! I sold everything I owned, even my computer to make another months rent. I was laid off from my job and couldn't get unemployment. I was makin' nothin' stocking shelves at a warehouse. And I couldn't ask for help. It would be like admitting that I couldn't make it on my own. But I told her no, I wasn't that desperate."

"So you knew about the deal. And I thought you were smart." Steve looked disgusted. "I'm not convinced you're not using. I know she was and so was the guy who stole the K from the veterinary clinic. It's still a small town...and word gets around- you are who your friends are."

"I haven't seen any of my friends since I moved back home, and I'm trying to figure things out. I don't know nothin' about it."

"I meant what I said. I'll rat you out in a heartbeat to save your life...and I won't think twice about it or who goes down with you."

"I'm trying to tell you. I want to stay home and maybe do something...I don't know, but I'm thinkin' about different things, like you learn on the job. School isn't for me, but maybe there's somthin' else I'm good at."

"You stupid moron. You're great at photography, at graphics and art stuff. You can figure stuff out on the computer. Animals freakin' love you," he motioned toward Toby who sat watching attentively. "I can't get those horses to come to me even when I have food. Even Toby here, where does he sleep? - never with me. Who does he try to protect? Not me!" His voice became stern again. "Don't screw this up with Mom. Pull it together. She needs you now!" Steve opened the door of the car. "How am I gonna know if everything is all right or if you need me? We should have a code or something. I'll pay for someone to get me home if I have to."

"If there's a problem, I'll call you and leave a message with something that has to do with..." he hesitated for a moment, "It will have something to do with a hawk, if you hear that word, then you'll know I need you right away. Get dropped off at the Semi Wild Club and I'll meet you near the clubhouse."

"Why of all places there?"

"It's safe. The cops park down the dirt road and don't bother me. Meantime, I'm outta' sight for as long as I want. I can have a friend pick me up at Crossroads Farm and return me hours later...they won't know the difference as long as my car is still at the clubhouse. We can talk, or I can get you into the car and out of there or have Mr. Alston pick you up. I've got a lot of choices." Bob sighed. "Are we straight then? Are we O.K?"

Steve looked at his watch. It was almost dawn. "You might as well stay for breakfast and drive me to Wal-Mart when it opens."

"Why?"

He winced a little, "I kind 'a need a new phone before you go back."

The slow rumble of the old John Deere tractor came to a breaking halt behind the retirement paddock at Elva's farm. Harold got off and left Frank behind to throw the bales of hay over the back fence. Harold tugged at his hat, a habit that had preceded the same routine for years. He opened the dented back gate letting the noisy metal latch signal another morning of farm chores. He looked at the retirement horses to make sure they were all standing and no fence was down. It saddened him to lose an animal, even from old age, and he could almost gauge his whole day based upon his first look over the pasture.

This morning was full of watchful, attentive horses waiting for their A.M. feed. It was going to be a good day. His eyes scanned the herd. His trained eye could spot a problem immediately. Any disinterest in food could indicate distress from a number of maladies, all of which had to be checked. But the most frequent problem with this herd was the open wounds, sometimes the result of aggressive play - or down right meanness. It was the internal turmoil of nature's pecking order. He had some trouble with the new resident, the old gray. She suffered the initiation treatment of nicks and bites and alienation, but this morning the old girl looked fine, in fact, he noted that she had made a friend. He glanced down at the water level in the trough and pulled up on the creaky lever to fill it.

He cleaned the tub and looked around the paddock as the clean water splashed happily into the basin, "yep...it's gonna be a good day," he muttered softly. He turned his attention back to the water tub when a small chestnut horse came up beside him and started to silently drink. Harold didn't notice him at first, then squinted and reached out to pat him, recognizing him as the one who befriended the lonely gray mare. "You don't look old and infirm, little horse," he said out loud. He squatted down as the horse drank and ran his hand down the legs. His eyes came to a lengthy rest on the rear left white sock.

"I'll be damned." He turned to Frank and called, "got any more of that paint up at the barn?"

Frank stopped throwing hay and yelled back, shaking his head. "Not again. Yeah, a couple of gallons or so."

"Go up and get one and bring it here."

The boy threw the last bale, jumped into the seat of the tractor and started back to the barn.

The tight-faced woman sat at her desk and made it a point not to look up from her typing. Bob stood directly in front of her forcing an uneasy silence between them until the words wanted to explode from him, "Excuse me! I have an appointment with Dr. Collins!"

"Take a seat." The woman replied, still not looking up from her typing.

Her lack of common respect infuriated him, and reconfirmed his hatred of college. This kind of treatment was at the core of his experience as a student. Every level of higher education, from secretaries to professors, had underscored his belief that academics were merely snobs who judged a person's importance by the number of letters after their name. He sat down in the waiting room and glanced at his watch, his anger still silently burning. He would only tolerate ten minutes of this.

Muffled voices stabbed at the air down the hall, pulling his attention to one of the offices in the rear. He could catch only fragments of the turbulent conversation filtering into the waiting area.

A door burst open and a woman's voice angrily retorted, "I'm filing a complaint! I'm not going to stand for this! I did the fieldwork, I did the background research, and I wrote the paper. You have no right to pass it off as your own work! I needed that publication on my CV, damn it!"

A calm, sarcastic reply spilled into the hallway after her, "You chose me as your mentor on this project. You're just a junior professor, and let me remind you, one that isn't tenured yet; your direction was based on my ideas and my guidance, therefore it becomes my credit. You work under me…you seem to forget that little fact."

The woman's voice became low and distinctly threatening, "You're nothing more than a leach, a has-been who wrote one important work. As far as I'm concerned, even that should be questioned; you probably stole that as well! This time you're not getting away with it. I'm going to make sure no one takes you seriously again, if it's the last thing I do."

"And just what are you going to do about it?" The reply was confident.

Bob leaned forward just enough to see the young woman's face, her eyes narrowed on the stubby figure with knife like precision, "Just wait and see," she murmured with distain. With that, she stormed down the hallway past Bob, creating a rush of air, banging the window blinds on the door as it slammed behind her.

Collins strolled out to the front desk and noticed the young man, "You're Winters?"

"Quite a show," Bob responded as he stood up. Collins didn't offer a handshake, or even real eye contact. It was in keeping with the first impression of this man.

The professor answered coyly, the corner of his mouth turning upward toward a smirk, "Yeah, well, probably her time of the month," he chuckled, "besides, there are a lot of disgruntled assistants who think they deserve credit for work they didn't do."

As they walked back to the office, Collins started to boast of his own accomplishments, pressing the importance of buying a copy of his book. It was a pitch wasted on Bob, who used the time to wonder why his father would tolerate even a minute of this man. He could almost picture his father's reaction to the *time of the month* remark, which probably would have landed a black eye on the little man.

Collins was a short, sweaty man. His slovenly appearance served to enhance his pale skin and receding scattered hairline. The power of his cheap cologne could not entirely mask the faint odor of alcohol. His shoes scuffed along the floor drudgingly as they walked; so pathetically worn and misshapen that Bob wondered what property of physics kept them on his feet.

That silly acknowledgment retrieved a sudden image of his mother that seemed oddly appropriate at that moment. *"Yeah, so I met this famous radiation physicist,"* he recalled her cynicism, *"the man could solve anything when it came to calculations, number one in his class, all kinds of awards, but all that fame and brilliance was negated by two simple facts; the man never tied his shoes or took a bath."* Bob eyed Collins with a grin, so much for the aura of genius that this man's peers once bestowed on him.

The office door closed behind them and the professor continued to revel in his own words of glory. Bob started to wonder why he needed to impress a twenty-year old kid. Finally, he could stand no more. "Look, Doc, I just need some information," he tossed the receipt on the desk, anxious to finish his inquiry and leave.

Collins stared down at it. "Did you find it?" He asked inquisitively.

"What is it?" Bob asked.

Collins eyes darted away as he spoke and his right index finger started to pick unconsciously at the receipt, "It was no big deal, a pendant that's most likely a hoax of some sort."

"A pendant?"

"Once plucked from the ground, it's totally out of context with the environment. No way to confirm its authenticity. It's interesting, but without the location of the site it came from – it's pretty much worthless." Collins was still flicking the corner of the receipt. "Maybe, if you knew your dad's habits…where he might have found it, then it might be a valuable find."

"I don't understand." Bob replied.

"Well, look at it this way," Collins pulled out a smooth half broken stone from the drawer of his desk, "take a look," he handed it to Bob, "see the way it fits in your hand?"

Bob let the item find the natural conformity of his palm and took notice of how the hammer type end would make a good, but primitive tool.

"If this had been found with other artifacts in a refuse pile or as part of a stratified layer of similar Native American artifacts, I would say with confidence, it's a hammering tool. However, this one item, brought to my office – might have been pulled from a pile of river washed landscaping stones in someone's back yard." Collins leaned back in the chair and smiled, "In fact, that's exactly where I got it. I use this stone to make a point to my students. I pulled it from the landscaping stones in my yard – it's nothing."

There was a pause while Bob considered the smooth oval shapes of river rock he used to spread during his landscaping days. He knew the professor was right.

Collins added, "So you can see my point. Without the site it came from, I can't truly determine much of anything." His chair creaked as he leaned forward, "So, you are the one who needs to answer the questions. What did your Dad do for a living?"

Bob's eyes dropped as he thought about his Dad. He replied almost apologetically, "He was an Operating Engineer, heavy equipment – ya' know, cranes and draglines. Why couldn't you just tell me this on the phone? Why all the secrecy?"

"Tell a hopeful client that his big find is probably a hoax? Tell me, do you have the pendant in your possession?"

Bob didn't want to admit he had it, he didn't trust this man, "So, my Dad...he wanted to know if the pendant was authentic – and it isn't?"

Collins sat back and crossed his legs, "I didn't say that. I said that without the rest of the site, I couldn't prove its authenticity. Alone, I would call it a hoax. What I can tell you is that your father brought me something that looked like a carved stone pendant, and I sent it to the lab for carbon dating. Right after, he had a sudden change of heart, because he went down to the University Lab and demanded it back before I even had the results. It's an interesting piece of workmanship, but like I said, worthless without preservation of the site."

Bob let his eyes float around the room, from one piece of tribal memorabilia to another. The bookshelves that lined the walls were warped and over burdened, smelling of years of dust, dingy and dated, right down to the flesh colored filing cabinet. It had a large metal bar hinged on the side of the unit. It was an odd design and Bob guessed that it locked by swinging the bar toward the front, securing the drawers into place with a padlock. He wondered what secrets this man had that would make a padlock necessary at all.

"Well, I guess you answered my questions," Bob replied. "But there is something I want to know about that famous site I read about in Marlton. How did the bones of those bodies not decay after all these centuries?"

The secretary opened the door without a knock and stepped deliberately into the room. She pursed her lips as she spoke, "Dr. Shandower's office called, he wants to see you A.S.A.P."

Collins frowned up at her and then casually glanced at his watch, "Tell him I'm in a meeting and then I have to teach a lab from six till nine. I'm not available."

"Why don't you call him? I don't want to tick off the Dean."

"That'll be enough," he dismissed her with a stony glare.

Collins eyes came back to the young man's, "When Native Americans cremated their dead, usually during the winter months, the fires were hot enough to burn the flesh and remove the carbon from the bones – but not hot enough to turn the bone to ash. Burning away the carbon protects the bone from the normal decay process. That's why they were preserved and eventually uncovered. So, you have been reading my books."

Bob stood up and went to the door, "Interesting, well, thanks for your time." As he faced the professor and spoke, his hand fumbled behind his back, pushing the interior button on the doorknob until it turned and popped out in the unlocked position.

Collins stood up with him. "From what your father told me, there were other items at the site of considerably more interest to me than the pendant. If that's true and you manage to find it, then you may have something here. I know the state would be interested in preserving the area. He reached for a book as he spoke, and started flipping through the pages. "One of the items he mentioned was a mask that seems to fit the time period of the pendant – *if it's real*. If you find the site, call me so as not to destroy or disturb anything, don't make the same mistake your father did by plucking it out and bringing it in. The depth at which the artifacts are found, and the other items unearthed, they're all critical to dating and identifying the origin." He turned the book around so Bob could see the picture of a round face with gaping holes as eyes and an open mouth.

"Who was this guy?" Bob asked, trying to sound out the strange name printed on the bottom of the page.

"His name is pronounced *Mee-sing*," Collins said, "Protector of the Forest Creatures, Keeper of the Game, Living Solid Face. He looked after the hunters and the game - provided harvest. He was one of the early Lenape people's most important gods. The face of the mask would have originally been painted red on the right side, and black on the left during its time period. This *is* worth finding. This is what your father said was still at the site."

Bob left the office, the empty eyes of the mask disturbed him deeply. Why was it painted in half black and red? He decided that it must be to symbolize dirt and blood. One side to denote the essence of life, and the other to the world we are reduced to after death; *one side feeding the other quite literally,* he supposed.

While he thought about the stony face, he wandered down the narrow hallway with its bland cinder block walls still the hue of yellowed dentures. He had walked this walk before. Every afternoon when he exited out the large automatic doors, he breathed a sigh of relief as if tasting freedom for the very first time. He had lasted only three weeks, then had stopped going to class. His father and he had fought bitterly about it.

At least now he knew he was on to something here. Someone thought that pendant, or the place it came from was valuable enough to kill for. As he turned the corner of the corridor, he caught a glimpse of Tate and Apple asking directions in the main lobby. Bob turned around and exited quietly out a side door, certain their presence confirmed that the professor knew more than he was letting on.

Collins picked up the phone and started to dial. There was a tap at the office door and he called out in its direction. "Come in."

The men entered and Tate sat down across from him while Apple slowly paced around the room examining the books on the shelf. Sensing the seriousness of his visitors, Collins hung up before the call went through.

"Can I help you?" He asked leaning back in his creaky wooden chair.

"Dr. Roy Collins?" Tate asked, pulling his badge from his coat pocket.

Collins nodded and Tate continued, "I'm Detective Tate and this is Detective MacIntosh." He stuffed the badge back into his coat and pulled out his pad. "We need to ask you a few questions. What was your relationship with Mark Winters?"

Collins didn't look surprised. "I didn't have a relationship. He brought in an artifact. I tried to get it carbon dated and the kid…was just here," He pointed toward the door, "he just left." Collins realized he had forgotten the boy's first name. "Well…what's this all about?"

"Did you know a Jerry Rabinowitz?"

"Yeah…works in the lab at the museum and does some work for me occasionally."

"You didn't know him personally? Your contact with him was all work related?"

"Not always, we didn't see each other much. Why?"

Apple answered from across the room. "He's dead. And we found that Winters had made some phone calls to your office. And, what a coincidence, we found Jerry had made some phone calls to your office too. That makes you the only link between two dead men and a missing woman."

"Wait a minute," Collins straightened up in his chair, "First, I didn't know anything about Mr. Winters' passing …and Jerry, what happened to him, and what did he have to do with this?"

"First of all," Apple cut in, "Mr. Winters didn't pass, as you put it. That would imply a natural, easy non-manmade death. No…he was murdered and in a very unusual fashion. When *was* the last time you spoke to Rabinowitz?"

"I'm not sure…maybe…no wait. He kept looking down at the desk like he was searching for answers. "I guess it was about ten days ago, when he called and told me Winters' picked up the artifact. I don't know exactly which day that was. Check the calls from his lab to my office, that will verify it." He looked nervously from one man to another. "I kept trying to get a hold of Mr. Winters but there wasn't any answer at the house for a couple of days…and then yesterday the kid called me. It's not exactly the kind of information you want to leave on someone's machine, you know."

"What kind of information are we talking about?" Tate was steady writing on his pad.

"Winters dropped off a pendant of unknown origin. I was hoping the kid knew where the site was, but he was clueless."

Tate scowled at him, "C'mon, Roy, who do you think you're talkin' to? People find arrowheads and shit all over this state. What's so special about this?"

"You have to understand," Collins started, "it was very well preserved and I figured it dated back to the late archaic period. There are two sites in this vicinity from this period and neither has burial items remotely tied to this style of artwork. Mark Winters described other things in the site as well, still very well preserved. The artwork looks like the hand of two different artists, so I would assume it's a hoax of some sort. We never got to carbon date it. I have to be very careful about this, especially after all the controversy surrounding the Holly Oak pendant."

"The what?" Tate replied.

"The Holly Oak pendant depicted an Indian and a mammoth. It's been pretty much accepted that although the carbon dating of the pendant was correct, the image had been carved on it much later in history. Winters' pendant is hand carved in a piece of stone and is almost three dimensional – that's unheard of in the time period in this area. But the other items that Winters described verbally to me could give it some credence – upon inspection. I need the rest of those items to qualify it or dismiss it."

"Where is this pendant now?" Tate asked.

"Winters demanded it back from the lab a few days after I sent it off. Drove there directly and took it. I don't know if the kid found it or what." He shrugged his shoulders.

"So, you're saying the picture on it doesn't match the time period." Tate stared at the picture of the mask, then flipped through the pages of a book sitting open on his desk.

Collins sat down in his chair again and folded his hands in front of him like he was praying. His fingers pressed lightly against one another in a thoughtful motion. "That's right. Maybe it's someone's idea of a practical joke. What I can tell you is this. I need the rest of the site to back up all the possible theories."

"What theories, spell them out for me," replied Tate.

"I can't answer that without the area it came from and other items that were buried with it."

Tate scribbled in his notes: *artifact is motive.* Then he resumed his conversation with Collins. "Now just how many people knew about this?"

"Just Jerry and I. The other lab techs only knew the artifact by number. There was no association with an owner's name."

There was a brief silence then Collins asked. "You just said that Winters was murdered. In the paper it said only that it was suspicious. May I ask how?"

"That's confidential information."

The secretary burst into the office startling the men, "Now he's demanding to see you immediately, says that he doesn't care if you have a class or not!"

Collins rolled his eyes and spoke directly to the officers, "I need to take care of a few things...if we're finished here. I really need to get back to work."

Tate and Apple started to step out into the hallway when Tate's eyes fell upon a photograph sitting on the bookshelf. He picked up the picture and examined the two orange clad men holding up two pheasants. A chocolate and white pointer sat at their feet. "You snagged some nice looking birds in this outing. Tell me, who owns the dog in this picture?"

Collins smiled. "Local outfitter – let me use one of his old dogs for the hunt because I don't own one," Collins shuffled some papers on his desk.

Tate set the picture back on the shelf, "We'll be in touch, Dr. Collins, don't go anywhere."

The secretary interrupted again, "He's still on the phone. What should I tell the Dean?"

"Ask what it's in reference to."

"Oh, I can tell you that. It's about his niece, your junior professor – she's filed a formal complaint."

Collins lowered himself into his chair as if he had been punched in the stomach. He whispered out loud, "She's his niece?"

The secretary raised her eyebrow slightly and her thin lips revealed a hint of pleasure, "Oh...you didn't know that?

Chapter Eleven

He moved with the roar of the wind through the pines, and she was compelled to reach into the blackness to save him. She felt weak and vulnerable in his presence, but knew his anger was not meant for her. She stretched out her hand to soothe his soul, and calm the searing heat of his brow. He took it and looked down at her callused hand in a gesture of tenderness and knowing. For a moment she felt consoled and peaceful as if she had taken his burden. But the wind grew louder and whipped around them. Her hand became a conduit for his rage, swelling inside her soul, surging like a torrent. The entity that connected the edge of reality held her by some fragile and tenuous bond tied to the marrow of her being. It left her gasping for breath, his undisputed power over her was clear. She awoke struggling for air, her sleep halted, and mumbling words that she could not pronounce in a language that meant nothing to her. She was sure that the meaning was clear to her in the dream. She struggled to repeat it, to force it from her memory to her lips, but could not piece the syllables together in her waking state.

She was startled at the sound of her own name, clear and crisp stinging the air.

"Well let's pack it up and resume the search for the elusive Mary Winters tonight. Coordinate the cars with spotlights. Can we get another dog unit out here?"

The second voice started to trail off, but it sounded like Tate's partner. "The local guy isn't cooperating, and the police hounds are over where she was last spotted this afternoon, on the northeast corridor of the state grounds. Thing is, folks that saw her claim the horse was jet black and big. Anyway, they're checking that area out and I understand the dogs have been running in circles all day."

"It's in a totally opposite direction from the Bozarth farm. Why would she circle around back to where she's been?"

"Maybe she's lost, disoriented." The men's voices faded into the distance until she could no longer hear their discussion.

She lay motionless underneath the sleeping bag afraid to breathe. She listened closely for the direction of the fragmented whispers and wondered if they had found her saddle in the woods or had discovered Shortstop. On foot, she wouldn't get far.

She heard Apple again, faintly. "My guess is she will stay put a few days but I wouldn't ease up in this quadrant. She seems to have a lot of friends in this town."

"I don't know," replied Tate. "We just searched this whole place yesterday." The voices continued to drift away again with barely audible discussion. Mary lay motionless until the darkness began to overtake the woods.

Her leg had started to throb again and she began to shiver from the pain of it. She pulled herself slowly into a sitting position. The deer stand was well concealed by the branches of the pines. She wrote a message on some paper and folded it again and again. Waves of nausea and heat passed over her and she wondered if her fever was the reason for the bizarre dream. It seemed so real and disturbing. She could almost feel the torrent of wind and dirt still whirling around her as if she were in the storm. She looked down at her callused hand, as if reliving the strength and comfort she felt from his touch. Her attention moved to the fields and she vowed to make it to Jack's tonight. She couldn't let anything stop her. Taking the last bird from the bird bag, she wrapped the note around the leg and secured it with a piece of duct tape. She needed to let him fly before dark. Tossing him into the air, she watched as he circled lazily in the last thin streak of evening twilight before heading south.

She covered herself back up and waited until the stars were clearly visible overhead and silence came with the dark. She rolled up the bag, clamping it tight and slowly descended from the stand. She counted the fence posts to retrieve her saddle from its hiding place and was almost surprised that it was still there under the damp leaves. She limped close to the woods line and listened for sounds of talking or rustling of leaves from movement, but heard nothing except her own breathing. Satisfied that she was alone, she cupped her hands and whistled in the same low muffled tone that called Shortstop and Butch in for the evening feed. She looked nervously around, but still heard nothing.

A black shadow of a small horse stepped to the edge of the fence, but it was not hers. She whistled the tone again. The same horse moved closer and stood patiently in front of her, staring with dark soft eyes. She quietly unlocked the back gate to take a closer look. He nuzzled her hand and she eyed him with awe. Shortstop now had four white socks and multiple splashes of white on his forehead, chest and hindquarters. A white trailing thunderbolt ran down his nose and veered playfully off to one side.

She slipped the bridle over his head and whispered in his ear, "Good disguise, ol' buddy…someday you can tell me about it." She laid the saddle over his back and tightened the girth. That effort alone was exhausting and she rested her fevered head against him to catch her breath.

As she led him through the gate, a shout from the far road and a spotlight blazed in her direction startling her into panic. She was blinded from its brilliance and threw the gate open wide, pulling herself onto Shortstop, swinging her reins and shouting in defense.

Two more lights blinded her vision, but she no longer needed to see. The retirement horses spilled from the paddock like a tidal wave set loose, crashing through the gate in torrents, their eyes wide with fear and excitement. And in that cloud of dust and light and choking dirt, thundered in the direction of the trooper's cars in a final magnificent explosion of fury and thick smoky yellow fog. She was lost among the churning hooves, and the sudden stampede for freedom. Knowing the bit was useless in a stampeding herd, she put her head down and held on for her life understanding that confusion would be the tool that saved her.

Officers ran for cover as the mass of old horses breathed the fresh air of freedom and were exhilarated by the memory of their youth. Horses, who had only moments before, limped stiffly in the field, shed their physical limitations with the new onset of adrenalin that surged through their system and the promise of open, virgin pasture.

"Get the woman!" Tate yelled from the patrol car as he shut the door and put his head down unable to see through the earthen smoke and hot yellow lights that rolled his way.

Mary held on with all her might as the brazen herd of fury stampeded past the patrol cars. The horses split, half galloped past the side of the barn, and the others across the paved road to an empty ruin of late summer's cornfield. She peeled her horse away from the group. Using the leather crack of her rein to hasten their exit, she headed through the barren field and into a strip of woods that paralleled a group of smaller private homes.

Elva and Harold heard the commotion and ran out screaming and waving their arms at the officers. Their antics also helped to fan the herd and create a little more excitement. Elva ranted and threatened a lawsuit that they would pay dearly for, but she knew her old horses wouldn't go far.

Officers scattered the area with small search parties, but couldn't find a trace of the woman. There were too many hoof marks in the dirt to determine any given direction at night.

When it was done, Elva calmly called the horses back with a clanking of grain buckets and the pleasant routine of food. The huge draft horse lifted his head in interest, his eyes bright with determination, as he slowly led the way back to the paddock, his constituents close behind. One by one each drifted into the safety of their familiar paddock. The offered bribe of an extra feeding held more allure than the memory of their youth and life in the wild. Slowly their demeanor returned to the aged and rigid state of their true years, as if the euphoria of their aphrodisiac had failed them. Elva accounted for them all and put a padlock on the back gate.

Shortstop loped through housing developments still heading northwest. They hid in back of a garage while cars passed, and cut across into small groups of trees where she stayed until all was quiet. She rode through backyards and even deflected a basketball lost by a young boy shooting hoops in the light of his driveway. The boy watched in awe and surprise while she rode by. Mary smiled and winked putting her finger up to her lips in a motion of silence.

She finally came out behind the local WaWa to catch her breath and let Shortstop take a rest. She did it more for herself than for him, and was feeling worse by the minute. A weakness seemed to penetrate her bones and her lower leg was hard and heavy. She breathed through her mouth and hoped she wouldn't faint. Police cars slowly rolled by her on the roads, splashing a wave of lights along the woods line that cast shadows across the ground.

Jack's house was only a few hours by horseback. But to accomplish that, she would have to cross more built up areas with residential housing developments, cut through the high school complex and cross the small wildlife management area to enter the Semi Wild grounds. She couldn't take another night of being pursued. She wanted this to end.

Ethan called Bob as soon as he heard it on the police band, but by the time Bob turned the Subaru into Elva's, it was a hotbed of commotion with cars circling the area and spotlights that lit up the night sky. At least she was still alive and seemed to be one step ahead of them. He wished he had been able to see her, to convince himself that she was O.K. He could only imagine all the chaos of her escape, and it spawned a new respect for her ability to evade capture.

He started back home down a long paved road that snaked through the pines and pulled the car into the dirt parking lot of a restaurant. Its large sign with a picture of a steaming coffeepot was the only light for miles on the seemingly endless wooded passage. The building was a run down log cabin, but the food was good and cheap. The locals were the only ones who knew this place. The young blond waitress didn't make eye contact as Bob stood at the cash register waiting to be seated.

"How many?" she asked, her eyes scanning over a room full of empty tables.

Bob looked around him as if she were speaking to someone else, "One," he replied, taking a map out of his coat.

She picked up a menu and started to lead him toward the corner of the room. "Smoking or non," she stated in a flat expressionless voice.

"Non."

She swiped the overflowing ashtray off the table and tossed the menu down. "Enjoy your meal."

Bob was amused but far too tired to care. He ordered a coffee and a sandwich and unfolded the map on the table. A shadow seemed to sweep over him as his mood deteriorated. He was exhausted. There was far too much happening to sleep.

On horseback in acres of woods, in a county of farms, she could continue to go unnoticed for a lengthy period of time. He took the artifact out of the inside of his coat pocket and rolled it over and over again in his hands. He marked on the map his home, then the cranberry bogs, the Bozarth Dairy Farm and the Matson's farm. He made a mark on Jack's house. He was certain it was where she was heading.

He overheard a man's voice mention the murder at the Winter's Morning Farm. His writing stopped and he slid lower into the seat to avoid being noticed. Still, he couldn't help but listen to the conversation. The table of men spoke back and forth to each other as if there was no one else to hear them.

"You heard about it. It's been in all the papers...someone killed her husband, broke into her house and then tried to kill her in the barn. Damn, you ask me I'd be on the run too. Peterson said that she impaled the guy through the throat."

"Damn, you don't say," added another man, "go away on a huntin' trip and you guys let a murder happen!" There was brief laughter from the group.

"Ya know, my wife left a note and food in the barn in case she comes while we ain't there. Hell, police ain't helpin' her."

"Weird."

"Did it say in the paper how the husband was killed out at the Semi-Wild?" A shaky old voice asked amongst the flurry of opinions.

"No, only that it was suspicious."

The same breathless voice hesitated then continued, "You know that's not the first murder out at the Semi Wild." There was a clanging noise as the coffee cup of the old man hit the saucer in an uncertain motion. "When I was a boy, my father told me a man was killed out there. Horrible death. The guy was found with part of his chest gone. Like they had cut somethin' out. Folks were afraid to go out of their house."

Bob straightened up in his booth. That information was deliberately left out of the paper, but Mom had told him how the murder looked and the results of the coroner's report.

He turned around to get a look at the old man, and broke his silence. "Excuse me, couldn't help but overhear your conversation. About what year do think that murder happened?"

All the men at the table put down their coffee and stared at the young man who intruded on their conversation. Bob felt compelled to introduce himself. "I'm Bob...Bob Winters. I wasn't aware that a murder had taken place out at the Semi Wild before. I'm interested. Can you tell me more?"

The old man smiled and glanced at his buddies for approval. "Your Mom's a good woman, we're glad to meet ya." A nod from the group was as good as a handshake. "Well, you heard jus''bout the whole thing. I was around seven at the time."

The younger old man sitting next to him laughed. "Pappy, how'd you remember what year it was, when you can't remember who I am some days." The other men chuckled, but the old man shakily continued.

"I remember," he nodded and looked down at the floor, his consciousness seeming to drift away, "Mom used to play the piano. The house was always filled with music. It was 1915. It was the year that Mom got real sick and was taken to her bed. Dad scraped together all the money we had, teamed up the horses and went all the way to Phil-er-delphia to get her a Victrola. Did I say she loved music? Anyhow, she died that Christmas. Dad wasn't the same man after that," he shook his head. "I was seven. It was nineteen fifteen." He frowned at the man who taunted him, but all the time his eyes had filled with his words. As if to shrug them off, he barked at the man next to him, "and don't be sassin' your Dad, boy!" He shook his cane at him and the men laughed again.

"How did the guy die?" Bob continued. "Do you remember who it was? Was the murderer ever found? What do you remember?"

The old man scratched his chin and smiled up at the blond waitress who refilled his coffee. His eyes drifted down to the level of her breasts as she leaned over to pour. "I remember that my Pop said it stopped the sale of the land."

The old man's old son broke in. "But the Well's farm ended up being sold anyway and became the Semi Wild Club."

"If you would let me finish," the old man frowned and turned toward Bob. "But the guy who was originally goin' to buy it – the dead guy- he was going to sell it off in parcels and make it part of the town. That guy dying let another buyer turn it into a private huntin' ground. When that owner died, it was passed down to the Club members to run – stayed pretty much untouched over the years. I don't recall if anyone was ever accused, rumor was gypsy's, but it not only stopped the sale, it was the talk of the town. Everyone was afraid they were next."

"Nineteen fifteen, you say." Bob threw some money down on his table and walked to the door. "Thanks. Interesting story."

"Somethin' else jus' occurred to me," the old man said as he leaned on his cane to turn himself around. "He was a rich guy and they couldn't have a wake."

"What do you mean?" The register clanked as the blond waitress rang up Bob's bill.

"His head was split clean open. They couldn't show the body."

When Bob got home, he studied the object of the hawk's talons until his eyes started to hurt. Still, he was fascinated by the story it held in its ancient drawing. Maybe it had something to do with *both* murders. They were similar. But who would copy an old murder? What was the point? No one would remember it to make a connection between the two. Still, it was a coincidence that intrigued him.

Deciding he couldn't sleep anyway, he went to the desk and pulled out a piece of thin tracing paper, then dampened it so that he could carefully wrap it around the pendant. He secured it with several pieces of tape to keep the parchment in place. He had learned this childlike technique on a third grade Halloween class trip. Only back then the object of mystery was much larger and easier to trace. Dampening the paper was his idea and he didn't know if it would even work, but he molded the paper as close as possible to the etching. As he slowly worked, he thought about the old graveyard near the grammar school, and how his teacher, had shown the class how to stretch paper across the old headstones and raise the words from the dead like magic. He took a fine piece of charcoal from his art supplies and carefully started to rub the side of the point over the paper in slow deliberate motion. A faint impression began to build. The hawk was clearly visible in all its stunning detail, the victim of the bird started to unfold line by line.

His excitement was replaced with disappointment. It was a primitive and oddly shaped object at the foot of the talons, nothing like the artwork in the hawk. The lines were boxy and seemed misaligned, like the drawing of a two year old placed next to a Renoir. He unwrapped the paper from the pendant and flattened the fragile surface out on the table. The styles were far too different. Had the pendant been carved by two different artists? Or, maybe the professor was right. It was a hoax. He studied the picture. It almost resembled the boxy lines of a ships sails. It didn't make any sense. One thing was clear, he had to find out what Collins was hiding.

He packed a few things and drove back out to the local college, knowing Collins would be at his evening class. He leaned up against the wall of the liberal arts building until students started to spill out the side door. It was break time. There were no cameras on the side entrances and the students pulled a trashcan in front of the door to keep it from closing behind them. Several students lit cigarettes and discussed their test results, as still others just came out to stretch their legs and gripe about the class. Bob put out his cigarette and walked inside, using the nearby stairwell to access the first floor offices. He waited until he saw Collins leave the waiting room of his office and walk back toward the lab to finish his class. If he was as distracted as he seemed, maybe he didn't notice that the lock on his door was disabled. Bob pulled down his skullcap and walked casually into the waiting room pulling his book bag behind him. As he suspected, there was no secretary during the evening. He turned the doorknob. Collins hadn't checked the door and with a sigh of relief, he stepped into the professor's office and closed the door silently behind him. He went to the file cabinet, which was locked down for the night. He set his backpack on the desk and pulled out a set of bolt cutters that he retrieved from the barn. He positioned himself in front of the cabinet in order to obtain the best leverage. Even with bolt cutters, the metal of the padlock was dense and resistant. But after several tries it gave way. Bob opened each drawer. The files had no names, just series of numbers and administrative titles. He went through each drawer trying to find something that would connect his father's find with the files. There was a familiarity of the numbers, not in the numbers themselves, but in their pattern. Three numbers, a dash, then four numbers following. It suddenly occurred to him, it was the same pattern of numbers as on the receipt. He rummaged through his backpack until he finally pulled the wrinkled paper from its black abyss. He pulled the file with the same number that was written on the receipt 399-0045.

There was a quiet rattle as the blind of the waiting room door knocked against the window. Someone was moving down the hallway. Bob moved toward the door, squatted down and pushed the button on the doorknob and held the knob from turning, just as a key was inserted in the outside lock.

"Damn it!" He heard Collins voice murmur from behind the door. He fumbled with different keys trying each one in the door. Bob braced himself, not allowing the door to give. Collins was cursing in a string now, "Where are the damn lazy security guards when you need them!" Finally, he turned away angrily and the blind swung heavily against the waiting room door.

Bob quietly returned to the file cabinet, grabbed the file and tucked it into his backpack. He swung the bar back across the drawers securing it with his high school padlock. It was his little joke on Collins. He cautiously let himself out into the hallway, and quickly strolled toward the nearby staircase exit. Collins had his back to him, and was yelling at a security guard about how he had a class to teach, and nothing worked right in this place. The security guard seemed to be tolerating the ranting although he acted like he didn't care. Bob breathed a sigh of relief as he exited out the side door and headed toward his car.

Mary and Shortstop moved in and out of the safety of the woods as quiet as deer through the black silk of night. Their shiftless forms were captured and then dismissed by each driver's weary imagination in a brief flash of headlights. Crossing the highway, they rode behind the brick buildings of the high school, around the high metal fence of the baseball field, and ducked in behind a row of large boxy houses that repeated their shape like trails of dominos. They had been riding for hours from one form of cover to another. An occasional barking dog heralded their late night passing, but it went unnoticed by their owners. The fastest way to Jack's house was to cut through the Crossroad's Farm. She never really noticed how vast and open their crop fields were. There were only thin patches of forest-lined borders. The farm was going to be more of a challenge than she thought.

The Crossroads Farm and Country Store was a large family owned crop farm that attracted people from miles around. They sold pies, fresh vegetables, and flowers. But they also sold a family outing on the farm that attracted families just looking for a quick way to satisfy the kids. They offered seasonal hayrides, pumpkin picking and Easter egg hunts. And after the rides, there was always the petting zoo and refreshments. There were paved parking areas with wide telescoping lights, and plenty of employees running around assisting customers. She decided to make a wide circle avoiding the lights and commotion, but at some point she would have to cross the strip of field that paralleled the road to the management area. The farm closed to customers at midnight, then it was only employees cleaning up and restocking until one in the morning. She waited behind a high fence that bordered the backyard of one house. She peered over the stockade style wood to the blackened house and beyond to the wide lit sky. She would wait for the dimming of the parking lot lights then make her move between the houses. It was the most direct route. Shortstop munched on some grass while she waited in the darkness.

The lights in the parking lots started to click off in groups, as the last of the customers began to leave. Lower lighting would remain for the employees restocking and closing up. Mary followed the edge of the fence as far as she could without being noticed by the headlights that drifted out of the parking lot. She laid her head on her horse. The cold night air seeped under her coat. Her body, hot and moist from the fever, responded in waves of uncontrollable shaking.

There were still a few cars in the farthest lot, but she couldn't wait any longer. If the police didn't get her first, she would die in the woods unconscious from the raging infection. Her leg felt thick and heavy. She was afraid to dismount for fear that the shear weight of it would prohibit her from getting back into the saddle.

She crossed the road quickly and moved into the wooded edge of the field staying within ten feet of the carefully groomed crop rows, but hidden by the sparse woods that separated one pumpkin field from the next. A few people were still meandering toward their cars with their purchases, but didn't seem to notice the large figure moving in the shadows.

Horse and rider stepped silently toward the last strip of field and the final obstacle to their destination. She could see the dense forest across the highway ahead. One more cornfield and one more hedgerow of trees, then the cover would subside and open up to acres of open fields. She kept her eyes in the distance, on the blackness of the management area and the promise of trails that led to the Semi Wild. They drifted silently across the pumpkin fields, behind the dead rattling cornfield that would soon be cut down for decorative Halloween cornstalks, and into yet another patch of trees separating another pumpkin field. She approached the nodding sunflowers that stood as rigid as a church congregation in the darkness, heads low and mumbling condemnation as she passed. She entered the farthest hedgerow when she noticed an orange glow up ahead. Shortstop froze in position. Mary urged him forward to get a closer look, convincing herself that nothing was going to stop her. The horse tried to look away, but at the same time he couldn't keep his eyes off it. It was an orange pumpkin set neatly on a stump. Its strange and macabre grin seemed to pull at the very last threads of her reasoning. A green glow stick had been placed inside and it's hollowed and puckered grin looked aged and tired. The edge of a lonely wood was a strange place for a lit pumpkin late at night. She peered into the darkness searching for whoever placed it in the wood. In the distance there were others too, faint glowing objects in the night and Mary's eyes fell on what appeared to be a human silhouette up in a nearby tree. She was silent and motionless while her heart pounded wildly in her chest. The person made no motion or recognition of seeing her. She was afraid to go forward, but it was too late to go back. Perhaps they hadn't seen her yet.

In the distance a low rumbling sound began to emerge from the darkness in waves of mechanical clanking. It echoed through the woods and she was helpless to tell which direction the sound was coming from. But Shortstop knew. He focused his attention down the woods line toward the farm store. Soon, bouncing lights and wild laughter brought the realization to her. She had stumbled onto the last run of Crossroads Haunted Halloween Hayride.

Laughter and screams filled the air as one spot light after another came on illuminating some Halloween figure or display in the woods. The tractor moved towards her…and the dummy in the tree swung out toward the group. More lights clicked on. There was nowhere to hide. She didn't have time to retreat unnoticed. She pulled down her hat and yanked up her collar. It was a stupid idea, but the only one that might save her.

She lowered her head and pulled again at her hat so none of her face was visible. The lights came on around her and a skeleton danced merrily on the edge of the field and sang strange and spooky lyrics. More lights came on and Mary swooped up the pumpkin pushing her fingers through the rotting eyes and pushing her horse forward, breaking into the field.

Shortstop reared as a white sheet ghost swung down from a tree and pure fear sent him galloping past the hayride. People pointed and screamed with delight as she tossed the glowing pumpkin in the direction of tractor and splattered its contents on the side. They rode across the field and disappeared into the darkness leaving the shrieks of laughter drifting far behind.

A young man at the wheel of the tractor turned around and shouted over the chaos to his co-worker on the hay bound trailer. "When did we get the headless horseman?" he yelled over the riotous commotion of the adults.

The young man shrugged. "Don't know. Get used to it!" he shouted back. "The last ride gets weirder every night." He turned his attention back to the people on the ride, reminding himself how much he hated this job. At least he wasn't cleaning up manure in the petting zoo.

Mary breathed a sigh of relief and felt safer once she crossed the invisible property line of the club. She wasn't worried about the hayride and figured they were enjoying themselves far too much to think anything was out of the ordinary. It was too late to worry about what the employees would do.

Jack's little farm backed right up to the trails of the Semi Wild. It was an area she knew well from training. She slowed Shortstop down to a walk and kept to the shadows around the fields making her way to his house. The dull aching pain all over her body had worsened and she was perspiring and cold at the same time. The burst of adrenalin in their flight across the field had taken the last of her stamina. She couldn't stop shaking.

She whispered to her horse. "It's almost over boy. We're almost there," but she said it to convince herself. She looked up at the stone clubhouse looming on the hill, a broken monument to every era of architecture since the date of its inception. Its massive contours out of place like a castle in the middle of nowhere. She followed the border of trees until she came upon the tunnel. Shortstop was alert but unafraid. Mary's eyes moved over the shadowy tunnel, now silent and still. She would do this and face whatever force in defiance of her own fear. She took a deep breath and nudged her horse into his shuffling gait. He moved confidently down the path without incident or hesitation, passed the foundation and toward an obscure foot trail that led up to Jack's house. His dogs barked when she approached, but there was no one to hear them. She dismounted and pushed the heavy door of the barn open. The front of his house and paddocks could easily be seen from the road. With Shortstops new paint job, she didn't want to chance someone recognizing his odd looking markings. Jack had filled a stall with wood chips put hay in a rack and left a bucket already filled with water.

She unsaddled Shortstop and slid the heavy leather off his back only to let it fall onto the floor. It was suddenly too heavy to lift. She gripped the stall door tightly as her head began to spin. She left the saddle on the floor and secured the door. Shortstop paid no attention as he took a long deserved drink, and hastily began pulling hay from the hayrack. She closed the outside barn door and leaned against it, all the time telling herself that she wasn't the type to faint. Stumbling up on the porch of the house, she gently knocked on the door. No one answered. If Jack thought she might try to hide here, perhaps he would leave a key. Her trembling hand fumbled above the doorframe, then checked under the mat. She stared at the dead geranium in the flowerpot by the door, finding the key under the planter. She let herself into the dark house.

A wall of warmth was the first thing to greet her as she turned on the light in the hallway. It hit her like a fire and she tugged recklessly at her coat and sweater pulling the layers off her body and throwing them next to the myriad of barn clothes already left in scattered piles on the floor. This entrance to the house went through the utility room where a variety of clothing Jack used for his barn work hung on heavy hooks or were thrown on the floor awaiting their next use.

The front door was rarely used, and certainly not by those who knew Jack. She hung her hat on the coat rack and sat down to pull off her boots. Her socks were stained from the water of the cranberry bogs and a rush of cold on her damp feet reminded her that her boots still weren't dry. She limped into the open kitchen and the small sunken living room beyond it. There was something odd about the place that took a few moments to occur to her. The house was stripped of every reminder of his previous marriage. There was nothing of feminine design in the place, right down to the dead plant on the front porch that stood out like a no trespassing sign. No carefully placed photographs or ornamental touches gave any clues to the owner. It looked like the furniture had been bought from some low rent hotel, benign and bland, lacking any inclination as to the man it possessed. It was as if no one lived there.

She grabbed the last apple out of a basket by the sink and opened the refrigerator. She bit into it letting the sweet juice fill her mouth and roll down her throat, firmly holding it in her teeth as she searched for more food. "Jesus, Jack, don't you eat?" she mumbled closing the door.

She took a long drink of water and finished the apple. She wasn't that hungry anyway, but anything in her stomach seemed to help the nausea. There was something more pressing she had to do first, before food and rest.

Mary limped into Jack's bedroom feeling as if she were dragging her leg behind her. She opened his chest of drawers until she found a pair of old green hospital scrubs, then to the bathroom to tend to her leg.

She caught her own reflection of the mirror and was shocked at what image was returned. Her face bore the scars from scraping branches and harsh cold weather. Her lips were pale and parched and dark rings had formed around her eyes. Her skin was rough from windburn. At the same time, she felt hot and sick and weak. She rifled through his medicine cabinet and set up what she needed to dress her leg.

Turning on the shower, she tried to convince herself that the wound across the front of her calf wasn't as bad as she had thought, and the fingers of red that had started to creep from the gash were manageable. Her shin was swollen and discolored giving it a grotesque shape. The hot steam started to roll behind the shower curtain and she stepped into it with antibacterial soap. The comfort of its heat would clean and purify her with this one simple pleasure, soothing her tired aching muscles and cleaning the wound. The bubbles of the shampoo slid over her shoulders and down her back while the smell of the outdoors and the cold that seemed to cling to her was replaced by the soft fragrance of chemically manufactured flowers.

She examined her fingernails under its pounding stream. They were rimmed with black dirt outlining the cuticle and throbbed from the heat of the shower. She scrubbed them over and over again with the coarse washcloth and kneaded them through the wet thickness of her dark soapy hair. She had to feel like a woman again and four days had gone without bathing, and without a warm soft bed and a sense of safety. As she stood beneath the hot water her body began to hurt, like it had never hurt before, right down to her fingertips. The steam radiated from her as she stepped from the shower patting the thick towel over her skin and ringing the water from her hair. Now that the dirt was removed, she examined the leg closely noticing how the jagged rip that crossed its surface was soft and yellow and fanning red streaks up her leg. It had begun oozing again. She pulled on the green scrubs and rolled up the pant leg above the knee. Sitting on the edge of the tub with her injured leg draped over, she poured the orange antibiotic liquid over the gash to clean it. It stung wildly and she cursed with tears in her eyes. It needed to be cleaned even better, but she couldn't stand the pain of touching it. She gingerly spread a layer of milky white antibiotic cream over it and pressed a light sterile pad on top. The cream was expensive and normally used on burn patients, but it was all she could find in Jack's cabinet. Before she could rest, she needed to find some kind of internal medicine to take to keep the infection at bay. Surely he had some penicillin or something strong on hand.

She rose from the edge of the tub to check beneath the sink, when her head started to spin, bringing her to her knees. She tossed up the seat of the toilet and began to wretch and her ears started to ring. The edges of her vision began to curl the darkness around her. She laid down on the floor, feeling the cool of the tile against her fevered head, telling herself that this would pass and she would rest for only a while.

Chapter Twelve

Jack pulled into the drive and shut off the car. The lights in the house were a dead giveaway. One quick look in the barn confirmed the presence of his visitor. He entered his home quietly, looked at his watch, and locked the latch to the door behind him. It was two in the morning. He had been held up in surgery for hours, and lost all track of time. The accident happened at dusk, and the elderly driver had never seen the young boy on his bike. Jack thought about the family and the old man, all with tear stained eyes, clinging to each other for support and comfort, certain that their sorrow would lead to an inevitable lawsuit. It was the way the system worked. The kid would be all right, and with a well-placed rod and some rehabilitation, his leg would heal just fine. But the old man would probably never recover from that one unfortunate moment when fate made their two paths collide.

He saw the light cascading under the bathroom door and into the hallway. He tapped lightly against it. "Mary...are you in there?" There was no answer and he called again into the silence. He pushed open the door and saw her on the floor. He knelt down and opened her eyes. Her pupils reacted, and rolled away as she smiled weakly up at him.

She moaned softly, "Mark...how could you do this to me?"

He put his arm behind her and lifted her to her feet. "Mary. It's not Mark. It's Jack." He could feel the intense heat of her body against his as he wrapped her arm around his neck and helped her over to the bed. "Mary...listen to me," he shook her gently as he spoke, "you're dehydrated and hurt." He winced as his eyes settled on the half-dressed leg wound. "I need to get you to a hospital." He got up and came back with a black bag and a basket filled with plastic lined pads, gloves and IV tubing. "I'm going to have to call an ambulance," he continued.

"No, Jack," she mumbled, "they're after me, they'll kill me. I'm only alive because they can't find me. The key is here...I just have to find it...don't leave me...don't let them hurt me." She grabbed his hand and for an instant her dark eyes focused sharply on his, "you owe me...damn you! You owe me this one favor!"

He was silent as he snapped opened the protective packaging of the saline bag and punctured it with the IV tubing. He watched, as the clear liquid traveled down the tube and dripped into the trashcan he had placed by the bed. He took hold of her arm and wiped it with an alcohol pad. "I'm going to start an IV, then I'll piggyback some antibiotics and give you something for the pain."

As he worked he contemplated her request. "You have to do everything I say, hear me? Are you allergic to anything?"

"No," she softly breathed through her mouth and had resumed her exhaustive state. Beads of perspiration had formed on her forehead and he placed a damp cloth on her brow.

"I'll have to go back to the office to get some more supplies, but if your fever is higher tomorrow, you're in the hospital. No questions asked. Do you hear me?"

"Just don't let them get me ...I didn't do it...I loved him, you know I wouldn't hurt him."

He taped the IV in place and hung the saline from a swing arm lamp over the bed by threading the loop of the bag on a clothes hanger. Then he drew up a small syringe and injected it into the line. "This will help. Or...at least it will make you not care. I'm going to clean that leg wound now."

A flush of warmth slowly crawled over her like a paralyzing blanket as she heard the vaguely familiar sound of packaging being torn and the snap of a new pair of gloves.

She felt the pain in her leg as if it were far away, detached, but Jack was right- she no longer cared.

When he finished, he sat on the edge of the bed and watched her sleep turning his options over and over again in his head. Some friend he was putting her life in danger. He had known her for years and cared for her deeply. He thought about their many dialogues and discussions at work. It was hard not to grow close working together. She knew more about his problems with Annette than he did. If she died in his home tonight he would have to answer a lot of questions about why he didn't call the police at the first sign of her. The pain medicine would have her out for a few hours and he could drive to the office, get more supplies, and be back before she woke. He only kept a minimal amount on hand just in case he would have an emergency with one of his own animals or stumble onto a car accident.

She looked peaceful in her artificially induced sleep. Her skin had a soft glow from the fever and her damp dark hair curled untamed around her face. She was right. He owed her. Their talks in the workplace were the only sanity he knew when his world was crumbling around him. He threw on his coat, grabbed his car keys and locked the door behind him. He gripped the steering wheel as he drove to the office. The white lines of the road glared up at him, and he thought about his ex-wife and what she would have done in the same circumstances. There would have been no comparison of course. Annette with her designer suits and perfect red nails would have never survived any of this. She spent most of her day looking into the mirror, concerned with party etiquette. Life with him must have been nothing like she imagined. She expected extravagant parties and important connections. What she got was a man who wanted to treat his patients and enjoy a hobby that gave him satisfaction in his time off.

Annette hated dogs, was deathly afraid of horses and despised his modest ranch house living. They had started to build a huge home in the finer section of town, but it burned before completion. She had taken everything from him, including what was left of his dignity. She wasn't going to finish the house and take it too. But none of that mattered to him now. It was merely a history lesson. He could have lived with the fact that they had different pursuits. What came between them was her embarrassment of his lifestyle. Her bitterness resounded in every word and action, when they were alone or with friends.

He had loved Annette for her classic beauty. That was what attracted him and held him. It was also what cursed him. She found another man that could give her the doctor's wife image and life. She left him without a word and without a tear. They had finished it through the courts without ever fully understanding the emotion and pain of their ending. No, there was no comparison between these two women.

He turned his Explorer into the office parking lot and walked up the steps to the back door. He fumbled with his keys, opened the door and punched at the alarm keypad just inside. The security lights in the hallway lead him to the supply closet. His eyes searched the closet of medications as he located the items he needed. He opened a case of saline bags and grabbed some sample packages of oral antibiotics and stuffed them into his pockets. He opened a small case of IV antibiotics, and was glad he had ordered it for emergencies. After he checked his take of the supply closet, he wrote a note for his office manager:

Had a sick horse last night. Please replace what I have taken, and I'll settle up when I see you.
Thanks Jack.

He felt it was plausible. His staff knew he had two horses and several dogs. It shouldn't raise suspicion.

He reactivated the alarm and locked the door behind him. As he stepped back out in the cold a police car blocked the drive.

Tate stepped forward from the darkness and into the security light of the backdoor. "Out a little late aren't you, Doc?" Tate glanced at his watch, then up at the doctor.

"Have a sick horse and I needed supplies," Jack replied curtly, trying to brush past him.

Tate took the bag out of his hand. "Then you wouldn't have any problem with us searching this would you?

Jack didn't argue. "Why are you harassing me?"

"Don't play dumb, Doc. I know the Winters woman is hurt and probably heading to your place. Got a call from the owner of Crossroads Farm tonight, said a couple of the kids were talking about the headless horseman on the last ride. Funny thing is –they don't have one. You're the only logical person she would go to in this area."

Jack stood quiet, not knowing what to say.

Tate handed the bag back to him. "Don't worry. She may have gotten the guy in the barn, but I don't think she killed her husband. The facts are starting to point elsewhere. Anyway, I think she's safer at your house and easier to keep an eye on. If I bring her in and arrest her, I'll never know for sure who it is."

"Why are you telling me this then?"

"Because we need you. You're going to let it leak that Mary is held up at your house. And we're going to keep an eye on things at your place."

"Like you did the night in her barn? I'm not letting you use her as bait."

"I like to think that we're protecting her. If she goes into the hospital and is subsequently released, she's fair game for whoever this joker is.

The ringing of Tate's cell phone interrupted their conversation and he swung the cover open as he spoke roughly into the receiver, "Hang on a minute!"

"Do you think it's a club member?" Jack asked walking toward his car.

"Oh, it's someone in your little circle all right, that I'm sure of. You keep her at your place, and we'll find out who did this."

Tate's attention went back to the phone as he and Apple watched Jack's Explorer roll out of the parking lot. "How many? Jesus! Put the reports…no we don't have any leads.

I'm on a murder case, damn it, isn't that more important?" He ended the conversation abruptly by snapping the cover of his phone shut.

Apple looked over at him concerned, "Now what?"

"Eight more freakin' sheep, and a swan shaped bird bath."

Apple snickered, "it's a real crime spree in this little town, maybe it's a full moon."

Tate rubbed his temples, "It's worse than that, it was lifted from the Mayor's house. His wife doesn't think we're takin' this seriously enough."

"Wait, the fancy thing - that's surrounded with flowers?"

"That's the one."

"They'd need a small crane for that wouldn't they?"

"They're gettin' more creative, and they yanked up the flowers too. What are they doing, holdin' all the lawn ornaments hostage?"

There was a brief moment of silence followed by the repressed squeak and cough of a quickly stifled chuckle. When the two men glanced at each other, their grins exploded into infectious rib splitting laughter that left them both breathless and sore.

Jack reached over and placed his hand on Mary's forehead. She opened her eyes slowly as he spoke, "You slept all night, but I think your fever is starting to come down. Want to tell me what's going on?" He shook a thermometer down and placed it into her mouth. He had decided not to tell her about Tate. She might try to run again, and she was in no kind of shape for that.

She tugged the thermometer out just enough to answer, "Just like a doc, ask me to talk and stick a thermometer in my mouth." She peered down at her now neatly wrapped leg, "I'm gonna have a nasty scar from all this."

"Tell me something I don't know. You should be in the hospital."

"No I shouldn't, and lucky for me I never had great legs to begin with."

Jack ignored her weak attempt at humor. He leaned back in the chair and put his feet up on the bed, "So how did you get here? Where have you been?"

Mary began to tell him what happened the night of the storm. She relived with him the chase through the state grounds and the old man and his wife who helped her. They laughed about the strange new paint job Shortstop got at Elva's place. She asked about Bob and if he had gotten her messages.

Jack told her what he knew. They talked for a while until her speech began to get drowsy and slow again. Jack pulled the blanket up around her neck and let her sleep.

Bob ate breakfast slowly. He was still tired from reading into the night, but couldn't stop thinking about the information in the file. The professor hadn't been completely honest about what he knew. In the file, there were notes and questions that Collins had written down that were far more fascinating than the examination report and pictures of the pendant. There were a series of scientific articles on the excavation of the prehistoric site not far from the Semi Wild. The notes scribbled in the margins alluded to possible connections between the pendant and other finds associated with that site. Collins had circled something about a stone mask and had printed his father's name and address on top of the article. Bob slowly read the paper entitled, *Archeological Survey and Long Term Management Plan*. It read like a building inspection, not an article about an ancient burial site or its historic significance. It was all about construction and limiting access to all the gray areas on the map marked sensitive. He tried to figure out the location based on how the general roads intersected. The sensitive areas were deliberately vague, and yet, he knew this area and it sounded strangely familiar. The proposal described a plan to preserve and protect the land and make it into a park of some sort. He took notice how the poles for the football fields were distanced from gray areas marked off on the map. When he turned the page and glanced at the layout of the baseball fields - it suddenly connected.

His thoughts whipped back to the day he and Steve stopped at the ball field on the way home. He remembered the strange feeling he had, the sadness and longing as if something were calling to him. It had to be the same place, there was no other.

Toby sat at the patio doors eyeing up the birds pecking at the bird feeder. His ears were set forward in interest and his gaze locked on one bird in particular clucking and pacing up and down the deck. Bob dropped a corn flake on the floor, "Toby, here boy." He tapped his foot on the floor to get the dogs attention.

Toby glanced with indifference at the fallen corn flake, returning his gaze to the brazen bird on the deck. Bob got up and walked to the dog stretching his arms toward the ceiling in one big yawn, looking to see what was so interesting that it defied food.

"Damn," he cut his stretch short. It was a large gray pigeon, its head bobbing in unison with its feet as it strutted and strolled up and down the deck railing. It was dragging a ragged piece of duck tape from its foot.

He grabbed his coat and after a few lame attempts to sneak up on the bird, he finally had a better idea. He walked out to the pigeon pen and flew open the door to let all the birds fly in widening circles over the property. The flapping whirl of their wings overhead sounded like sheets whipping in the wind, and soon the lone bird on the deck joined his own kind in the air. Bob watched as one by one, the pigeons landed on the coop, entered through the one-way door, and merrily helped themselves to an additional feeding.

Bob caught the bird inside the pen and gently dislodged the note from its leg.

I'm heading to Jacks. I'm O.K. Don't get followed. Love Mom

He gathered up the books, stuffing them in his book bag, and set off for the Semi Wild Club. But there was one stop he had to make first.

The county library was a large one-floor office building whose contemporary lines seemed out of place in the rural field that it rose from. Bob strolled through the library feeling the hushed, artificial silence surround him. He felt out of place among the intellectuals that frequented here. He walked up to the reference counter and smiled at an attractive Asian woman frantically tapping on her computer. "How would I find what papers published in nineteen fifteen?"

The woman reached under her desk and pulled out an orange notebook. She thumbed through it without expression or interest, never asking a reason and not interested in one, then turned the book around and put it in front of him. "Here is a list of newspapers. Looks like six were current between nineteen hundred and nineteen twenty-five. These four were publishing in nineteen fifteen. What area do you want to focus on?"

He surveyed the list before him. "But the event I'm looking for took place in the vicinity of Indian Mills."

"Then I would suggest the Central Recorder." She sat down and her fingers began tapping on her computer again, then she looked back at him. "The Recorder is on microfilm."

The librarian disappeared for a while then returned with small boxes of film. She walked him over to the machine and instructed him on all its adjustments.

The librarian clicked the machine on and fed the microfilm through as she spoke. "They're so old. Sometimes it's best to look at several newspapers anyway. So if you don't find what you need here, still check the other newspapers in the area. If it's big news, they'll probably cover it."

Bob sat down and the tape started sliding past him on the screen 1887, 1897, 1898. Pictures of women in ankle length dresses and ads for blacksmiths flew past him. The motion of the machine was hypnotizing. He stopped when he saw an ad for a Victrola, remembering the old man in the restaurant, and slowed to read each paper that rotated in front of him. There was nothing news worthy happening in the area. The paper covered blurbs about local people who traveled to nearby towns. It spat out who was sick, who was better, and who was having a good year with crops. He wondered how one woman visiting her nearby sister could be put in the paper as news. They must have struggled for legitimate material. There were ads for automobile parts, ladies shoes and horses and mules bought and sold at a good price, or so the ad read. He read August, September and finally November when his eyes came onto a large one-column article. It read:

Gypsy Convicted of Murder

Elija Harris, a member of a tribe of gypsies camping in the Atsion -Hammonton area was arrested in connection to the deceased John Morganstern, owner and proprietor of Morganstern Mills. It is alleged that Mr. Harris encountered Mr. Morganstern while poaching on the Wells farm and that afterward a physical altercation ensued. Mr. Harris allegedly attempted to conceal his crime by making it appear to be a hunting accident. The murder weapon was later found in his possession.

Mr. Morganstern had proposed to purchase the four hundred acre Wells farm for division into smaller farms and businesses. A charge of murder was preferred and bail was denied. Elija Harris is a member of the tribe that had some trouble with another tribe at the fair grounds two years ago, when there was a fierce fight between two men.

Bob wondered if the man had been a victim of circumstance. He suspected that the police had focused on him because Gypsies were different, like Native Americans, like Hippies, like him and his friends. He imagined the nomad's surprise when arrested for possession of a bloody arrow and a deer over the fire. That would have been reason enough to convict him back then.

He returned the microfilm to the front desk and set off toward the Semi-Wild Club...or the old Wells farm.

Apple moved along the shelving as if he were looking for a book, "What would make a kid who hated high school suddenly go the library?"

"The same thing that would make him go to a college professor," Tate replied watching the boy leave. "You follow him and I'll find out what he was doing here."
The two men went their separate ways, one to the microfilm on the reference desk, and the other toward the exit.

"Excuse me ma'am," Tate spilled his badge on the counter in front of Asian woman, "can you tell me what that kid was looking for?"

The woman looked down at the badge. "I'll show you, officer," she replied. "The young man was interested in a particular date, in a particular area. In fact, he printed out an article from the microfilm, so I can save you some time." She went to the printer and reached into the waste paper basket. "The first copy is always so light, that you have to increase the density to see it better." She unrolled a paper with light gray print. It was good enough to read and she handed it to him.

Tate read the article. "This is strange."

"In what way?" She asked.

He looked up and smiled at her, "I need to know where the Wells farm was located in nineteen fifteen. As she led him to the dusty room of old township maps. He wondered if a copy of the original police report would still be in the old police archives.

Mary awoke in the same position she had fallen asleep in. She smiled at Jack, who was resting in the chair across from her. "I really slept."

"I guess you did," he replied. "The swellings gone down a little, and I think if we leave the IV in today, hang maybe...two more of the antibiotic, and you do nothing but rest, we can go to oral antibiotics by tomorrow night."

"You know, for a bone doc...you're all right." The corners of her mouth curled into a knowing smirk. "Why didn't you go into ER medicine?"

He shook his head and glanced up at her, "They work you like a dog and you have no control over anything." He looked down at his watch as he spoke. "And how about you – why radiology?"

"I thought the lighting was rather becoming"

Jack responded with a laugh, but it was abruptly cut short by his seriousness. "I have to have office hours today. If I reschedule my patients, well...it may look suspicious. Besides, you don't need me. You have to sleep and let this thing heal." He went to wash his hands then returned with a tray of cereal and warm tea. He set it down on the bed table and checked the IV site on her arm. "Is your arm hurting? Sometimes these antibiotics can irritate the veins and become real painful down the arm."

"No, I can live through two more. I'll be fine. Just leave me a bag and I'll hook it up when this one runs out."

Jack continued to check the IV. "I checked your horse this morning and he's fine. But I got to tell you he's a pretty ugly sight. Looks like he fell into a paint can."

Mary reached for the cereal. "I guess I'll never find out what happened there, but someday, I'll find a way to thank Elva."

Jack pulled on his overcoat and briefly returned to her side. He bent over and kissed her on the forehead and a moment of awkwardness passed between them. "I'm glad you're all right...and I'm glad you're here. We'll figure this thing out." He left the room still speaking as he walked toward the kitchen, "Now, stay put," he called, "keep the door locked, and I'll be back around seven with some real food."

Bob pulled his Subaru up to the clubhouse. The police would think he was just walking the dog, but no one had driven in behind him - at least from what he could tell. Tate's car seemed to have its share of problems on the winding dirt road that led up to the club. It was probably easier to park on the main road and wait, rather than take a chance of getting stuck hopelessly in the mud.

It had started to drizzle and he and Toby walked around the grounds, slipped into the woods, and circled around to the trail that backed up to Jack's house. He watched from the edge of trees to make sure that no one followed him on foot. The going was tough and the mud seemed to suck noisily at the sole of his boots. The club was abandoned during the workweek and even the old retired dog handlers weren't using the grounds on this cold damp day. Satisfied that he wasn't followed, he walked up the footpath to the back of Jack's house.

Mary heard a soft rapping on the door and it woke her. She rolled off the bed, grabbed the IV from the lamp above her and crept up to the kitchen window to get a look.
She threw open the door and grabbed her son to hug him, "I missed you! It's so good to see you. I guess you got my messages!" She saw the concern in his face as his eyes took in the tubing leading to her arm, but she quickly explained about how much better she was feeling and that it was nothing to worry about.

Bob pulled his boots off as Toby happily licked his missing mistress and ran around the house. They caught up on the events of the last few days, as Bob cleared the coffee table, and spread the books out across it. "This was what Dad got from the library," pulling out the pendant and recounting the conversation with the professor at the college and the questions he had about the image.

Mary positioned herself on the sofa pulling a blanket up to her chin. She gazed down at the material. "So – you read it. What's your impression? Is the professor the other guy? Peterson said there were two asking questions."

Bob frowned as if considering the idea for the first time. "I don't know. After all, he needs the site to back up the find. From what I've read, the artifact isn't much good without site stratification."

"What?" Mary asked.

"Stratification. They need to look at how deep the site is, and other artifacts that collaborate the same time period in order to verify its authenticity."

"So you're saying that without the area where it came from, this in itself isn't enough to be important?" Mary marveled at the young man before her. "You did good." She smiled at him lovingly. "And to think you fixed the barn roof and got Old Butch walking pretty good now too."

"Ornery as ever." He replied with a laugh. "I've been walking him around with a saddle and tomorrow I'm gonna' try to ride him and see how he does on that foot. Oh, and we have a goat now."

"A goat?"

Bob shook his head and he retold the story as they both burst into laughter.

Bob decided not to tell her about the old murder on the grounds. There was no sense in weighting his mother down with more information than she needed. Besides, he wasn't sure of its importance yet. He noticed how frail and tired she looked.

He shuffled through the books. "I've been reading this stuff, Mom. It's pretty interesting. Did you know that Indian Mills used to be a Lenape reservation called Brotherton? It was news to me. Anyway, now most of the tribe live in Oklahoma. Seems we pushed 'em out of New Jersey." He turned the pendant over in his hands as he spoke, "Nobody did this kind of art, ya' know, most images were just scratched, not raised and in three dimensions like this."

He sat back in the chair and looked at his watch. They had been talking with no interest in the time and it was getting late in the day. He explained that he had taken a part time job at the local feed store unloading trucks. "I have to get back," he started, "A shipment is coming in around four and I need the pocket change."

Mary managed a tired but lovingly smile at her son. She could see so much of Mark and her in him. "Your father would be proud of you," she started. "He always admired your independence, your will. This last week has proven that you can do anything. He was right."

Bob touched the compass at his neck, "Well, working our place has given me a new appreciation, too. I mean, he worked all day – and hard work, physical work, and came home to pitch hay, fix fence, and take care of animals."

"But for him it was his sanctuary, his little space of peace and simplicity in a crazy world. I know your father didn't show it much, but he respected the way you ran your own life. You weren't afraid to explore or experience on your own. He was always worried for you…that maybe you would get into some kind of trouble. But I never worried. I always knew you were the strong one. You would find your way back to us."

Toby had curled up next to the gas fireplace and rain started to peck against the window.

Bob stood and pulled on his coat. He glanced at Toby who had worked his head under the couch in an effort to hide himself. "It'll take a while to get through the woods in this mud. Do you want me to leave him?" He motioned in the direction of the sleeping dog.

"Yeah, he looks comfortable and I like his company. He can stay. I need some time to look at all this stuff. Will you come back in a few days?"

Mary stretched across the couch and closed her eyes feeling the comfort of the gas fireplace. Soon after, she felt the weight of the dog gently step up on the couch and find a narrow spot between her and the back of the sofa. He climbed in softly, as if afraid to wake her, and rested his head on her shoulder. She stroked his head and both closed their eyes drifting to sleep with the rhythmical sound of the driving rain as their lullaby.

Kevin cleaned the floor of the kennels, and satisfied that the dogs were taken care of, turned his attention to his equipment. He slid the heavy saddle off the trailer rack and placed it over the fence for inspection. Saturating a soft rag with Lexoyl, he lovingly caressed its tired surface. The years of use had conformed to every part of his backside and legs like a velvety pair of jeans. He thought about his dad and his granddad as he carefully smeared the protective coating over the soft conditioned leather.

He had never gotten along with his father. It was his Pappy who had taught him the most. He considered his childhood as he worked, how Pappy treated him like an adult. They went to every field trial together, and some he had even ditched school for. He heard his father's words warning him – *You can skip school, son, but the first time your grades slip – I won't look the other way, Pappy or not. You'll stay home.* So, he worked hard to stay ahead in order to sneak off to an occasional trial. Pappy was always happy to call him in sick to school.

Dad always said Pappy was a crazy old coot. But to a child, the man seemed huge and invincible. Even into his seventies, with two hip replacements, he still rode a horse at every event. And that was the way he finally died. The gallery of spectators had found his horse standing quietly on the trail, as if waiting for his rider's direction, Pappy's large body slumped forward, one arm around the animal's neck. A heart attack had taken him with calm, quick resolution. Kevin smiled, that's how he would have wanted to go – doing what he loved most.

As his hands worked the leather, he recalled how stiff and shiny new the saddle had once looked. It was part of a first place purse Pappy had won, thanks to a stylish little pointer named Rocket. He remembered that dog well.

Rocket knew how to play the game, and was wise to it. He was a seasoned All Age Champion who would run far ahead of the handler and onlookers, and when out of sight, would sniff around, lift his leg on a few bushes, and carefully return to full hunt status before his handler and judges caught up. The dog was brilliant and clever. He knew when he was being watched, and put on a classy show with unwavering style in front of the judges.

However, as life would have it, after many years and many wins, Rocket was retired when he started to go blind. He remembered his Pappy telling the vet, *the dog must be seein' something because he can still run in the field.* But even a little kid could see that it was more like a fast limp with no real direction. Pappy faced his denial the day Rocket ran head on into a tree and knocked himself unconscious on the ground.

Pappy never let a dog get bad, but he had trouble saying goodbye to Rocket. It was the only time he had ever seen the big man cry. Twelve at the time, he had come running around the corner of the barn, to see the hulking old man bent next to Rocket's kennel, sobbing uncontrollably, one hand pressed to his face – the other dangling the dog's empty collar.

That collar now rested in Kevin's trophy case, as sacred as an athlete's number - retired in memory of a great contender, and never to be worn again. There would never be another dog like Rocket.

He sighed heavily as he worked, his eyes blurred with recollections of the past and questions about his future. He was almost thankful when a car pulled into the driveway and distracted him from his thoughts.

The disheveled man dragged himself out of the car and waved as he called, "Hey, Alston, you remember me?"

Kevin squinted at him, trying to put a name with the man's face. He called back to the stranger, "Yeah, you came with another guy – wanted a guide and a dog for a day – I don't do that anymore." His impression now was the same as then, an occasional sportsman who hunted only to brag to his friends.

"You do remember me," Collins stated.

"What do you want?" Kevin returned his attention to his saddle, and decided right then, that he had no time or interest in this man.

Collins was unaffected by his disposition, "I know you train out at that club on route 541, where Mark Winters was killed. Did you know him well?"

"What's it to you?"

"I'm just an interested party who thinks we can help each other."

"How so?" Kevin was amused that this man would think he needed any help from him.

"I suspect there's something important out there. Collins carefully retold the story of his meeting with Mark, the artifact, and his guess that the site was on the Semi Wild grounds. He was careful to add, "I only came to you because I thought you might want to know. If the site is discovered there – well, it might affect how the land could be used down the road. Best to not let it be discovered and made public."

Kevin straightened in sudden interest. "So, if it was to be found there, and I'm not sayin' it is – the state might take the grounds, or would they protect it?

Collins hesitated, knowing he had hit on something here, "Both, they would protect it from being developed." He went on to describe how the state had prevented development of other sites where significant artifacts were found. "Help me find what I need, and we'll work on a plan for preserving the grounds, but I need to find it first."

"Wait." Kevin glared at Collins as he considered his alternatives. He pursed his lips, torn between hating this man, and the remote possibility that if Collins were right, whatever he was looking for might keep the Semi Wild undeveloped in the future. He vacillated for a few moments between his desire - the need to save his training grounds and every revolting instinct that warned him not to trust this man. As Kevin's hand slowly swept across the cold brass nameplate engraved with his grandfather's name – he turned to the professor with firm resolution, "What do I have to do?"

Chapter Thirteen

The faces that circled the table looked grim. Kevin and Jack sat side by side in the old clubhouse dining room, while Susan tugged at her glasses and shuffled through a stack of papers in front of her. All the board members were present and most of the membership crowded the room around them.

"So that's it," Jack concluded closing his leather notebook. "I think that Susan here has made some good points and if you have any additional suggestions, well...we'd be happy to hear them."

Susan started to pass the packets of papers out to the members. I'm going to send one to those folks who couldn't attend tonight," she added.

A gruff, deep voice came from the back of the room and a bearded man stepped forward. "So, I just want to make sure I understand this, our alternatives are to find a philanthropist to buy this trustee out or come up with the money among the members? Can't we just increase the dues to cover the costs?"

Susan responded, "We couldn't get the money in time by increasing dues, and a lot of the members simply can't afford it."

Words of agreement spread through the crowded room. Jack watched as the people he knew started to talk angrily between themselves. He hoped that he had motivated them enough to get someone to come up with a good idea in the eleventh hour of this problem. They were running out of time. He stood and tapped on the table. "Before we break, I'd like to talk a moment about a different subject." His face looked tired as he addressed the members. "After the unfortunate death of Mark Winters, I have talked to a lawyer to assess our liability here at the Club along with the possibility of purchasing the ground. Now don't get me wrong, we can't stop accidents from happening, and everyone who rides accepts the responsibility for injury under the equine state liability law. But I can't help thinking that if Mark had been here by himself, or come in the winter time to run his dogs – well, it might have been twenty-four hours or better before someone looked for him out there." He shifted his weight uneasily, unsure of the reaction to his next suggestion. "If we come out of this thing, we need to let a caretaker live here on the grounds fulltime. That way, someone can keep an eye on things and organize the work here." He looked into the faces of his colleagues. "It could have happened to any of us. I think we owe it to Mary and the rest of our membership to at least have someone connected with management of the grounds, on a full time basis. My lawyer and I are still trying to work out all the details, but I think it'll benefit everybody to have someone here."

Kevin spoke for the first time that evening, "We're talking a lot of money to be part owner in the club. I don't know any takers, do you?" He looked around the room, then continued, "If we take on a caretaker, they wouldn't have to pay property tax or utilities or even for minor house renovations. The club has the funds for that from the dues sector. But to live for free on four hundred acres of backyard and a free residence might be some incentive. We'd be lookin' to have someone with equipment knowledge, who could do minor repairs and run a tractor. Someone who is willing to stay in this old place and keep things maintained up here. But it has to be someone who has a loyalty and interest in what we do."

"The place would need some major fixing." Susan added, "but it isn't impossible. The bedrooms upstairs just need some paint and new windows. The kitchen, well…maybe some new appliances – and definitely rodent extermination." Her eyes and those of all the other women in the room looked wearily around them."

Jack agreed, "Ideally, I would like someone to work with environmentalists on planting warm grasses in the fields, so that the quail had more feeding areas than we currently provide."

The members seemed to agree and were considering the proposition. A woman piped in, "It's a historic house, we shouldn't let it fall apart. Having a caretaker would keep it up." The members talked as they filed out the building, leaving the three sitting silently at the wooden table.

Jack quietly whispered to Kevin and Susan, "Mary's showed up at my place. She's pretty shook up, but she'll be fine."

"What are you gonna do? Susan replied, "She can't hide at your place forever."

"I don't know. I don't know what I'm doing anymore," Jack put his head in his hands.

"Well, maybe the police have come up with something new in the case," she started, trying to console him.

Jack glanced down at his watch, and started to gather up the papers in his notebook. "Well, I'd better go."

"Jack," Susan added, "At least she's safe with you."

He tried to smile, but wondered how safe she really was.

Jack arrived home late and was surprised to see Mary on the living room couch, reading. He was also surprised that she hadn't pulled the IV out herself. He half suspected that she would. It was confirmation to him that she was more concerned about her leg than she let on. He noted her better color and she seemed to be more alert.

He put the Chinese take out on the kitchen table and took off his coat. "Feeling better, I see?" He smiled, grabbing up the handles of the boxes and joining her in the living room. "Nothing like a little MSG to make you feel better. Get any rest?"

"Bob came by and brought me these," she gestured toward the books. "It's pretty interesting. You learn about this stuff when you're a kid in school, but it never seems real...it's like a story being told with no connection with reality. Did you know that there was an archaic period Native American burial site found right near here?

"What does that have to do with anything?" Jack sorted through the variety of books as she spoke.

Mary continued as if she hadn't heard him, "I really knew so very little about their lifestyle and beliefs...and I have their blood. Well, at least I know what my stalkers are after." She handed Jack the stone pendant. "Be careful with it, but this is it. Mark knew it was valuable."

He examined it under the light, "So why the books then?"

"Apparently there is more wherever this was found, and Mark was trying to get some insight into its value. At least that's our guess."

"If he knew this, then why not tell you about it?"

She became suddenly somber, "I don't know...unless he wasn't sure it was real or on some level, he didn't trust me."

"Maybe he knew it could potentially put your life in danger," he replied thoughtfully. "You can't know what was going through his mind during all this. So what have you found out?" He motioned toward the piles of books wishing to change the subject.

"I've read a lot, but I'm not sure if what I have read is important. Compound that with dozing off here and there, and I have a brain full of scattered information. One thing is that they trusted their dreams and acted on them. They felt that their visions were messages from the gods to direct the future of their actions. So, lets say if one warrior had a vision of a bear attacking a deer, it could be interpreted as an upcoming battle between two tribes." She continued. "And, when they made their weapons they adorned them with plumes from birds, because they believed that the weapon would take on some power of flight and listen to this...they were often buried with their domesticated animals." She looked at him and shrugged. "I didn't know they had domesticated animals, did you? Dogs mostly, sometimes deer."

"Now what were you saying about a burial site?" Jack sipped at his drink.

"Cremated human remains and stone artifacts like axes and spearheads were uncovered." She flipped through the pages as if summarizing the information. "I suppose that the hawk on the pendant is one of those power symbols, you know, the predator attacking what Bob believes is something that is pretty hard to make out – looks like a box."

Jack was still staring at the depiction in stone. "How old is it?"

"The local expert, that Mark consulted, estimated this at approximately four thousand years old, but it was never verified. Trying to find much data in that era and in this area is pretty tricky. Still it's an interesting read."

"That's long before recorded settlers in this country, or much of anything else." Jack handed her the paper box and a fork and she set down the book to eat. The light from the gas fireplace played upon her hair and he decided that he felt comforted having her here. She was interesting and real. She told him about Bob's visit and the details of what he had found out.

"What's your impression?" He finally asked poking his fork around the inside of the little box until he found the last piece of shrimp. "So you think the professor is the guy after you? Do you think we should go to the police and tell them?"

Mary shook her head. "No, not yet. Tate wouldn't believe me, and he would just make me a sitting duck for whoever this guy is. I've got nothing on this Collins guy. For all I know his interest might be legitimate. But I think," she hesitated, "the site might be here…on the grounds."

"What makes you think that?"

"A feeling, a premonition, I don't know…I needed to come back here, even my dreams were based here. Every part of me tells me that I have a connection here that's left undone."

Jack smiled. "You'll think more clearly after I pull your pain meds. You know you've been reading too much." A chuckle left his throat.

She smiled back, but knew he was wrong.

Jack finished his food and picked up one of the books. Page after page of photographs depicted strong featured, dark skinned men with black shiny hair and animal skin clothes. There was a disturbing sadness in their eyes that was evident in every photograph. He couldn't define it but felt its presence in every image. Mary had the same kind of look, an inner sadness that he would capture when she thought no one was looking. He glanced up from his reading, "Well...let's start with what we know. Do you have the book on weapons?" he asked.

"Yep..." she continued reading.

"How did they kill their adversaries?"

"Arrow or spear, I suppose, until the gun entered the trading scene...again much later than the estimate on the pendant."

"No. I mean describe the typical warrior killing during the time period of the pendant, according to the history books. How would it play out?"

Mary rested the book across her chest trying to remember an earlier section of her reading. "The experts speculate that they would hide or sneak up on their prey in the woods, fire an arrow or spear and then follow up..." she hesitated, "with a blow to the head, either with a rock or a hand crafted stone instrument." Their eyes met.

Jack put his feet up on the ottoman and started flipping through the pages, "Do you think someone else found this site, and used what they found to kill Mark before he could tell anyone else?"

"...and somewhere in one of these books," Mary responded, "I read that arrows were so difficult and time consuming to make, that the warrior would attempt to retrieve it after the kill. So was the way Mark died supposed to be a message to me? This person must assume that Mark told me - that I know where the site is."

They both sat in silence for a moment and Mary felt a wave of exhaustion and sadness sweep over her. "It finally makes sense, why they came after me in the barn. Where was the hawk – that's what the guy yelled at me." She closed her eyes and rested her head back against the sofa. Toby put his head in her lap.

Jack watched her closely, and at first he thought she was in pain, "Are you all right?"

She began slowly not opening her eyes, "Twenty-one years, Jack," a tear rolled down her cheek. "I've never been with another man, never thought about being with another man. We met right out of high school and married." She brushed the tear from under her eyes to have another one take its place. "Sure, Mark and I had our ups and downs, but he was a good man, an honest, hard working man. All he wanted was the best for his family. That's not to say, that he didn't have his faults. God knows, I have mine. But our fights were always petty and solvable, part of being married. Most the time they were about the boys. He tried to make them into responsible men, or his idea of responsible. Especially Bob. Bob wanted no part of his father's world, and I think Mark was hurt by that." She shook her head. "He would have given me or the boys anything we asked for. He would have laid his life down for us. That was the kind of husband and father he was. God! -it wasn't supposed to be like this. We were supposed to retire and enjoy our grandchildren."

Jack handed her a tissue. He wanted to console her, but didn't want her to think he was taking advantage of the moment. "He was a good man," he began, leaning back into the chair, "and twenty-one years of marriage is a badge most people don't get to wear. I envy you and Mark for that. You two had a kind of teamwork about your partnership. You counted on one another through whatever life handed you." His mind started to drift into his own sadness. "My marriage lasted five years and she took most of my income with her in the breakup. In the end, there was no respect or common ground between us, and I would never care for anyone again.

I just don't have it in me anymore." He ended his conversation abruptly like he had said more than he intended.

"Jack," she said softly, her voice quaking, "I can't think about this anymore. I need to shut it off, just for a little while, just to clear my mind." She hesitated, "Can...can I stay with you tonight? I know this is an awkward request...but I just want to feel cared for one more time. Not in a sexual way you understand...I just don't want to be alone tonight. I just want to know it will be O.K."

Jack reached over and gently took her hand. She was asking him to be Mark tonight. He looked down at the lines in her hands and turned it over in his. He touched the tender calluses on the palms, and still with all its strength, it felt helpless and trembled in his. They were the hands of a teammate, a partner, a friend, but still the hands of a woman. He knew she did not make this request easily. He kissed the inside of her hand pressing his lips softly against the roughened texture of her palm. He released it and wrapped his arms around her feeling the warm wet of her tears as her face pressed against his shoulder. "You're safe with me tonight," he stroked her hair, "Sleep...and I won't let anything hurt you." If he could be Mark for her one last time, then she would be Annette for him - and maybe they could each find a small moment of peace in the solitude of night.

Bob awoke suddenly to a tapping at his bedroom window. He rolled off his bed and poked his fingers through the blinds at the figure outside. He recognized her as the young woman who smiled in the feed store, only now, he realized that he had known her all along.

"Melissa?" He spoke through the window. The young woman's smile revealed perfect white teeth where heavy metal braces had once laid stripes of black. The coarse red hair that defied the laws of physics in high school, now fell past her shoulders into twisting tendrils to the middle of her back. She wasn't anything like the girl he felt sorry for in school. The broken down kid sobbing uncontrollably in the girl's room was just a memory. She was the most beautiful woman he had ever seen. How could he have ever thought she was homely?

He shouted through the window pane, "Give me a minute, I'll be right out!" He clumsily tugged on his jeans and pulled a clean T-shirt and fleece over his torso. Whatever she wanted, he couldn't go out there looking like a slob.

He pulled open the front door and she whirled around to face him.

Her green eyes laughed as she watched him scan her slender figure taking in the new woman before him. "Ethan said you needed riding lessons. So I came over to get you started."

Her smile warmed him as she spoke and the freckles that once dotted her face had faded behind some light makeup, and that magnificent smile. It stunned him. "I don't get it. I'm confused," he babbled, "Why did Ethan send you?"

"Well, he's going to be doing a little local farm work for the next few weeks."

It was the way she said it that made him realize that Ethan was in trouble again.

"And…he told my Uncle Joe that he promised you lessons," she added, "so, I was called to help you out."

Bob looked down at his watch. "It's nine A.M, isn't that a little early?"

"It's better early. I have a lot to teach you." She pulled her hair back with her hands and wrapped a cloth band around it letting the sunlight catch and ignite it like fire.

Bob realized that she wasn't going to take no for an answer. He noticed her horse tied to a tree. "Come on in and I'll get some boots on." He knew Melissa would never be interested in him, but what the hell, she was nice and he needed to get Butch moving again.

"Wow have you changed!" Bob shouted from the bathroom as he combed his hair in the mirror.

"Yeah, you could say that," she called back, looking at the books spread lazily across the floor of the living room. She ran her fingers over some of the pages and wondered why he was interested in this stuff. "What's with all the Indian history?"

Bob rinsed his mouth free of toothpaste, coming up from the sink to answer, "Did you know that when young Indian boys became men, they were sent into the woods all alone to find their spirit gods?" He came around the corner into the living room.

"Who's this guy?" She pointed at the picture of the mask, "He looks pretty scary."

Bob smiled at her interest, "Oh, he was the god who gave them a good harvest, lots of game – kept them through the winter."

"Then he's the one you want as your spirit god so you wouldn't starve," she added casually.

He leaned over her shoulder. He could smell the scent of herbal shampoo that lingered in her hair, "Actually, if he was your spirit god you had to pay tribute to him forever. Even after you die, your family had to continue giving feasts and honoring him. If you didn't, he might turn his back on you, or spite your whole tribe with a horrible plague."

Melissa closed the book, "Kinda' needy, isn't he?"

Bob grinned, "Guess so, but it's kinda' cool when you draw the comparisons."

"How so?" She asked.

"They kinda' used herbs and drugs to find their spiritual mentor of sorts. Dreams were roadmaps that guided their decisions and their lives. I wonder if that's the real reason why drugs are so popular. I mean, think about it, maybe our generation is looking for a kind of spiritual peace and we've disguised it as recreation." He suddenly felt a pang of embarrassment, revealing his private insights to practically a stranger.

She looked up at him, "Interesting theory. So you're saying that kids don't even realize it, but they aren't trying to escape reality, they're trying to find inner peace and spirituality through chemical experimentation."

He laughed, "Too deep, huh?"

They walked together out to the barn. Within the hour, Butch was saddled, and Bob knew by heart every item of tack, and how to fit it properly to the horse. She explained the pressure points to look for on a saddle, and how to check if it's fitting properly.

Bob was up and in control and the two of them turned the horses behind the barn and down the trail into the woods. Melissa was a good and patient teacher encouraging him to relax and feel the movement of the animal beneath him. They talked as they rode and soon the conversation left horsemanship, and gravitated to their experiences in high school and what they had done since graduation.

Bob knew she was related to Ethan but was never really sure how. Melissa was Old Joe's niece, and Ethan was Joe's grandson. There were plenty of problems in the Peterson family. But when Melissa's dad claimed he and his new wife didn't have room to take her in – Old Joe stepped up and offered her some normalcy. He helped sell her mom's house, put the money away for her education, and gave her a place to stay.

"You're uncle is running a house for teenagers," he chuckled.

She smiled sweetly, "I think Uncle Joe, in his small way, is hoping to make amends for his own teenage years. I hear stories that he was quite a trouble maker growing up."

Listening to her, Bob felt as though his problems were small and insignificant in comparison with hers. And yet, she managed to smile about her past as if it were someone else's story, knowing the ending would justify the conflict.

In school, she was always made fun of and had a small group of friends. Her carrot red hair and densely freckled bony figure made her the target for mean jokes. Back then she always stayed to herself, rarely venturing to look anyone in the eyes. As they continued to talk, he was surprised at how much they had in common. She hadn't dated much, or even gone to the prom. How could one year have transformed her into such a beauty? He couldn't take his eyes off her. She was so easy to speak to, pleasant and attentive, as if she was almost interested in him. She talked about her classes at the community college and Bob confided that it wasn't for him. She asked about Steve and how he was doing. And with that question, a wave of disappointment swept over him as he wondered if her interest had to do with his brother.

They rode past the old rusted car and headed down along the fields to Old Joe's place. Melissa laughed at the sight of Ethan struggling with a manual fence post digger. "Oh!" she grinned, "we can't let this go by without some fun." They veered toward the small figure twisting the post digger into the hard earth.

"Doesn't Old Joe have a hydraulic digger for that?" Her voice was laced with chiding sarcasm.

Ethan didn't look up. His short figure struggled as if he were twisting a large corkscrew into the ground with every muscle he had. "Great!" He frowned, "I need your crap today."

"Don't be botherin' the farm help!" Joe called as he turned the corner of the barn.

Melissa flashed a smile at her Uncle. "So what dastardly deed is Ethan being accused of this week?"

Old Joe grumbled, and took off his hat to survey the job progress. "When you're done there, boy, put the wire back up and there's two more broken posts down further." His crooked finger led the way for their gaze.

Ethan glanced up at Melissa, "It was worth it," a faint grin swept into the corners of his mouth, just as Old Joe's hand slapped him upside his head with a whack.

"I'll show ya!" Joe stormed towards the barn, "C'mon...it's this way."

Melissa rode over, but Bob stayed behind. "Would it do any good for me to help ya?"

"No. It's not really work that needs to be done. It's just get even time...I'm used to it. Go take a look!" He returned his strong wide hands to the metal handles.

Bob rode over to the barn and came up next to Melissa. Old Joe whipped back a blue tarp and revealed piles and piles of ugly dirty lawn sheep.

Melissa reacted first. "You gotta be kiddin'. He's the idiot whose been stealin' these things from all over the county? He's a legend, a hero!"

Old Joe frowned, "Well if you ask me he's been doin' the people a favor – butt ugly."

"How ya gonna get rid of them, Uncle Joe?" she asked.

Joe grinned and a silent twinkle came to his eyes. "I got an idea that'll make everybody happy and keep the boy from getting' in trouble with the law." His eyes found Bob's. "You game, Winters?"

The day had moved on and Bob turned Butch back out to pasture. Melissa had shown him several exercises to improve his balance, giving Butch frequent breaks in between. He watched as she slid a firm gentle hand down Butch's leg and then demonstrated how to clean his hooves. The horse seemed to let her do whatever she wanted, never challenging her authority.

As she prepared to leave, she seemed to be waiting for something more. She mounted her horse to go home, but then turned suddenly and trotted back to him.

"Aren't you going to ask me out?" She asked leaning down toward him.

The question had taken him aback and he replied quicker than he thought, "If you're interested in me to meet my brother, then don't waste your time - he'll be away at college until Thanksgiving." The moment it spilled from his mouth he hated himself for saying it.

Anger crossed her face like a sudden thunderstorm and she jumped off her horse to approach him, "I'll ignore that and ask again. Aren't you going to ask me out?"

"I just got out of a bad relationship," he stumbled, "I don't need to be dragged through the mill again," he answered almost embarrassed, this girl wasn't going to give up. "Besides, I'm not the athlete..."

With that, she grabbed him by the front of his fleece and pulled him close. Her physical confidence amazed and startled him. "I'm not interested in your jock brother. I'm lookin' for a man – only a real man could step in and run a farm – hell, you did it without missing a heartbeat," she smiled mockingly, the playful sparkle returning to her eyes.

Before he realized what was happening, she kissed him longingly - letting her lips trail over his in a tender almost taunting release.

"I've changed a lot since high school and you have too," she whispered. And just as abruptly, she walked away, turning only once to wink. She remounted her horse. "I'd love too...see you on Saturday at eight," she said with a wave. "I'll bring dinner."

Bob watched her leave still feeling the sensation of her kiss drift over him in a wave of desire that left him heated and breathless. She was like an impending tornado, one part of him wanted to run and still he stood dumbfounded and in awe of the danger and power that possessed him.

She was well out of sight.

"Eight then..." He mumbled staring after her.

Bob finished his chores and returned to the house. He sprawled out onto the floor and clicked on the TV, then picked up a piece of paper. Using a blue pen, he began to sketch. He remembered his dream of flying and the aerial view of the land he passed over. He tried to bring back that feeling, the hill, the field, the swooping speed, the air moving beneath him in torrents.

After a while he bored and flipped the page. He tried to sketch the stone hawk and then the boxy shape beneath the talons. What was missing in this puzzle? His version looked nothing like the real pendant even with all his talent. Art and photography class were the only A's he had ever received in high school. He found it troubling that his memory of every detail of the pendant was clearly distorted by its absence. He looked critically at his work, disgusted that the final result of both pictures was so poor.

He tossed the pad aside and closed his eyes. An odd but strangely plausible idea came to him. What if the artist had seen the image as a vision, then transposing it correctly in stone would be difficult from mere memory. The hawk would be easy to reproduce, available to the eye – but a vision was like a fleeting moving veil with indistinct edges and odd distorted perspective. The more he considered it, the more plausible the theory became. He gave up on the picture of the hawk, but returned his attention to the memory of his flying dream, continuing to fill in the land as it swept beneath him. As his pen began to run dry, it started to skip and blob in irregular lines, but before it emptied, it left a large thick pool of blue ink in the right hand corner of the hill. Bob reached into his box to retrieve another pen, and as he considered how to improve his drawing, his brow furrowed at what the pen had left behind.

He grabbed the phone and dialed furiously. He was breathless when the answering machine picked up, "Steve – I've got it – I've got the hawk!"

Chapter Fourteen

Mary peered out the window into the milky morning mist. Jack was gone. His work was probably what destroyed his marriage, or perhaps, the night together had made their relationship too awkward for him to face. She dressed, threw on her coat and let Toby out. He ran to a tree while she limped stiffly to the barn and saddled up Shortstop. She needed to take a better look around, and this morning's fog would hide her presence. She would start at the tunnel. Jack had been good enough to wash the paint off her horse and he looked like himself again- although the faint remnant of a thunderbolt still remained down his nose. There was a warm front moving in, and it clashed with the cold from the icy rain of the day before. It created a rolling fog and smoky mist that lay across the fields in a thick low moist blanket. She headed off in the direction of the foundation and further toward the tunnel.

She tugged at her hat and took a deep breath as she passed the foundation. The corridor of the tunnel kept resurfacing in her mind. It looked friendlier than the last time she had come through here. The now sparse leaves that remained made the difference. The bare branches clicked together sounding a dry rhythm in the cold restless air, casting momentary skeletal shadows that danced merrily along the ground then disappeared in the overcast of the trying sun.

It no longer resembled the tunnel on that ominous October evening, just the open, pathetic remains of another lost year. The clacking arc of trees that formed the open network above them seemed benign and tame, beating out a random song- empty and sad. It held no new mystery.

To her left she could see through the wall of scrub pines and across the open field. There were deer trails tangling across the trampled brush. The accident kept repeating over and over in her mind. She dismounted and dropped Shortstop's reins. She patted him on the neck and he seemed uninterested in this place. He dropped his head and swayed back and forth, searching for one tender blade of grass left from the summer.

She walked through the tunnel, around the trees and went to the area that played out the struggle in the mud. Its memory long since gone, choppy from rain and deeply churned hoof marks. But in her mind she relived that night, seeing the indentation it had left and the way Mark looked at her with that empty dead stare. She remounted and headed through the woods. There was still a lot of land to cover.

Overhead, a hawk slowly circled above her, his call the solo echo of the wild. Shortstop halted and his eyes followed the bird as its graceful sweep cut across the fields and upward toward the clubhouse – eventually disappearing in the lifting fog.

As she turned him along the tree line and back toward the foundation, a smoky figure on horseback hesitantly moved out of the woods and drifted in the same direction, angling as if not to be seen. She followed the figure staying hidden by the pines. The horse ahead came to a stop and when the rider turned his head she realized its familiarity. It was Bob. She hastened Shortstop's trot to catch up and the horses neighed and snorted in recognition. She was relieved for the company, "Guess we both have the same idea."

Bob looked around cautiously, "Tate's car is out on the entrance road, but he normally doesn't get out and follow me, just keeps track of my comings and goings. The road's so washed out right now that coming up here with anything less than a horse or a four wheel truck is an invitation to be towed."

Mary reached over and patted Butch on the neck looking down at his legs. His fluid movement was back and his high stepping elegance had returned. "You did good with him, ya know." She turned in her seat looking for Toby as she spoke, "You're turning into a real farm boy!"

"God, not that! he chuckled, but saw the concern in her distraction. "Toby will find us, he knows his way around here. Let's go this way, I have an idea I need to check out."

They rode through the backfields with its scattered brush and broken hedgerows, toward the rear of the hill where the clubhouse drifted in and out of the shifting fog. The fields held onto the mist and there were pockets of cold and warm as they made their way across the muddy grounds. The place was abandoned. The sloshing of the horse's hooves and the gentle swish of the tall brown grass was softened only by the chatter of birds, and the occasional call of a distant quail.

The back of the stone club house bore out of the fog, its old chimneys seeming to have no end as they disappeared into the heavy sky.

Both horses startled and froze in their place. Mary and Bob squinted into the mist to see what the animals sensed. Up on the hill at the back edge of the cemetery was movement born from the mist and fog. It rose swirling and mystical then in a whirlwind pattern, disappeared.

"Did you see that?" Bob whispered.

"Illusion, nothing else. The fog, the wind...weird. Do you think somebody's up there?"

The horses seemed to draw strength from each other and with the immediate danger past, they moved toward the base of the hill. They stopped again when the old blue Ford tractor started to take shape midway up the rear of the slope.

"That's the tractor Dad used on the work day. This is what I wanted to check out." Bob pressed Butch on and they started to walk up the hill toward the back of the cemetery grounds. He dismounted and kicked his boot across the low thick brush where the tractor tires had left their indelible mark.

"What are you looking for?" Mary asked.

"Dad was pulling a stump back here and couldn't get it loose. Kevin and he had bet him that he couldn't get it out..." He looked up at his Mom. "When did you ever know

Dad to give up on a bet, especially with Kevin?" He followed the tire tracks from the tractor to the huge old knotted stump on the top edge of the hill.

Mary dismounted in curiosity. They walked around the stump examining the chain marks that marred its woody surface. Mary's foot slid beneath the stump and Bob pulled her back as they heard the dropping of dirt onto something hard.

"Do you think we can move it?" She asked.

"The trunk must be five foot around...maybe if Dad got the roots loose."

They positioned themselves on one side of the tree and on the count of three pushed the stump. It didn't budge. Bob scavenged the woods and found a long thick branch to use as a wedge. He worked it back and forth under a corner of the massive roots and soon it was wedged enough to create a small opening.

"I'll go in." Bob volunteered, "I don't want both of us in there in case this branch goes." He stopped for a moment. "Did you bring the pendant? I might need it, if there's drawings in there."

Mary fished through her saddlebag and pulled out a flashlight and the artifact."

Bob took them both and squeezed her hand. "It'll be all right." He pushed himself through the opening, cautiously contorting his slender body into the hole, working the branch tighter into place with his shoulders. He lowered himself until he felt his feet on the ground. Standing, he could almost poke his head out.

He crouched down slightly and scanned the shallow pocket of earth with the flashlight. The formation of root systems from the large tree above had created a small space in the earth. It smelled stale and musty and the roots dangled like ominous tentacles around him. First the light settled on a discolored skull. He moved toward it and noticed the bones lay in an ordered pile - as if at rest. The person had been cremated and the bones interred here. Just like the description in the books.

He squatted down to take a closer look. His eyes adjusted as he concentrated the beam of the flashlight, noting the fact that there were no shells or debris. This was truly a conscious tomb. The skull lay to the south and the hands in position to it, no longer covering the face, but in alignment with the face. The bones of the legs were bent and brought up to the chest and the soles of the feet faced the west.

His light fell upon the variety of stone items placed near the body. A dirt-covered stone axe of sorts, what appeared to be long sharp spearheads, rested in the dirt, next to a chiseled stone container.

He turned his attention to the item. It clearly wasn't an article of everyday use. It was made for a special and specific purpose; perhaps a ritual.

He knelt down and shined the flashlight on its elaborate carving barely visible with its coating of dirt. It must have been ceremonial, that he was sure of. He blew on the lid and a familiar face appeared. Gapping eyes and an open mouth of a large stone oval face.

The pocket of earth had managed to leave its treasures relatively unscathed over time. He picked up the mask. There was no color any longer, but he knew that once, the right side of the face had been red, and the other black. It's large-life size expression and eerie gaping holes for eyes stared blank as if trying to whisper some secret knowledge.

He brushed it carefully with his hands. The mask was acting as a lid to a hollowed out rock of a container. The sides of the rock had been etched with animals of power, a hawk, a bear, a deer. He marveled at their detail. It must have taken years to chip and rub and polish. Every detail of the hawk was etched with their eyes curiously dead staring, following the beholder.

He ran his hand along the hawk feeling for every line of its beauty and brushing off the remaining dirt as gently as possible. A quiet sensation began to surge through his soul and held him to the article as if in a trance. His eyes became glazed over and vacant as he let his imagination and intuition take over. It frightened him at first. It tugged at him against his will and a knowledge washed over him in waves of emotion without words or recognition. He couldn't take his hands from the container or the mask. He was paralyzed as it filled his mind with images. In the distance, he vaguely heard voices on the surface, but was held helplessly to the carving, unable and unwilling to free himself from the history unfolding before him.

Mary had retreated behind some brush when she heard the sound of someone approaching. She was relieved that it wasn't Tate. "Kevin," she said, "I'm glad to see you." He must have been the misty image in the fog she had seen earlier. She started to walk toward her friend.

His eyes went from the uprooted stump to her and back again. "This is it, isn't it?"

Another man stepped out of the woods and startled her, but it was too late, she had been seen.

Kevin spoke to Collins. "This is it, we found it."

Collins moved toward the stump, "Like I said, if anyone could find it, it would be the people who knew him best. That's why I came to you."

Kevin glared at the hole by the stump, "When you asked me to help you, I wasn't planning on it being here. I thought following Mary would lead somewhere else...anywhere else...take a look, make sure."

Collins frowned at him and clearly didn't like taking orders. "There's been a change in plans. I have to produce the site the artifact came from...or it means pretty much nothing. Not only that, there could be a lot more information found if we excavate the whole site – not just raid it like grave robbers. That could mean the whole top of this plateau." Collins eyes scanned the overgrown plateau and the clubhouse beyond.

Mary felt a cold panic and confusion start to climb through her limbs and into her chest. Her voice was ragged and angry, "You killed Mark? Is this why you killed Mark? For money? For some useless piece of stone?" Her eyes grew wide and she could feel herself shaking with anger, the adrenalin coursing through her as it did that night in the barn. "My God, Kevin…you were his friend...our friend."

Kevin yelled defensively, "Collins said this could be worth a lot of money and save the grounds. Money can buy more land for the Club, and now it's about survival. They can't touch us if we own the land – and if we can't own it – this might protect it!" He turned angrily toward Collins, "It's all we got left. You said the state would protect it!"

"Why are you doing this? Why are you working with him?" She shouted.

"Collins came to me for help. When I found out you were at Jack's, I figured I had nothin' to lose. If you found it – it was a way to save the club!"

"Then *he* killed Mark?" She turned on Collins as she spoke.

Collins shook his head, "I'm no killer."

"What about your friend in my barn?"

"I just wanted the location of the site, and Jerry –when we came up with nothing on the break-in, had to try something more forceful. But instead, you killed him. I had to go to someone who knew you - and Kevin knew you."

"I don't believe this." Mary looked around her eyes plotting her escape.

Kevin stared at Collins. He realized that he was a pawn, an unwilling player. He could feel himself shaking with raw uncontrollable anger, his hand deliberately groping the inside of his coat. His eyes weren't focused on anything. He was thinking with an intense determination that blocked everything else out. "But I *could* kill if it meant losing the land. We aren't going to give up our grounds…to anybody, for any reason, and certainly not for some dead Indian!" His voice was directed toward Collins. "Now get this crap and get it out of here. You got what you wanted!"

"This site could change history and you're going to deny it exists? You stupid fool! This find is mine. This find is going to be bigger than your little dog trials. One call to the state and this land becomes a historical site! They'll restrict its use and I dare say that this area will be entirely banned.

All I have to do is submit my survey and findings to the state." He got down on his knees to lower himself into the opening.

Kevin pulled a gun from his pocket. "No one is takin' this land or any part of it away. We had a deal..." He silenced the arrogant grin that had pushed him over the edge. Collins fell limp from the shot, blocking the hole to the tomb.

Bob felt released and took a deep breath as if he breathed for the first time in his life. He focused his eyes in the dark, dazed by the images that had been passed over him and the knowledge that consoled him.

Inside the stone container, there were small deer and bearskin pouches with powder in them. Beneath them a single bear claw, several hawk feathers and a pile of broken arrowheads on top of a dried out deer skin quiver.

He was now acutely aware of the conversation on the surface. He patted his pocket and found the red handkerchief that Kevin had given him the night in the barn. With it, he gently picked up one of the broken arrowheads, crusty and discolored with time. He wrapped it up and put it in his pocket. The light from the flashlight started to flicker and he tapped it against the ground. When he pushed the arrowhead into his pocket, his hand found the pendant. Without hesitation, he took it out and placed it back in the container with the remainder of its ancient contents.

There was a shot fired above and someone fell halfway in blocking the light from the surface.

Bob frantically pulled and pushed at Collins body, until finally he fell into the hole. He shook him into a brief period of consciousness. Collins slowly turned his head and his eyes fell onto the mask. For a moment a glimmer appeared in his fading eyes and he reached for it, "Mesingw," he muttered, his voice throaty and liquid, filling with blood. He began to choke on the fluid filling his lungs and his eyes went still.

A plan started to take shape in Bob's mind as he pulled the mask from Collins' hands.

Mary turned and ran for her life, darting into the woods, fighting the slope of the hill and ignoring the pain of her leg. Her heart was pounding as she fought her way to the plateau and bolted toward the clubhouse, running with all her might. Kevin followed in strong hurried steps. She frantically reached and tugged at the clubhouse door, but found it was locked. She ran across the plateau and started down the other side toward the next thick cluster of woods. There were areas were she could hide if she could just reach the trees. Her leg felt heavy and clumsy. She stumbled toward the trees letting the downward slope of the hill propel her body forward.

A shot rang out behind her. The pain was instant, sharp and crippling. It ripped into her left ear and through her head, spinning her around and sending her face first into the dirt.

Bob tossed the mask on the surface and reached for the axe head on the floor of the tomb. He struggled to pull himself out of the hole, when a heavy hand grabbed his arm, and he looked up into the face of his brother.

"Jesus what the hell's going on here?" Steve asked. "Is this the way you help Mom? I got let out down the road and was walking up to the clubhouse- heard arguing, then gunshots. There are a couple of cops down on the road. What the hell's goin' on?"

Bob turned to his brother, "Just do as I say." He put his fingers to his mouth and whistled for the horses, then pushed the red handkerchief with the arrowhead into Steve's hand. "Put this in the bag on Kevin's four-wheeler." They both disappeared into different directions of the woods.

The lone sound of the familiar whistle made Kevin halt. He spun around from the edge of the plateau and away from the motionless body that lay at the base of the hill. He knew that whistle. He turned his attention toward the area of its origin. His eyes searched for Mary's horses and their movement toward the sound. He'd come back for her. Someone else was here.

The large figures of the horses moved toward the cemetery in search of the food the whistle promised. The fog obscured the nearby foliage in opaque sheets of floating mists. Kevin brushed past the shrubs and walked into the open heart of the cemetery area. His eyes moved carefully over the thick brush of the grounds and the larger stones that might hide a human. It had to be the kid and he couldn't have a gun, or he would have used it by now.

The horses froze in their tracks, their huge bodies, rigid and balking, wanting to flee but unable to look away. Kevin saw it, a glowing set of yellow eyes emerging from the fog sending his imagination reeling in the commotion of the startled horses. He aimed his gun at the stone face then moved closer to get a better look. The bizarre face with glowing eyes had a flashlight behind it, and stood guard from a tombstone like a mystical warning.

The brothers watched from below the rim of the hill, "Let me have it, I can hit him with it," whispered Steve as he tried to pull the axe head from his brother's hands. Bob refused to let go and tugged it back, "This is somethin' I have to do, let go – it's mine."

Kevin turned toward the whispers as he grabbed the mask angrily from the monument and threw it across the cemetery. He raised his gun, letting the barrel follow the direction of his hearing. As Bob stood up to take aim, a dark figure rushed forward releasing a piercing cry of rage that echoed through the grounds. Kevin whirled around to come face to face with Mary, her face distorted with rage, caked with blood and dirt from her wound. She slammed against him with the full force of her momentum, her yell shrill and inhuman, the weight of her body knocking him off balance sending him twisting and turning from the impact.

Kevin tried to regain his legs and the stability to fire in retaliation. He hit with a thud as his head landed on the corner of a headstone. His death was instant.

Mary collapsed in a heap on the ground.

Bob stood in the bushes dazed, the power and madness rapidly draining from his body, trying to take in what his eyes had seen as Tate and Apple, breathless from running, appeared with their guns pulled. He backed away from the commotion, slipping silently down toward the rotting tree trunk.

Steve hissed to gain his brother's attention and tossed the mask into his waiting hands. Bob snatched it out of the air and dropped it into the hole following it with the heavy axe head still in his hands.

As the ceremonial mask fell onto the sandy dirt floor, it was shattered into pieces by the weight of the pursuing axe. That one frantic action defined his destiny, and the destiny of his children. With a final pull on the branch, Bob returned the stump back to its place. He rushed up the hill to the police and his mother.

"Is she all right?" Bob asked, everyone's silence confirmed the answer without the need for verbal exchange. He stared down at her face; the distinct contrast of the red blood covered the right side of her face, and dark streaks of dirt were roughly etched on the left.

Her eyes stared blankly up at the sky, her face expressionless and Bob knew her final purpose was done.

Chapter Fifteen

Tate left for the office early, there was a lot of paperwork and loose ends to tie up. The sun was just starting to come up and frost clung to the windows of his car. The sound of his cell phone interrupted the radio and he fumbled with it as he drove, "Yeah, Tate here."

"Yeah, it's Apple. Are you on your way in?"

"ETA about ten minutes. What's up?"

"No...I want you to see this for yourself."

"I don't like surprises. Want to tell me what this is about?"

"And ruin it? No way, I gotta' see your reaction to this."

Tate turned toward the police station and glanced at his watch. It was five-thirty in the morning. He wondered what new problem awaited him. He turned the wide cone of his car lights into the small rural police station and coasted into his parking spot. As he threw his car into park, he slowly looked up into the silent piercing eyes of hundreds of fake, fuzzy, farm animals - sheep to be exact - a quiet mob pretending to graze on the police station lawn.

The entrance to the station was imitation sheepskin of all shapes, colors and sizes. They were carefully placed in various positions, some merely grazing and still others committing obscene acts with one another. They were flanked by several wooden wishing wells and at the center of the silent meandering herd - the mayor's swan, surrounded by flowers.

Someone was mocking them and the scene flew in the face of all the law enforcement officers who stood staring at the benign beasts. Reporters were snapping pictures and laughing with coffee in their hands.

Tate got out of his car, "What kind of sick dumb...idiots are we dealing with? And what kind of security was goin' on here last night?" he snapped.

Apple smiled, "I don't know, pulled up and it was all here. Guys inside didn't hear a thing."

Tate grabbed his partner by the arm as he continued to stare at the scene. He spoke in hardly a whisper so the reporters couldn't hear, "Apple, ...*Who* are these people?"

"Why," Apple grinned, "They're Pineys, Tate."

Tate doodled on the pad in front of him as he and his partner reluctantly phoned each robbery victim. "Yes, this is Detective Tate. Early this morning in a predawn bust, we recovered hundreds of contraband imitation livestock. You will need to come down to the station to identify your ...er...sheep....yes sir, we have reason to believe the rampage has finally ended."

The men were almost relieved when the wide smile of Angie Simone, interrupted their work. Angolina asked for the conference room, an indication it was serious. She sat at the end of the table watching their reaction. When none came, she noisily opened her purse, pulled out a mirror, and began to reapply her red lipstick in a slow deliberate and sensual manner. She grinned as the two men pondered, "Want to rethink this?"

"What's there to rethink? We both saw the whole thing. We reported it like we saw it." Tate picked up the pictures of the crime scenes again.

Apple laid two prints side by side, "Are you sure you're right about this?"

"I'm as sure as honey bees make honey," she replied, snapping her pocketbook shut and standing up. The weight of her robust figure pushed the chair harshly behind her, "Then I'll file my report, Nathaniel. But I'm tellin' you it don't make sense." She exited with a smile and a wink, "I want to show you both somethin' else. I'll be right back, boys."

"Is she messin' with us?" Apple mumbled after the door closed behind her.

"Look at them," Tate placed the post-mortem picture of Kevin's face next to the picture of Marks. "The head wounds appear to be at the same angle, same depth, and at the same area of the head. But so what – coincidence!"

The door opened again and Angie stepped back in, "Here we go. Now it gets real in-ter-estin'." She clicked the light on at the view box and hung two skull x-rays. "Here's Mr. Winters' skull fracture, and here's Mr. Alstons. Everybody's skull is shaped a little different. Now look at the two head wounds." Her fingers traveled to the wide gray line that trailed down the two skulls like a carbon copy, "The skulls are different but the fracture is the same diameter at every topographical landmark of the frontal bone, same length, depth and diameter. If you boys didn't give me an eyewitness, reliable account- from two fine upstandin' officers…I'd have to say it's scientifically impossible to recreate the same exact injury in two different people - but this one is as close as it gets." She hesitated not being fond of the word, impossible, but continued, "Then there's the woman…now that's a whole other problem. By all medical accounts the bullet should have killed her on impact. You said she was shot at the base of the hill, but there's no blood trail leading up to the cemetery from where she was hit," she smiled exposing her straight white teeth, "I'm tellin' you – this is some weird voodoo shit you got goin' on here, boys – no blood trail means no heart was beatin'. That bullet took a transventricular trajectory severin' the mid-brain…"

Tate raised his hand, "English please…"

"It entered behind her left ear and exited the right temple. Considerable damage to the midbrain; ya know, it's that little connection of nerves…you need to…I don't know…just breathe, think and coordinate any body movement!" She laughed at her own sarcasm watching Tate's reaction. "There's not one case report I can find that's left anyone standin' after a bullet has severed the midbrain." She shifted her weight from one leg to another as she began

225

to whisper, "I'd say you got some serious zombie action goin' on in this littl' town, honey. Why would a dead woman need to get up that hill anyway?"

"To save her son from a bullet."

Angie lifted one eyebrow, "Well my Mama used to say that women are powerful creatures - conduits of the gods. I can tell ya science can't explain it."

Tate rolled his eyes, "You Bayou women- you're all alike. You're a scientist, damn it, it's coincidence."

Angie acted pleasantly annoyed, "You obviously never had a Bayou woman, honey, or you'd never go back to those skinny white butt women you date. Let me tell you somthin'- dogs like bones, men like meat!"

Tate had already turned his back to her and rolled his eyes sadly at Apple. The sensuality of this woman was the biggest unsolved mystery, and he was helpless to understand the aura of his attraction to her.

"Oh! The arrowhead in the four wheeler is old, but the DNA is a go, and it connects our buddy Kevin to the crime scene - sweet cheeks. We'll talk again in a few days." She slapped Tate on the rump, and he jerked to rigid attention. She laughed heartily as the door closed behind her.

"I told you smokin' weed would fry your brain someday!" Steve's words stabbed sharply at Bob's story as they rode the horses up the trail toward the old clubhouse.

Bob retorted, "I told you, butthead...I don't do that anymore."

"Well, I only believe what I saw. Like what the hell was that weird mask thing about anyway?"

"It was the *Keeper of the Game*. He protects the game and the land. The mask was a ceremonial thing. It was a big deal. Anyway, the guy who was blessed with him as his spirit god...well he got to be responsible to him the rest of his life."

"Jesus...sounds like a lot of work."

"It was."

"Could you get out of it?"

"Never. And if you broke the mask at any point in your life, you ended up taking on the responsibility forever and then passing the task on to your family for all of eternity."

Steve's gaze drifted up to the clubhouse as he bored of the history lesson. "I can't believe it. Why did they choose you to be caretaker. A free house...a great view...you stepped in some lucky horseshit somewhere.

"Well, it seemed like a good investment buying into the Club. I can't think of anything better to do with my inheritance than to help purchase the ground and expand future grounds – I know it's what Mom and Dad would've wanted and I'll always have a place to live, and look at that view. How many people have a backyard like this? And it's not free. I have to mow, clear, help keep an eye on the place, and monitor game management. I have a lot of work as caretaker. I'm thinkin' about taking some wildlife management courses. Can you believe that?"

"You're smart enough. If you want it – you'll do it."

They rode the horses up to the gray tub full of water. Shortstop barely broke the glassy surface and made no noise as he sipped. Butch plunged his head up and down into the liquid, snorting and splashing until he was up to his eyes in the water.

Bob smiled at his antics and patted his horse on the neck. "Ain't dainty, is he?" He laughed as he spoke. "You know, Steve, we can never talk about what really happened here that day. Not to our future wives or years from now to our grandchildren. This has to remain a secret between us forever."

Steve shook his head in agreement, "Got news for ya', nobody would believe you anyway, dipshit. We did the right thing, I have no regrets about it. Kevin killed Mom, he deserves the rap for Dad.."

The two men reached over and shook on it.

A pickup truck slowly rumbled down the road toward them and they both waved when they saw Melissa's brilliant smile. Tate's car slinked silently in behind her, the road now hard from the cold. He drove past and parked near the horse trailer.

Bob kept his eye on Tate as he leaned down and gave Melissa a kiss. Why don't you get on Shortstop and we'll take a little trail ride? I think my wussy brother here has had enough. He's complaining his balls hurt."

Steve frowned but then started to laugh. "When you're as well endowed as I am – well you have these problems." As he began to dismount, his foot caught in the stirrup and he fell backward helplessly on the ground - one foot still held by the horse. Shortstop stood motionless, turning only his head to stare down at his fallen rider.

"You're lucky he's a good mount," Melissa giggled, "he may have taken off with you like a one legged rag doll in a five legged race."

Steve struggled to free his foot from the stirrup, but by now they were laughing so hard they were all helpless.

Bob's attention returned to Tate, and he rode away leaving Melissa to give his brother a lesson in dismounting. It was good to watch his little brother struggle at something.

"Hello Detective." Bob's voice was mature and emotionless. He wondered what new information the officer brought him.

"So I hear you're goin' to be takin' care of this place now." Tate extended his hand and Bob took it.

"That's right."

"Hope you're going to fix that road."

"Hope you're gonna get a real car," Bob jumped down and started to adjust Butch's bridle.

Tate flipped open his notebook. "Well, I got to tell you, this was the strangest case I've ever worked on. Everyone who can tell us what happened is dead or missing. And you boys here can't fill in enough to tie up all the loose ends. But the good news is that when we went through Kevin's things we found the murder weapon in his fourwheeler. So based on that we can assume that Kevin had the motive, and the opportunity. Was the location of the site ever found?" He looked over the vast fields that lay before him.

"No." Bob answered, "and I hope it never is."

Tate leaned against the trailer. The sun felt good and combined with the brisk fresh air and the beauty of this place it made all his questions seem small. "I suspect that he used an arrowhead from the site so your mom would take it as a warning. I guess we'll never really know."

Bob squeezed another hole into the bridle with a leather punch and pretended he was uninterested in the findings, "The more I learn, the more I realize how very little I understand, Detective."

Tate scratched his chin knowing the kid had a point after his meeting with Angie. "Anyway," Tate returned to the subject, "the tangible evidence is the only thing that matters in court. So we can wrap this up."

Bob continued to adjust the bridle, undeterred.

Tate sighed heavily, "The coroner's report has confirmed the DNA from the arrowhead found in Kevin's four wheeler matches your father's blood."

The next evening Bob stood on the hill by the clubhouse. There was one more thing he had to do. He lifted his mother's saddle onto Shortstop and pulled the girth snug. He placed her riding boots into the stirrups backward, and duct taped them into place…a rider's tribute to the dead. Then he looped the nylon saddlebag to the rings at the back of the saddle.

Butch stood ready next to Shortstop, tacked up and patiently waiting. Finished, Bob finally stood back and slipped the bridle and bit off Shortstop, freeing the animal from human control.

He pronounced his intentions out loud to the wind, "Your last ride, Mom," he patted the horse on the neck, tears filling his eyes, "You once told me that riding made you weightless and free of the earth. I know this is what you would've wanted." With that, he pulled a knife from his belt and punctured a hole in the bottom of the nylon saddlebag. Immediately, the course heavy ash began to spill from its contents, returning his mother's remains to the earth. He mounted Butch and started down the hill, slowly at first, Shortstop following close behind them. As the horses moved faster, Butch and Shortstop gained speed and freedom as if in some unspoken race - until their rhythm escalated into a heated gallop across the barren fields. Bob looked behind him and could almost imagine his mother in the saddle, her smile breaking into uncontrollable laughter. He turned back to feel the speed of the wind through his hair, and the sound of the coarse grass being beaten by the rhythmical gait of the steeds.

He closed his eyes for a second and let the exhilaration fill him, overwhelm him, as it did in his dream – all knowing, powerful, in control of his domain. A smile crossed his face as the joy of pure freedom filled his spirit until he thought he would explode in laughter from the pleasure of it. He opened his eyes and glanced behind him.

Shortstop had disappeared down a distant trail, leaving only the restless pines swaying behind his path - and the soft beating gait that would make his rider-less voyage a whispered legend.

Six Years Later

Toby eased himself off the couch, the stiffness of his body subsiding as he moved toward the door. A Brittany puppy with ears much larger than its proportioned body yapped playfully at his heels, but Toby ignored the request to play. He spent a great deal of the day on the couch now. Melissa recognized this cue and looked up from her dishes and out the window. "Daddy's home."

Little Robbie jumped from his seat at the table forgetting about the new pack of crayons in front of him. He used both hands on the doorknob, and twisted his whole body as he turned it, throwing the front door open with a bang. His cowboy boots clacked on the old wood planks of the front porch. Toby followed him obediently outside and waited at attention, the puppy spilling out after him.

Bob's pickup rolled slowly up the dirt road, passed a few people training their dogs, and parked in the driveway of the clubhouse. Melissa walked out onto the porch wiping her hands with a dishtowel.

"How was your day?" she called with a smile.

Bob shut the truck door and greeted his little boy by lifting him onto his shoulders. "Good. I ran the combination of grasses by some naturalists, and I think it will work. I'll do the planting and the Club is purchasing the seed. It should expand our usage time and improve nesting. It'll work out just fine." He bent over awkwardly to kiss her on the cheek at the same time balancing the squirming five-year old on his shoulders. He whispered affectionately in her ear as he patted her protruding belly, "You know it's another boy."

She smiled and smoothed her blouse over her stomach, "How do you know that?"

"I just know," there was a sparkle in his eyes.

"I'll be outnumbered then," she laughed. "It will be awhile before dinner, why don't you guys take a walk?"

Bob tugged at Robbie's little arms, "So little man what should the men do while Mommy is busy?"

"Can we have an ad-ven-ture?" He struggled with the word, not knowing it's meaning, but understanding that having one was always fun.

"Mm...how about I tell you an Indian adventure story that was told to me once?" He began to walk around the back of the old clubhouse following the well-worn footpath down to the cemetery.

Butch and Martin were posturing over a pile of hay, but Butch came quickly over to his master. Bob patted his horse on the head. He still wondered what happened to Shortstop. The horse had never been recovered, but somehow, he knew that he was O.K. Sometimes, at night, he would wake to hear the familiar four beat gait of his trot echo on the trails, but like the rumors of the riderless horse – he could never substantiate it. Bob threw a bridle over Butch's head and pushed Robbie up onto the back of the horse. "How's your balance?"

"Good! Mommy says I'm a natural. Give me the reins, Daddy."

Bob gave him the reins and Butch walked slowly by Bob's side while the little boy giggled and rocked on the horses back.

Well, there were once two Indian brothers who lived near here a long time ago. The youngest boy was a great warrior and hunter, who emulated his father's great deeds..."

"What's em-u-lated?"

"It means copied. He and his father were alike- both great warriors. Anyway, the father was very pleased with this son and showed him great respect. However, the older brother could not hunt very well and seemed to fail at every task. The oldest son grew up certain that his father was very disappointed in him. He tried and tried, but could not compete with the younger brothers boastful conquests..."

"What's that?"

"O.K." Bob drew in a big sigh, "he grew tired of his brother always being the favorite and being the one who everyone loved and respected for his great deeds. So he started to question everything about their way of life, their gods and their beliefs. He would shun his work, draw and daydream, leaving his chores for the others. His father grew angry and inpatient with the older son, certain that he would never provide for his own family or survive the hard life they lived in the wilderness. Well, when the boys were of age, they had to prove they were men. It was their tradition. As a test of manhood, both brothers had to go into the woods until they found their spirit gods. They had to return with gifts for the elder members of the tribe. It was a very important ritual."

"They had to sleep all alone in the woods at night?"

"Yep. The younger brother returned to the tribe with a nice buck as a gift to the elders. He was accepted as a man. There was a great celebration and the father was very pleased and proud of his son.

When the older son returned, his gift to the elders was a carved stone pendant. The image of a hawk rose from the surface of the stone as if it were alive. It made the elders afraid. They had never seen a carving like it before – as if the hawk were trying to free itself from the stone. The oldest son told the tribal elders that the Keeper of the Game, their most respected god, had spoken to him and given him a vision. The god had come to him in the form of a hawk and revealed to him that this enemy would first take their spirit, kill their game and destroy their land. And that he must protect it."

"Why did he make the pendant, Daddy?"

"He carved this picture into the pendant so that they would always know who their predator -or who their enemy would be. After all, many years might pass, and he wanted the image to be known by all generations. Anyway, the father and the elders became very angry. Some believed the carving was trickery and the boy was mocking…or making fun, of their gods. See, the hawk on the pendant was attacking something they didn't understand and had never seen, it was a picture of a ship with sails. So anyway, the father was ashamed of his older son and banished him from the tribe. He sent him away and told him never to return."

"That was mean."

"Well, that's not the end. Their mother was a strong warrior herself. She loved both her sons. When the father banished the older son she was very angry and sad. Soon after, the game disappeared and a plague started to sicken and kill their people. She knew the god was punishing them for not believing the message he sent to the boy. It was believed that god himself had taken revenge on their people. And when her husband died, she vowed to make amends... make things right."

"He was mean anyway."

Bob smiled at his son's youthful innocence, "No. He wasn't mean." He continued undeterred, knowing that was another story- for another day.

"She sent her youngest son to find his brother, but he could not be found. When most of the tribe had died from the plague and the remainder wanted to move on, she refused to leave this place. She worked every night by the fire, teaching herself how to carve the stone, like her son's pendant. She rubbed and chipped the hawk and other animals of power as a tribute, and made a bowl and covered it with the carved face of the god. She used it to hold great offerings to beg forgiveness from the Keeper of the Game. She filled the container with sacred herbs, talons, and claws from the animals they respected, believing that the animal's power would give her strength to protect their hunting ground and keep it safe until the return of the chosen son. When she died, her younger son honored her by cremating her body, so her spirit would be carried up to the heavens. He buried what was left of her bones on the hill where his brother had the vision. Then he put his father's weapons with her so she could fight as fiercely as the strongest warriors in the next world.

Some say her spirit protected these grounds for many years and kept it as a game preserve, like their tribes tradition. It is believed that she kept her promise to save it from all who would try to destroy it- or her power over it."

Bob's hands opened to the hill of the cemetery with its odd monuments and overgrown brush, "And it is told that she defended it without mercy, until her oldest son finally found his way back home. This is that hill…"

"Wow. I like that story, Daddy." Robbie squirmed in excitement, "Can I be the warrior who protects the land?"

"You sure can." Bob helped his son down and he immediately picked up a stick and pretended to fight a demon beast in a nearby pine tree. The puppy rushed into the brush beside him and barked at the thrashing branches. He watched his little boy do battle knowing that the demons of today were harder to slaughter and far more difficult to ascertain. His own father had known it too. His hand went instinctively to the compass at his neck and a pang of longing filled him. He wondered if he could avoid the pitfalls that seemed to fan the conflicts between fathers and sons.

A lonely mournful call cut through the air and across the barren fields embracing Bob's attention and pulling it toward the sky.

Above the cemetery, with its circle of fallen monuments and rim of tangling trees reaching upward toward the heavens - hung a single hawk, held motionless against the peaceful blue of the eternal sky. Its wings spread wide and still, defying every boundary set by the limits of man …playing on the fingers of the wind.

The End